# THE LIBRARIAN AND HER ALPHAS

*An Omegaverse Reverse Harem Romance*

LAYLA SPARKS

Copyright © 2025 by Layla Sparks

All rights reserved.

No part of this book may be reproduced in any form or by any electronic or mechanical means, including information storage and retrieval systems, without written permission from the author, except for the use of brief quotations in a book review.

CONTENT GUIDE

- Domestic Abuse (not by her new pack)
- Pregnancy

# PROLOGUE

### Lena

"Ouch," I say as Zorin's hand wraps tightly around my hip as we enter the mansion. I try not to cry out at how hard he's gripping me, and I'm scared it might leave a bruise.

The grandeur of the mansion hosting the Omega-Alpha Ball takes my breath away.

I've never been to an event like this before, and I can't believe my alphas finally allowed me to attend after keeping me at home for years. The high ceilings adorned with crystal chandeliers make the ballroom seem like it's from a fairy tale.

"Stay here," Zorin commands, his tone cold and unyielding as he, Aleks, Raul, and Thomas abandon me to get drinks.

I watch them walk away, laughing with each other, leaving me alone amid swirling colors and the soft rustle of silk.

Nervously, I adjust the mask on my face to make it more comfortable.

Everyone is wearing one, but mine feels like it's suffocating me since my alphas have abandoned me on the sidelines of the dance floor.

I bite my lip and wring my gloved hands, feeling the weight of embarrassment settle in my chest.

My eyes dart around the room as I try to look like I belong there. I hadn't belonged anywhere, especially since I had chosen to stay with Zorin and his pack instead of living on Howl's Edge Island with my family. My sisters weren't happy with my decision to stay with Zorin, but I assured them a million times that I was fine.

Suddenly, an alpha with curly red hair peeking out from beneath his mask approaches me with a smile.

"Beautiful event, isn't it?" he says, his voice warm and inviting.

"Y-yes," I stammer, relieved to have someone to talk to. Being alone was embarrassing for any omega. "It's my first time being here. It's amazing."

"Well, let me tell you," he says, smiling. "It's the same old thing, over and over."

I laugh, feeling more at ease in his company.

But my happiness is short-lived when Zorin's sharp gaze falls on me from across the room—a silent reminder of his dominance over me.

My heart pounds faster with fear. The only reason I was still with him was the thought that he would change and love me again like he used to.

Every omega's dream is to be marked by her pack, and everything would be a million times better. I just have to be patient with Zorin.

"Are you alright there?" the red-haired alpha asks, concern lacing his words when he sees my laughter die on my lips.

"Uh, yes," I reply, forcing a smile and trying to remove myself from his presence, but he suddenly takes my hand.

"How about a dance?" he asks. His green eyes are

sparkling from behind the mask, and I can't help but feel the compulsion from the alpha that omegas were never immune to.

"Sure," I say, not wanting to be rude, even though I don't want my alpha to get even madder.

Confusion swirls through my mind as we dance. It's my first time leaving the house after pleading with Zorin to accompany him. I should take advantage and have fun while I'm out.

But I can't shake the feeling that Zorin is waiting for me to make a mistake.

The laughter and music of the ball fade into the background as my heart races in my chest while the red-haired alpha tries to converse with me.

※

After we dance, the stranger alpha pulls out his phone and shows me a funny video, our shoulders touching as we lean closer to watch. Being with a kind friend like him is like a balm to my frayed nerves, and for a moment, I forget about Zorin's disapproving glare.

"Tell me about your pack," he asks curiously, shooting me a smile. I can't help but feel drawn to his calm demeanor—so different from the harshness I've grown accustomed to.

"Well," I hesitate, unsure if I should reveal too much. But something about him makes me want to trust him. "My alphas...they haven't bonded with me. None of them has marked me. I think it's because I haven't been able to get pregnant."

It feels nice to finally talk to someone about this instead of spending endless days quietly doing chores and pleasing the alphas while getting stressed out thinking about not being able to get pregnant.

The words slip out before I can stop myself, and I instantly regret it when a low growl from behind catches me off guard.

Zorin's towering figure looms over us, his steel-gray eyes burning angrily, and my heart jumps in my throat.

"Lena, what are you doing?"

"We were just talking," I whisper, fear clawing at my insides.

"Omegas don't disclose pack business," he snarls, his voice cold and menacing. "It's time to go home."

He grips my forearm tightly, lifting me from the chair, and I wince in pain.

"You're hurting her," says the stranger alpha, standing up to defend me as he tries to intervene. My pulse is racing, knowing that fighting Zorin will only worsen things.

"Get out of my way. She is my omega," Zorin warns, cutting him off with a deadly glare.

Just before I'm pulled away, I see Thomas step forward from the shadows behind Zorin. His expression is smooth, calm, but his voice is colder than all of theirs.

"Making friends now, Lena?" he murmurs, his tone like ice. "I suppose we left you alone too long. You always were a bit... attention-starved."

My heart is pounding as Zorin practically drags me outside, my legs trembling beneath me as we approach the car. I try to keep my balance since he's moving fast, and walking in heels isn't easy. The night air is chilly against my skin, a stark contrast to the warmth inside the ballroom.

Zorin yanks the car door open and shoves me inside like utter trash. My head collides with the seat in front of me, a sharp pain spreading across my forehead.

I let out a cry of pain as I clutched at the throbbing spot. The alphas never physically hurt me, and now I am in shock at how he is treating me right now.

"Please," I whisper, tears streaming down my face. "I didn't mean to tell him anything about us."

But it's no use. My door slams shut. He's angry as hell as he stomps to the driver's side, closing the door quietly as he enters.

Tears roll down my face as the car engine roars to life.

Raul, Aleks, and Thomas climb into the backseat. Zorin's face is a mask of fury as he starts shouting at them about what I said at the ball and how I've embarrassed the entire pack.

My heart hammers in my chest, fear gripping me tightly, making it hard to breathe.

"Look at her," Zorin spits, gesturing toward me with disgust. "Clueless and useless. She's so deformed that even her eyes are a different color. No wonder he couldn't stay away."

"Don't think for a second he was interested in you, Lena," says Aleks coldly as I stare straight ahead at the street signs zooming past us, trying to hold back my tears as my arm throbs with lingering pain.

Thomas leans forward slightly, his voice low and emotionless. "If you had any real value, we would've marked you already."

I shrink further into myself, wishing I could disappear.

I've never felt so humiliated or frightened with Zorin and his pack. As we drive through a dark road, I'm silently praying to just get to my room once we reach home without any of them knotting me.

---

Suddenly, the car screeches to a halt. Zorin yanks the door open and grabs me by my hair, dragging me out of the vehicle and into the cold air.

We weren't at home but in an unfamiliar place.

The rain pelts against my face as I cry out in terror, forced onto the ground by his brutal strength.

"What are you doing?!" I shriek, tears streaming down my face. "I didn't mean to talk to another alpha at all. You are the only alpha I care about."

"Silence," Zorin barks, his voice crackling like the thunder around us. "This will be the last time you ever embarrass the pack."

Raul and Aleks step forward, towering over me ominously. Their expressions of cold, calculated cruelty send shivers down my spine.

Thomas stands behind them, arms crossed, raindrops dripping from his neatly styled hair.

"Maybe this will finally teach you not to talk without your pack leader's permission," he says flatly. "Omegas like you forget their place far too easily."

I try to crawl away, but Zorin's hand slaps me across the face with lightning speed. My face is burning as I try to pull away, but he's gripping my hair so tightly.

"Zorin, please," I whimper, pleading with my eyes, but all there is is hate behind his gaze. "You chose me as your omega for a reason. You said you loved me."

I don't remember him being such a monster as he's acting right now. Granted, he was slowly turning more and more violent toward me, but I never forgot the dates, flowers, and the first time we met.

Suddenly, their fists rain down upon me, striking my face, my body, and my limbs. The pain is excruciating, each blow tearing through me like fire. Desperation claws at my insides, and I can't do anything but curl up and try to protect myself from the onslaught.

I conjure up an image in my mind to get away from this brutality.

I try to remember my sisters, Carmen and Francine. But remembering their faces makes me cry even harder.

I wish I had listened to them.

"Remember this," Zorin says quietly, his voice dripping with contempt after they are satisfied with the beating, and I'm hurting all over. "If you survive this, don't you dare return to our home. You're nothing to us."

With that final threat, they leave me lying on the cold, unforgiving ground.

The sound of the car engine fades into the distance as darkness begins to claim me.

My bones feel like chipped ice.

I cling to consciousness for as long as I can, staring at the stream of blood on the cement ground—but eventually, the pain becomes too much, and I can't stay awake any longer.

✦

The sharp crack of thunder jolts me awake, my body trembling as I struggle to make sense of my surroundings.

Rain pours down, soaking me and chilling me to the bone. The taste of blood fills my mouth, but I notice strong arms around me. I can hear his harsh breathing as he runs with me in his arms.

There's a scent, but it's faint—like black pepper mixed with cedar.

"Don't move," he commands when I stir in his arms. Fear is rising within me, and I wonder if a different alpha pack will claim me now.

An omega is always vulnerable without a pack. But in my case, my pack tried to *kill* me.

"Where are you taking me?" I manage to croak out through bloody lips.

"To a hospital," he says gruffly. "I don't know who the fuck did this to you—but they're going to pay."

My breathing is harsh as I feel the pain from my broken rib. Zorin tried to kill me. He and his pack wanted me dead.

The realization hits me hard as the rain continues to pour down, drenching me and the mysterious alpha holding me.

Everyone cautioned me that they were bad news, but I believed the promises of the alphas. Their gifts and presents to woo me, just to destroy my life in the end.

My heart aches with betrayal, and I can't help but wonder if there was ever any genuine affection between us. *Were they just waiting for the perfect opportunity to get rid of me? Or did my actions at the party truly push them over the edge?*

# CHAPTER 1
## FOUR YEARS LATER

**Lena**

"Shit," I mutter, frantically slathering my scent blocker lotion all over my body. I'm late for work, and it's my turn to read to the kids at the library today.

I tug on a soft blue dress with one hand while rubbing lotion into the back of my knee with the other. The fabric sticks slightly from the leftover residue, but there's not much time to care. I have to make sure my scent stays hidden from the humans I work with because I'm not prepared to answer a bunch of questions, which would probably end up with me being poked and prodded at a lab.

This morning I overslept, having woken up from a nightmare at three a.m. The nightmare was so vivid, and I woke up in tears, believing Zorin was still beating me in the rain.

As I run my fingers along the large scar on my left arm, memories come flooding back—the night Zorin and his pack attacked me, leaving me broken and bleeding.

Four years later, I'm here, living in hiding, passing off as a human, but the pain still lingers.

Turning my gaze to the picture frame on my dresser, I see the smiling faces of my sisters, Carmen and Francine. The photo was taken at a friend's barbecue, our laughter and goofy antics frozen in time. The glass is shattered, a stark reminder of the distance between us now. I miss them, but I know it's too dangerous to follow them to Howl's Edge Island, where Zorin might have moved to.

I wish they could be here with me so I'm not alone.

My mother, on the other hand, is a different story. She was never particularly kind to us girls growing up, and her harsh words and cold demeanor left me feeling unwanted and unworthy. Maybe it was one of the reasons I stuck with Zorin's pack for so long, waiting for love or any sign of affection.

"Focus, Lena," I tell myself, pushing the memories away. "Today is going to be a great day at work."

---

Later that day, I'm in the library and take a deep breath as I open the worn copy of *Red Riding Hood*.

The children sit cross-legged on the colorful rug, their eyes wide with anticipation.

"Once upon a time," I begin, my voice chirpy and filled with enthusiasm, "there was a little girl named Little Red Riding Hood who lived in a village near the forest."

The children listen intently as I read the tale of the little girl and her journey through the woods.

"Miss Lena," a small boy with thick glasses interrupts, raising his hand. "If the wolf is so big and bad, why doesn't he just eat everyone in the village?"

Giggles erupt from the other children, and I can't help but smile at the innocence of his question.

"Well, you see," I explain gently, "the wolf isn't interested in eating everyone. He's just trying to survive like anyone else. And besides, it would be a very short story if he did that, don't you think?"

The children nod in agreement, and I continue the story until its thrilling conclusion.

As I close the book, Paige, my co-worker, guides the children toward the shelves where they can choose their own books to take home. She's petite, with a pixie-like face framed by dark curls, her green eyes always sparkling with energy, but her energy reminds me of my sister Francine.

"Great job today, Lena," she whispers with a smile before returning to the eager young readers.

"Thanks," I say, smiling as I watch the children fighting over a book on the shelves. "Good luck."

"I could use some of that," Paige sighs, but she quickly inserts herself into the argument between the children. "Shh, don't cry! I have more of those books in the back."

Carrying the now-closed book in my hands, I head to where it belongs, not wanting to pile it up with the other books in the containers we didn't get around to organizing.

I quickly slide the book back into its place so I could help Paige out.

"Your reading was quite captivating," a deep male voice says from behind me, and alarm goes through me, knowing immediately that he isn't human.

My chest tightens as I whirl around to face the unexpected voice.

He's an alpha right here in my library, and it doesn't help that he's breathtaking. His steel-gray eyes are intense beneath dark blonde hair that falls effortlessly across his forehead, framing a chiseled jawline that could cut glass.

"Uhm... are you a father with a child here?" I stammer, trying to maintain my composure as my heart races. This is the fucking last place I ever thought I would see a wolf like myself. Alphas were much bigger than omegas and usually came in packs, with an omega as their mate to share between them.

"No," he replies, his voice smooth and rich like melted chocolate. "I was looking for a book on military tactics. Your voice caught my attention, and I had to stop and listen. The sound of your voice is very...captivating."

"Thank you," I say, forcing a smile despite the unease curling in my stomach. I can't help but feel exposed, vulnerable under his gaze. My scent blockers should be working, but being this close to an alpha has me on edge.

I instinctively want to flee, but politeness keeps me rooted to the spot. Plus, if I run, he will know I'm hiding something. Alphas don't like to be kept in the dark about anything.

"Could you help me find the book I'm looking for?" he asks, eyes scouring my body. God, he isn't even discreet about it. He must not have a mate.

I wonder if he has a pack. *No, I can't let my mind go there.*

"Of course," I reply, swallowing hard. As we walk through the library, he follows closely behind me, his presence practically radiating heat. My heart hammers against my ribs, and I concentrate on keeping my breathing steady.

But my pussy is clenching as I try to keep my slick from releasing. Alphas could sense when an omega is horny, and I can't let him suspect me for a second.

After my horrible experience with Zorin and his pack, I need to push him away.

"Sometimes these books can be a bit disorganized," I blurt out nervously as we arrive at the correct shelf, trying to fill the silence between us. "But I'm sure we'll find it in no time."

"Your dedication to this library is admirable," he says,

joining me in scanning the shelves. We reach up to touch the spine of the same book, our hands colliding.

A sudden bolt of electricity goes through me, and my breathing stops as he sharply looks at me.

*Shit, he must have felt that too.*

"Oh! Here it is," I announce, distracting him by pulling the book from its hiding place. "This should be what you're looking for."

"Thank you," he murmurs, his fingers brushing mine as he takes the book. The contact sends another shiver down my spine.

"You're welcome," I say softly, unable to meet his intense gaze any longer.

My heart races as he pauses and sniffs the air, his steel-gray eyes suddenly locking onto mine with the intensity of a thousand stares. Panic bubbles in my chest, and I freeze, wondering if he can sense that I'm really an omega beneath the scent blockers.

If an alpha pack discovered an omega was around, they wouldn't waste any time claiming them.

"Very nice," he says, holding the book, but his eyes are still on me.

"Uh, this is the general area for the books you're looking for," I stammer, making a hasty excuse to leave him there.

As I move away, I can feel his eyes on my body, my blue dress swishing around my thighs. My heart pounds so hard I'm sure he can hear it.

---

Ten minutes later, I'm chatting with my co-worker at the front desk when the alpha approaches, a stack of books cradled in his arms.

"Whoa, he's hot," whispers Annabelle.

"Don't stare," I hiss as he deliberately approaches my side of the desk, placing the books down.

My heart races as I try to act nonchalant, focusing on scanning the books.

Suddenly, the alpha places his hand on top of mine, stopping my movements and sending lightning spikes through my body.

"Have you lived here your whole life?" he asks, his question coming out of nowhere. But I know he's trying to figure me out and getting frustrated.

I laugh nervously, trying to hide my discomfort.

"Yes, of course," I lie, my breathing labored as slick seeps from my pussy. My underwear is probably wet as hell. It's been years since I've been around an alpha, and his presence is affecting me on another level.

I turn my attention back to the computer screen as he checks me out. His name is Gunnar Thorne, and I file it in my mind, planning to look him up later on social media.

Relief washes over me as he gathers his books and leaves with one last look at me.

"What was that about?" asks Annabelle, her eyebrows raising as we watch the hot alpha saunter his way to the exit doors.

"Sometimes we get the odd ones," I shrug, feigning nonchalance. "I'm not too worried."

But deep down, I'm worried.

Alphas don't like to be confused, and something tells me he'll be back for answers.

---

The downpour outside is relentless as I organize the books in the library before locking up for the night. The books are a hot mess, and I don't want to drive outside right now, so I might as well make use of my time.

As I organize the romance novels from the returned stack, I can't help but flip open the pages and read some of the chapters.

I might as well pass the time until the storm passes.

The sound of thunder echoes in the distance, and I glance out the giant window. The storm is moving faster than expected, already cloaking the world outside in almost pitch-black darkness. Rain doesn't usually bother me, but the heavy downpour sends unease snaking through me, reminding me of that fateful night when my previous pack left me for dead in the rain.

"They're not here anymore. I'm okay," I whisper to myself to stay grounded.

Putting away the book, I hug myself as I shiver. Standing before a bookshelf, I take deep breaths, attempting to push away the memories that threaten to consume me.

My phone buzzes in my pocket, startling me out of my reverie. I pull it out and see a tornado warning alert on the screen.

With a sigh, I realize it's too late to drive home. Being stranded out there sounds like a total nightmare.

Luckily, I have a bag in the employee break room with snacks and a blanket in my car. I hope I don't have to spend the entire night in the library because that would be uncomfortable.

"Guess it's just us tonight," I murmur to the rows of books surrounding me. Ever since my ex-pack left me for dead, I think back on why I stayed with them for so long. Zorin never cared about me after charming me to be their omega. And I had fallen for them hard, which was a big mistake.

As I continue organizing the shelves, I can't help but

think about Gunnar, the alpha who had visited the library earlier.

My heart races as I recall our brief encounter, his touch lingering on my skin. I had lied to him, telling him I had lived here my whole life. *Would he find out the truth? What would he do if he discovered that I was an omega?*

I shake my head at the sudden, intrusive thoughts because there's no point in worrying about that now.

Instead, I focus on the task at hand, finding solace in the familiar rhythm of organizing the books. The storm outside rages on, but inside these walls, surrounded by stories, I feel a sense of safety, even if it's only temporary.

---

After organizing the shelves and reordering the books as much as possible, I grab the thickest book to read for the night after retrieving the blanket from my car.

It was horrible outside—my clothes were mildly drenched, even from how fast I ran. I can't imagine driving in the storm.

I settle onto the large couch in the middle of the library, lying on my back as I read.

The thunder rumbles overhead, a deafening clap that makes me shiver as I wrap the blanket tighter around me.

This is one of those moments when I hate being alone.

*I wish I had a pack.*

"But that's not safe," I whisper, trying to focus on the book. Alphas are enticing at first and then pure monsters after they snare an omega.

My heart races as I listen to the rain pounding against the windows. I can't shake the horrible memories of the beating —the fear I felt that night for my life.

I try reading again, hoping to escape into the pages of a

world where love conquers all. The words blur together as my mind races, unable to focus on anything but the thunderstorm outside.

Suddenly, a loud banging at the library's front door startles me, and I jump, dropping the book to the floor.

Panic seizes me as I struggle to breathe.

"Oh my god," I whisper to myself—my voice barely audible above the howling wind. A single thought pounds through my brain relentlessly.

It could just be my co-workers coming back briefly. Or even... *Gunnar?*

# CHAPTER 2

**Damon**

Waiting for my next kill has never felt so exciting.

Thunder rolls overhead, and rain falls in heavy sheets, drenching me to the bone as I stand outside the IT Solutions building. It's a miserable night, but my anger keeps me focused, my mind occupied with thoughts of killing him tonight.

The man, a waste of space, isn't innocent at all, and now it's time to put an end to him. Water streams from my black hair, dripping onto my face and obscuring my vision, but it doesn't bother me.

I can still see the entrance to the building.

"We finally tracked him down," Max says, standing next to me, his bright red hair visible in the rain. "Took us long enough."

Gunnar grunts in agreement, his steel-gray eyes gazing intently at the building. "Now that we know it's him, he's not getting away."

My blood boils every time I think about the man who

works inside these walls—a child abuser, the lowest form of scum. My pack and I have been surveilling him for weeks, and tonight, we'll make sure he pays for his crimes.

A civilian had taken a risk and contacted us, hoping we could do what the police had so far failed to do.

"The man you're after," he had whispered over the phone earlier in the day, "he's not just another thug. He's running a trafficking operation that's tearing the city apart. Children have gone missing, and I can send you a photo of him."

His voice quivered with fear and anger—he knew what was at stake if this man was allowed to roam the streets.

My pack and I are ready for him. This is our livelihood, but I do it mostly for myself.

A roll of thunder sounds overhead, snapping me back to reality. I take a deep breath and steel myself for what is to come.

"Can't afford to make any mistakes," I say. "We need to confirm it's him and that he matches the picture we have. I don't want anyone else to suffer because of this piece of shit."

The human had provided us with valuable information, but we've also hijacked the town's police system, cross-referencing records to ensure the people we're after are indeed criminals. Our pack only hunts those who deserve it, and we need to be sure we're pursuing the correct targets.

"Don't worry, we've double-checked everything, Damon. This guy's got a record as long as my arm," Max assures me.

"Let's just hope he gets out soon," Gunnar mutters, his gaze fixed on the entrance. "I think that's him."

"Oh yes, that's him," I growl, fury coursing through my veins, heating my blood when I see him leaving the building. The stories I've read about this guy sicken me to the core. I clench my fists at my sides, my nails digging into my palms.

"Here he comes," Gunnar murmurs, his voice low as Max stiffens beside me.

We all focus on our target. He's tall, broad-shouldered, moving with a confidence that sets my teeth on edge.

*Thomas.*

His name is seared into my memory from endless nights of research, a dark stain on my conscience that won't be removed until justice is served.

I know without a doubt that it's him.

"That's him. He looks exactly like his picture," I say, my voice barely audible over the rain. My packmates nod, their faces set with grim determination.

Thomas walks toward his car, glancing around as if sensing something's off. We still have the element of surprise, for now. I nod as he reaches for the door handle, and Gunnar moves like a shadow, ambushing him from behind. He clamps a hand over Thomas's mouth—

—and Thomas *explodes.*

He slams Gunnar backward with brute strength, his eyes flashing amber, claws extending.

"Fucking mutts," he snarls, his voice a guttural growl that confirms what we feared: he's not human. He's a rogue alpha.

Max lunges, catching Thomas's arm before he can shift completely, but Thomas twists violently, sending Max crashing into a parked car. Metal crunches.

I don't hesitate.

I charge in and ram him into the building wall, snarling in his face. We grapple, claws slashing, our strength evenly matched in the downpour.

"You came for me? You have no idea what you're dealing with," he spits, fangs bared.

"I know exactly what you are," I snarl, ramming my knee into his gut. "And I've killed stronger."

With Gunnar back in the fight and Max shaking it off, we overpower him—barely. The three of us take him down hard, using every ounce of our combined strength to keep him pinned.

"You're making a huge mistake," Thomas pants, his eyes wild.

"Mess with someone your own size," I snap. "You're the lowest scum on the planet preying on innocent children."

We gag him, bind his hands in silver cuffs we brought for this exact reason, and haul him into the backseat.

"You can't do this!" he growls, thrashing like a wild animal.

"Shut him up," I bark.

Gunnar shoves a rag into his mouth, and I gun the engine.

---

The drive to the quarry is a tense blur. Thomas doesn't stop moving, straining against his restraints with a strength that would tear a human's limbs out of their sockets.

"Careful," Max mutters. "He's got fight in him."

"Let him," I say. "I want to rip it out of him when we shift."

The rain intensifies as we reach the woods. It's the perfect place to finish this.

We kill the engine, and I bark, "Let's get this done."

We strip and shift, our massive wolf forms towering in the shadows. Thomas doesn't flinch—he *smirks*.

Then he shifts.

A monstrous silver wolf now stands before us—larger than we expected, scarred and wild-eyed.

He bolts into the woods.

"Go," I growl, launching after him.

Thomas is fast, agile, and experienced. Every now and then, we catch his scent, then it vanishes again, lost in the rain. But he's bleeding from earlier, and that's what gives him away.

Gunnar howls. He's spotted him.

We converge, fangs bared, muscles surging with power. I catch sight of Thomas ducking under a branch, but I'm faster. I leap, slam him to the ground, and my teeth sink into his neck.

He fights like hell.

His jaws snap at me, claws raking my side, but Max and Gunnar dive in too. We tear through fur and flesh until there's nothing left of him but blood and broken pieces.

Together, we tear the abuser apart, limbs reduced to oblivion. When the attack is over, Thomas's lifeless body lies in pieces before us, and the red haze covering my vision begins to disappear as my heartbeat returns to normal.

Justice has been served.

We shift back into our alpha forms, but a long, eerie siren pierces the air, stopping us from congratulating each other on a job well done. We freeze, recognizing the sound as a tornado warning.

*Shit*.

"Guys, we need to find shelter now," I growl through clenched teeth.

I'm covered in blood, and Max and Gunnar are no better off, but we won't survive out in the storm. The rain seems to fall harder, washing some blood off my skin. I can think about what we've done later, but we need to get somewhere safe right now.

"Agreed," Gunnar says, scanning the area. "We can't stay out here."

"Let's grab our clothes and get moving," Max suggests, urgency lacing his voice. We wash ourselves haphazardly in the rain, trying to clean as much blood off our skin as possible before grabbing the spare change of clothes from the car and changing into them.

"Aren't we going to get rid of the body?" Gunnar asks.

"I don't give a fuck about that," I reply darkly. No one would ever track us down, and it looked like a wild animal had gotten to Thomas.

The storm is picking up, the wind whipping around and causing the trees to sway wildly. It won't be long before the tornado arrives. I glance at the sky and hurriedly gesture to the car, pulling open the driver's side door.

"Everyone in," I order, climbing back behind the wheel.

"Sure thing," Gunnar replies as he and Max quickly pile into the car to prevent their clean clothes from getting soaked. The engine roars to life, and I push my foot on the accelerator, getting us moving.

We drive through the darkened forest and onto the main road just outside the quarry in search of refuge. The storm is worsening, and at this point, any building with a basement will do—even a shopping mall.

It's almost impossible to see anything beyond the windshield.

As we head back into town, the mile markers blur, and I squint, trying to make out landmarks along the road. My pulse races, a mixture of adrenaline and anxiety coursing through my veins from our recent execution and the storm. It's almost poetic justice that we killed Thomas on a night like tonight.

The bastard didn't deserve any better.

"Hey, there's a building with a light on over there," Max points out, his voice snapping me from my thoughts. "Maybe we can wait out this storm there."

"Ah, the library," Gunnar says slowly, his tone tinged with excitement. "I met the librarian earlier today. She's... interesting, to put it mildly."

"Oh really?" Max smirks, raising an eyebrow at Gunnar. "So you read books now?"

"I guess so," Gunnar says, lost in thought. I can tell his

mind is elsewhere as he thinks about this mysterious woman. "There's just something different about her, all right?"

"Like what?" I ask, intrigued despite myself.

"When our hands touched, I felt a spark. It was strange, but it felt like fate," says Gunnar after hesitating.

I'm surprised by Gunnar—he's usually the most serious of us, so for him to say something like that must mean the experience jarred him.

I scoff at the idea but remain silent. Mating with a human would be impossible, especially for our pack.

We haven't had a mate in years, and it's unlikely one would just walk into our lives like that. But as the rain continues to pelt down and the wind roars, rocking the car from side to side, I shove my skepticism aside. We need shelter, and we need to find it now.

The tornado is fast approaching.

"Fine, we'll go there," I say, turning toward the library. It's a short drive, and soon enough, I'm approaching the building. I cut the engine, and we hurried out of the car, slamming the doors behind us as we sprinted toward the front door.

I bang on the door again, ready to break it down and barge inside, when the door swings open to reveal a small, pretty woman in a blue dress.

Her eyes widen in shock at the sight of us, and she moves to close the door immediately upon seeing us.

"Wait!" I call out, quickly stopping the door with my boot.

As soon as I see her face, I'm captivated by this woman, even more so than Gunnar's story had led me to believe.

# CHAPTER 3

### Lena

Three alpha werewolves at my doorstep.

*Fuck my life.* I never expected to see three huge alphas standing in the rain, soaked, and looking for a place to stay.

I recognize one of them from earlier in the day, Gunnar, but I don't know the others. Judging by how they're gathered together, it must be his pack. I wonder who's in charge, but I push that thought away.

I can't be thinking those kinds of things.

Alphas are dangerous, no matter how good they look, and these alphas, well, they look quite yummy.

I rub the inside of my wrist absentmindedly, hoping my scent blockers continue to work. As an added precaution, I also take heat suppressants, but it's been a few days since my last dose, and I know by now that the pills are wearing off.

*If they come inside, I'm screwed.*

Anxiety swirls in my stomach as I stand there, blocking

their entrance into the library. If they find out I'm an omega, my freedom is over.

"This storm is only getting worse, and we need a place to shelter. Let us stay here with you until it passes," says the dark-haired alpha. He pauses, then adds, "Please."

That familiar tug pulls at my belly, the one that aches to obey the commands of an alpha.

By now, I know it's useless to ignore it, even though my pride doesn't want me to. Besides, ignoring a direct order from an alpha will only make him angry, and this one looks like the type I don't want to cross.

"Alright," I sigh, opening the door wider for them to enter the library. "You can stay here, but only until the storm passes. We're not allowed to have visitors after hours."

"Thank you," says Gunnar, making eye contact with me while his two packmates walk in, dripping rainwater all over the floors.

"You're welcome," I say, but I start to feel my face heat up when he stays beside me until I lock the door. "I see that you're back."

"Yeah, I wasn't far from the library when I met up with my friends," says Gunnar slowly, watching my every expression. A wave of fear washes over me. He brought his freaking pack here.

*What if he knows that I'm an omega?*

But that's not possible. I take a deep breath to see if my omega scent is noticeable, but it's not. We follow the other two alphas into the library, and I barely refrain from rolling my eyes at the mess they're making on my clean floors.

I shiver as another ominous roll of thunder sounds overhead.

"Are you okay?" asks Gunnar, and I nod, biting my lip. I haven't quite shaken the anxiety that weighed on me before the alphas showed up, and I watch them make themselves comfortable in the reading area.

Being alone with alphas here is such a bad idea. But it's not like I have a choice.

A flash of lightning illuminates the space, and I glance outside again, a sinking feeling settling in my gut as I see how the weather has turned.

I would have to stay overnight here.

I'm stuck here with the alphas, and the realization makes my heart race. I need to calm down, knowing that if I'm not careful, they will pick up on the slightest scent that I'm uneasy. I find some comfort in the fact that the library is large, and I'm not confined to the same space as the men.

Sure, they might be getting comfortable in the reading area where I planned to sleep, but I can always lock myself in the staff room. My eyebrows rise when the red-headed alpha kicks off his shoes and puts his feet on the couch.

The dark-haired male shoots him a glare and then turns to me, his expression apologetic.

"I'm sorry about my friend here," he says. "He's clearly forgotten his manners. Allow me to introduce myself. I am Damon, and this is my pa—, I mean friends, Max and Gunnar. Thank you for allowing us to shelter here in the library with you."

"Of course," I say, giving Damon a tentative smile. His intense gaze takes me aback, and I feel a tingle race across my skin from how he looks at me. "My name is Lena. I work here at Willowstone Library. You're welcome to stay until the storm passes."

"Thanks, Lena," says the one named Max, running his hand through his curly red hair. *Oh my god, his voice sounds familiar.* "Beautiful name."

I nod, blushing as I wonder why he has such an effect on me.

A strange coppery scent reaches my nose, and I sniff the air gently, trying to place it. It's coming from one of the alphas, and I stare at them more intently, wondering what the smell is. In the dim light of the library, I see a small splash of red across Max's neck, and it clicks into place- it's blood that I can smell on him.

"Are you hurt?" I ask abruptly, wondering if I should get the first aid kit. Alphas can generally care for themselves, but I need to pretend that I think they're human, so a first aid kit would seem more realistic. Max frowns at the question, and I gesture to his neck. "You have some blood on your neck. Did you injure yourself?"

"You're observant," Damon comments, raising an inquisitive eyebrow. I shrug, trying to play it off as nothing.

"Just 20/20 vision," I lie. "Should I get you a bandage, Max?"

He wipes the blood off his neck and then onto his pants.

"Nah," he says with a grin. "I guess I missed a spot after all my hard work today."

Gunnar glances at him with a scowl, and I frown, choosing to ignore his comment.

I can't get involved with them in any way, period. Whatever they were up to before they showed up at my library is their business, not mine, and it needs to stay that way.

"Oh, okay," I say quickly, trying to end the topic.

"A bandage is not necessary," Max says. "I appreciate your concern."

Something about his voice pulls at a memory tucked away in the back of my mind. I try to remember why his voice would be familiar, but I can't quite place it. The memory is out of reach, and it eludes me.

I pushed it aside for now, figuring I would rack my brain later when I was alone.

Damon is staring at me and into my eyes, which makes me flinch. He's disgusted by my different eye colors.

"Is something wrong?" I ask, wringing my hands.

"You have beautiful eyes," he compliments, and my face heats. If he keeps scrutinizing me like this, I might as well take off my panties and offer myself to him this very minute.

*God, it's been so long.*

"Can I get anyone anything to eat or drink?" I ask, suddenly getting up to shake off the feeling. "We have some snacks and drinks in the break room that I would be happy to share if you guys are hungry."

"No thanks, love," Gunnar says with a shake of his head, making my stomach somersault. "We're all good, thank you."

He's just as handsome as I remember, but the fact that he found his way back to me after I had politely brushed him off makes me uneasy. I had been right to think he would be back for more and wouldn't leave me alone until he found out who I was. Damon may have that dangerous vibe, but I knew that Gunnar was the one to watch out for.

He probably already told his pack about me, and I need to tread carefully for the next couple few hours.

"Are you sure? It's no problem for me to get the snacks," I blurt out.

I want nothing more than to hide away from these alphas at the back of the library, but my nature as an omega makes me want to please them. I need to be a good host.

"Lena, darling, we're fine," Damon growls, and I hate how my skin tingles at the term of endearment. "You're doing enough just letting us shelter here, I assure you."

"Let me just show you what we've got," I babble, backing away towards the break room, needing an excuse to leave.

"I promise you we don't need anything," Max protests, but I shake my head, refusing to take no for an answer.

"I'll be right back. I'm sure you'll change your mind," I stammer. "Besides, I just want you to be comfortable!"

I turn and hurry deeper into the library, secretly relieved to no longer be in their presence.

I keep looking back as I go, checking to ensure the alphas aren't following me, but the passage behind me is clear. My pussy clenches at the thought of all of them rutting me and knotting deep inside me.

I shake my head, trying to clear the image away. Because if I continue down that line of thought, everything will go to hell.

The break room is blessedly quiet and empty. I start rummaging through the old boxes we keep there in search of food. I know we can get drinks from the vending machine, but there must be something else I can offer the alphas.

As much as it pains me, I want to please them. I want them to like me.

*No, Lena*, I tell my inner omega wolf. *Why am I even trying to get them to like me? Leave well enough alone. Packs are trouble.*

I wish I could listen to my inner self, but I was never very good at it. I can't hide here forever, and I groan, wondering what the fuck I'm going to do now with these alphas in my library.

# CHAPTER 4

**Damon**

"She's beautiful," Max breathes as the librarian hurries away from us.

I can agree with him. I'm intrigued by Lena and her unusual eye color, one blue and the other green. Heterochromia is rare among humans and even more so among wolf-kind.

I watch her long, wavy, auburn hair bounce as she rushes to get us snacks.

"I told you there's something about her," says Gunnar when she's out of earshot.

"We're not mating her," I reply in a low voice. "It would be a waste of time. Frankly, a human cannot get pregnant from us."

It's simple biology. And our knots would make it impossible to conceal our wolf nature.

"True," says Max.

The library is quiet for a moment as we all contemplate Lena while thunder cracks outside.

"Lena is gorgeous, I won't lie, but we can't get involved with her," I say, getting up and pacing around. I pick out a random book and flip through its colorful pages.

"How about just one night?" Gunnar suggests, and we all look in the direction she had run off toward.

"Absolutely not," I growl, narrowing my eyes at him. "As much as I want to rut her right now, I can't. She's let us into her sanctuary out of the kindness of her heart, and I won't have her feeling we're taking advantage of her. She has no place for monsters like us in her life."

"We can show her," says Gunnar with a devilish glint in his eye and a hard-on in his pants.

I place the book back on the shelf and return to my comfortable chair, crossing one leg over the other. I start to remember the events of the night and decide to give my pack credit before they start fixating on the little human librarian.

"Glad we finally got rid of that piece of shit, Thomas. We did good work tonight."

"Tearing him to shreds was the least we could do. You might call us monsters, Damon, but he's the real monster," Gunnar growls.

"Very true," I nod in agreement. If blessed with a child, I would protect it with my life. But I would need an omega for that. My thoughts drift to the pretty human librarian, and I quickly shake them away.

It's not good to dwell on something we can never have.

"I found the snacks!" Lena calls out in her lilting voice as she hurries over to us, arms full of snacks and drinks.

My mood brightens at the sight of her, though I don't quite understand why. Max and Gunnar also perk up when they see her.

I let my eyes roam over her shapely form, swallowing hard when I noticed how her large, creamy breasts seemed ready to spill from the front of her dress. All it would take is one swipe from my claw, and her dress would be in ribbons on the floor, exposing her to me. My desire hardens within my pants, and it takes all my willpower not to act on it.

She would be horrified by my thoughts, and I can sense that Max and Gunnar are also holding back.

---

Lena places the snacks on the small table in front of us, and I look away, trying to avoid staring at her juicy cleavage as she bends over.

"Help yourselves," she says, waving to the snacks with a flourish. "I'm sorry there isn't more. This was all I could find."

"Don't worry about it," Max replies, smiling at her. Her cheeks turn pink, and she looks away. The food doesn't interest me- all I want to eat is *her*.

But I have to play the part of a human, so I pretend to be interested in the disgusting array of expired or on the verge of expiring snacks.

"Alright, I'll leave you all to talk," she says, ready to escape again.

"Sit with us for a while," Gunnar invites, and I nearly let out a growl of frustration. *Does he not understand how much restraint it takes not to rip her little blue dress into shreds?*

"Um, do you mind if I sit here with you?" Lena asks nervously, glancing over at Max. He jumps up from where he's lounging on the couch, scooting over to make room for her.

"Of course!" he says, patting the seat beside him. "Make yourself comfortable."

She sits next to him, nervously smoothing her dress over her thighs. I focus on the shape of her thighs beneath the fabric, my mouth watering at the thought of having them wrapped around my head as I pleasure her. She swallows nervously, and I clear my throat, trying to regain my focus.

"So, Lena, are you from around here?" I ask in a friendly tone.

"Yes," she stammers. "I've only been working at Willowstone Library for two years."

"What made you decide to work here? You look pretty young. I figured it would be a job for someone much older."

She blushes, and I grin.

"I know," she says. "But I've always loved reading. I went to college for this, and I love my job here so much."

"What do you like about it?" Max asks, and her face brightens immediately. Gunnar stares at her intently, just like I am. We're enraptured by her every second she's here.

"Oh, I just love that I get to introduce people to their new favorite stories," she gushes, her eyes sparkling excitedly. "Especially the children. The best part of my week is story time with them, and today, I read Little Red Riding Hood to them. It's when I met Gunnar here."

"Yes, that's true," says Gunnar, who is also looking at her intensely.

"Was Gunnar being the big bad wolf in the library today?" Max asks cheekily, and Gunnar kicks at his shoe, shooting him a glare. Max shrugs and grins at Lena, her face turning even redder.

I roll my eyes at my pack's antics.

Even after being reprimanded, Max is trying to cross the line. I watch as Lena sinks deeper into the couch, finally relaxing as her initial apprehension seems to wear off.

"So, do you have any kids of your own?" Max asks.

"Not yet. I would love to have children one day, but I don't think the time is right now," Lena replies, shaking her head.

"What about a boyfriend?" he probes, and my heart drops

at his blatant question. *What the hell is wrong with Max?* I can't bark orders to shut him up in front of her, so I must keep my cool. "Are you dating anyone, Lena?"

"No," she says in a low voice, her face paling. "I haven't dated anyone in quite some time."

"Why? You're hot as fuck and guys are probably falling over themselves to be with you."

She shrugs halfheartedly and stares at her legs, fiddling with the hem of her dress. Max continues to ask her questions about herself, but I notice she doesn't share much beyond basic, surface-level details.

I raise an eyebrow in interest, my suspicions piqued. Asking about a boyfriend is invasive, but her reluctance to elaborate makes me wonder if she's hiding something.

Curiosity about her grows as I observe her secretive demeanor. Humans typically love to talk about themselves when prompted.

"What about your family?" I ask, hoping to change the topic and encourage her to open up. "Are they also from around here?"

"Yes, I mean no," Lena stammers, breathing hard. "They moved here when I was y-young." She brushes a trembling strand of hair away from her face.

"Do you have any siblings?"

She shrugs noncommittally, tucking another strand of hair behind her ears. Her leg begins to bounce ever so slightly, the hem of her dress inching over her thighs with each movement.

"Do you see your family often? I'm sure it must be great to all live so close together," I say gently, trying to coax her into sharing more. The pink blush on her face deepens with her silence, and I watch her curiously, wondering if there's more to her story.

Just then, a strange scent hits my nose, and I tilt my head

slightly, sniffing the air. It's sweet but mingled with something I can't quite identify.

Max and Gunnar also seem to notice the smell.

They exchange puzzled glances before looking at me, their nostrils flaring as they take it in. I glance at Lena and see her biting her lip, her brow furrowed in anxiety.

Then it hits me.

The smell is Lena's scent.

She's nervous, and the more anxious she becomes, the stronger her scent grows. And right now, it's bordering on overpowering.

*She's an omega.*

### Lena

"Um, so how about you guys? Where are you all from?" I ask, desperately trying to change the subject. I place a hand on my knee to stop my leg from shaking with nervousness.

My scent is rising, but I can't just leave abruptly. Not yet, or else it'll make them wonder.

"Lived here all our lives," says Damon, raising an eyebrow at the sudden change in conversation.

"How about girlfriends?" I ask, and Max chuckles.

"Not in years," says Max, winking at me as he pops a health bar into his mouth. Suddenly, I remember as I look into his eyes.

It hits me like a lightning bolt.

He's the alpha from four years ago at the dance. He's the alpha I talked to before Zorin yanked me away from him.

Shaken, I grab a chocolate chip cookie from the packet on the coffee table.

I need something to do with my hands, and I need to fill

my mouth to make sure I don't say anything I shouldn't. The cookie is stale and slightly bland, but it's better than nothing.

I know it's him, his voice and humor.

Even the hint of his warm cinnamon scent is there. Even though we both wore masks during the party, I knew it was him, and I would be embarrassed if he knew I was the helpless omega that night.

I focus on the barely-there flavor of the chocolate chips, flinching when Max's knee brushes against mine. He makes me nervous—they all do—and I don't understand the electricity that seems to pulse between us.

My pussy clenches as slick gathers between my inner thighs.

But suddenly, I glance up to find all three alphas watching me intently. They have serious expressions, and Damon's eyebrows are drawn together in thought. Max shifts slightly next to me again, and I hear his sharp intake of breath.

My stomach sinks.

Based on their reactions, my inhibitors and scent blockers are starting to wear off. Panic pools in my gut when I notice my vanilla scent getting stronger in the presence of these alphas.

I can't be around them anymore. I need to hide.

"Gosh, I'm suddenly exhausted," I say, jumping from the couch. Their eyes follow me as I smooth down my dress. "I think I'll head to the other section of the library to get some rest. I'll leave the snacks with you in case you get hungry. Goodnight!"

"Lena," Damon tries to protest, but I quickly rush away before they can stop me. I power-walk toward the back of the library and into the storage room.

The storage room is just a few doors down from the break room, but it's the furthest space from where the alphas are sitting, and I think it will be the safest. Hopefully, the smell of dusty, damaged books and stale air will mask my scent so the alphas out there won't detect me. Part of me knows their sense of smell is stronger than that, but I can only hope they will leave me alone.

I open the door to the storage room and turn on the light.

It flickers as another ominous roll of thunder sounds overhead. I shudder and sink to the floor, wrapping my arms around myself.

This night couldn't have gone any worse.

The storm has awakened my nightmares from the night I was attacked by my old pack, and now I'm stuck in the library, my safe place, with three new alphas whose intentions I can't be sure of.

I try not to cry, knowing it will only cause my scent blockers to wear off faster due to strong emotions, but a tear rolls down my cheek anyway.

I swipe it away, trying not to dwell on my past.

After all these years, I'm not immune to an alpha's charm. I thought I would be, but I can't stop thinking about them.

I can't deny how attractive Damon, Max, and Gunnar are. I don't want to think about my attraction to them, but my skin tingles, and my body responds when I picture Damon's dark eyes staring at me. It's been so long since I've been in heat, and with my inhibitors wearing off, I know nothing can block my true omega nature.

The throbbing intensifies, a heartbeat between my thighs. The feeling is almost overwhelming, and I can't resist the urge any longer.

Before I can second-guess myself, I lift my dress and slide my panties down my legs, my thighs parting to expose my slick pussy to the cool air in the storage room.

Tentatively, I touch myself, gasping at how wet I am. Sliding two fingers around my pussy, I sigh, imagining it's Damon, Max, or Gunnar touching me.

# CHAPTER 5

**Damon**

"She's hiding something," Max says, scratching his head in confusion.

"I think we know why," Gunnar adds, staring in the direction Lena disappeared, as if willing her to reappear before us.

*She has a scent.*

Humans aren't supposed to emit a natural scent like us wolves.

"It can't be," I mutter. She wouldn't live in seclusion without an alpha pack if she were an omega. She would need a wolf pack of her own to survive her heat. Something about Lena and the secrets she's hiding intrigues me. I want to know more about her, but I know I'll have to work to get to know her.

Nothing about her makes sense right now.

The storm rages outside, and the lights in the library flicker with the thunder overhead. A flash of lightning crosses the sky, illuminating the trees and whipping wildly in the wind. The tornado should be passing through or already passed, and I hope the building is sturdy enough to withstand the strong winds and pelting rain.

Thirty minutes pass when I realize Lena is not returning to this part of the library. Max is stretched out on the couch, playing on his phone, while Gunnar reads a manual.

Maybe she slept, but I sense that she's avoiding us. Her nervous behavior and her unwillingness to open up about herself are odd.

The instinct to protect her and ensure she's okay washes over me.

"We need to talk to her," I say after contemplating for a while. Standing up from my chair, I stretch, and my joints crack. "She's avoiding us."

"If she's an omega, it doesn't make sense for her to avoid us," Gunnar says. "She should want to be knotted and mated. She doesn't have a pack."

"And if she does?" Max counters.

"Highly unlikely," I say, sniffing the air, searching for her fading scent as I walk in the direction she ran off to.

We wander through the library, looking into all the tiny nooks and crannies where Lena may have crawled to hide from the storm and get some sleep. Eventually, we move toward the back of the building and the staff break room.

To my surprise, she's not in there, but a delicious scent of vanilla wafts towards me from down the hallway.

"There's her scent. Fuck," Gunnar says, eyes widening with the realization that we're dealing with an actual omega. Omegas are rare and even rarer out here without wolf packs for protection.

"Well, goddamn, Damon's right," Max says, breathing heavily when he notices her scent floating down the hallway. I sniff the air hungrily and follow the smell all the way to what looks like a storage room just down from the break room.

There's a light coming from under the door.

The door is closed, but I can hear faint whimpers coming from beyond the wood. Only one person could be emanating such a sweet perfume.

*Lena.*

I rap sharply on the door, the sound echoing in the small hallway.

"Lena?" I call loudly. "Are you okay in there, honey?"

The whimpers stop momentarily, and Lena's sweet voice calls back to me.

"I'm fine!" she replies, but my keen hearing picks up that she sounds out of breath. "Just dropped some books, and I'm organizing them."

I quirk an eyebrow in interest.

"Are you sure?" I ask. "Sounds like you're struggling in there. Do you need some help?"

"No, I'm fine," she says, sounding preoccupied with something.

The smell in the hallway strengthens, heady vanilla notes overwhelming my senses.

I can feel Max and Gunnar still behind me as they, too, catch a whiff of Lena's scent. My nostrils flare as I take a deep breath, and I feel my cock stir behind the zipper of my pants, fascinated and aroused by the delicious smell.

*How is it possible that a human could emit such a powerful fragrance?*

I'm almost certain that she's an omega. In all my time as an alpha, and with all the humans I've encountered, I've never met someone I had such a visceral reaction to.

My pants suddenly tighten, and I quickly unzip, letting my hardening dick swing free. The others are also affected by her.

Gunnar lets out a low growl, and I turn to look at him.

"What?" I ask.

He shakes his head, adjusting himself as his cock tents the front of his pants.

"I just don't get it," he mutters. "Humans aren't supposed to smell like this. I couldn't smell her when I met her in the library earlier today. I've never met a human female that I've…"

"Wanted to fuck so badly?" Max groans. "I've gotta agree with you, man. Something about the way she smells is driving me crazy. I can almost taste her sweet pussy on my tongue."

She's affecting all three of us alphas. Only an omega can make an alpha drop to his knees for her.

"Do you think she just sprayed a bunch of perfume everywhere? We need to make sure before we scare her," Gunnar suggests.

"It's her," I grunt as I palm myself. "Her natural scent."

"Fuck, I just want to eat her," Max growls, his mind on the rut that's bound to happen.

She whimpers again. I turn back to the door, breathing hard, wondering what to do and how to approach her with this.

I suddenly notice the gap between the door and the doorframe.

The storage room is old, and the wood has warped over time, creating a space big enough to see through, even with the door closed. I lean forward to peek through the opening, unable to help myself. I am curious about this omega and the effect she has on my pack and me.

My eyes widen at the sight before me.

Lena is sitting on the storeroom floor, her legs spread wide open and her fingers plunging in and out of her drenched pussy. Her head is thrown back in ecstasy, and she thrusts her hips in time with the movement of her hand.

"Oh God," she whines, dragging her fingers out from her hole and spreading her pussy lips.

"She's touching herself," I breathe. Max and Gunnar crowd around me urgently to see what she's doing. I have the best view from where I'm standing.

My mouth waters as I see the pink of her cunt, shiny and glistening with her arousal. I instantly grip my hard cock as I watch.

She drags her fingers around her opening and up towards her clit, flicking and pinching the hard little nub before rubbing it vigorously, then shoving her fingers back inside herself, her back arching at the sensation.

"Fuck," Max whispers. "Look at that gorgeous pussy."

Her pussy lets out a squelch, her juices coating her fingers and dripping onto the floor. She's so wet, and her inner thighs, glistening with her arousal, shine under the weak fluorescent light hanging from the ceiling.

"Oh," she moans, scissoring her fingers inside her cunt, making sure to rub the sensitive spot within. She gasps at the feeling as I rub my cock up and down, breathing heavily.

She continues to finger-fuck herself, unaware that I'm standing a few feet away with an aching cock that had hardened like steel the moment I smelled her.

She looks delicious, ripe for fucking, and it takes every ounce of self-control I have not to burst in there and shove my rod deep inside what would undoubtedly be a slick and fertile pussy. Instead, my hand is inside my pants as I continue to stroke myself, the tip of my cock already leaking precum.

Gunnar stiffens, his gaze laser-focused on Lena's hand between her legs, while Max lets out a groan and begins to rub himself over his pants.

A small wet patch appears on his crotch the moment he touches himself, and I'm glad to know that I'm not the only one so fucking turned on by Lena's behavior.

"Fucking hell, baby girl," Max murmurs, his breaths becoming labored as he strokes himself.

Gunnar doesn't move, his erection straining against the front of his jeans, yet he doesn't touch it. He just continues to watch Lena, soaking in the frenzied movements of her hand and the little whimpers she lets out.

Lena pulls down the front of her dress, exposing her creamy tits.

"What the..." growls Gunnar.

She tugs on her nipple with her other hand, and I fucking lose it completely, rubbing up and down maniacally, holding back my urge to rut her.

Her nipples are pink and rosy, just begging for my tongue and teeth to lick and nip at them. She moans while pinching her nipples and her sounds shoot straight to my cock.

*She has no idea we're watching her.*

And the thought turns me on even more.

I fist my cock in my hand and begin to stroke myself more earnestly. Precum leaks from the tip, and I use it as lube while I masturbate.

I've always been proud of my size, but now I want nothing more than to watch Lena take it in her pussy and have it stretch her out. I don't care that we are in a public library where anyone could walk in. All I care about is watching Lena pleasure herself.

Nothing else matters at this moment.

I want to watch her orgasm. I need it like I need my next breath.

If I were in there with her, I would be rutting while she's on all fours, shoving my cock into her while pulling her head back by her hair, baring her neck for me.

Her cunt would be hot and tight, so drenched with her desire for me that it would be hard not to cum instantly. When I did cum, I would be sure to knot deep inside her, spilling my hot load into her fertile womb. And even after I came, I would continue fucking her, milking her for every last drop of pleasure she could take.

My balls tighten, and my dick gets impossibly harder as I imagine fucking her ass as well. She spreads her legs even wider as she leans back, giving us a good view of her little asshole.

As I stare at her tiny hole, I wonder if she's ever had an alpha's dick inside it. It doesn't look like it, judging by the way her tight asshole puckers with every clench of her delicious pussy.

She looks like she's an anal virgin, but with me, she won't be that way for long. I would take every hole and make it mine.

"Fucking beautiful," Max says, breathing harder, and I know he's thinking the same thing.

Lena cries out when her orgasm washes over her, her pussy flooding with her arousal and soaking the floor beneath her.

I grit my teeth as I watch her, not quite ready to cum yet despite the scene before me. I need just one more moment to admire her. Her breasts are heaving with each breath she takes and her cunt spasming around nothing as she comes down from her high.

I'm desperate to fill her with my seed and impregnate her. This omega needs to be knotted and bred immediately.

# CHAPTER 6

**Lena**

"Oh," I gasp as my pussy suddenly clenches while I rub my clit urgently. I can smell the alphas on the other side of this door, and it's making me even hornier.

I can't believe how wet I am, and it's because of them.

But as I rub my clit harder, instead of the spike of pleasure I crave, a stab of pain shoots through my center.

A deep, empty ache resonates within my womb.

*Fuck. Fuck. Fuck.*

I'm in heat. When an omega goes into heat, she needs an alpha's knot to fill the emptiness and relieve her from the mindless pain, which could last up to a week.

I jam a finger inside, trying to ease this burning ache in my core, but all it does is intensify the pain.

Teasing myself has never been a problem before, but with my scent blockers wearing off, all I want is to be rutted and knotted by an alpha.

An image of Damon crosses my mind, and I whine as my

pussy clenches around nothing, imagining him ramming his thick shaft inside me and filling me with his big, juicy knot.

A gush of moisture rushes from my pussy, and I attempt to squeeze my legs closed, trying to contain the flood of slick. It's useless; the whole room is thick with my scent, and I can smell myself. There's no way the alphas haven't detected me by now.

Suddenly, I hear grunting on the other side of the door, and I catch my breath in shock.

*Were they pleasuring themselves, too?*

A thrill snakes down my spine at the sound, and despite the terror of knowing they've found me, I can't help but feel unbearably horny.

I want them. *Now.*

Their low grunts are affecting me, and I should feel mortified that they heard me masturbating. I wonder if they know what I'm doing here, but I'm sure their keen alpha senses can pick up my scent.

I kick my panties off my feet and crawl closer to the door, determined to hear the sounds they're making more clearly. I press my head against the door near the crack in the doorframe and take a deep breath. Whoever is standing closest to the door smells delicious, like smoked cedarwood. The scent tugs at my memory, but I'm too aroused to care right now.

Their grunts fill the passageway, and I can hear the rhythmic thumping of them pleasuring themselves.

Knowing they're on the other side of the door, driven wild by the sound of me and the scent of my arousal, sends me into a frenzy. I squeeze my thighs tightly together, trying to ease the growing ache in my core.

Heat pools in my belly, spreading like fire throughout my entire body.

The feeling is almost unbearable.

If I thought I was aroused before, it's nothing compared to what I feel now. I know for sure that my scent blockers have worn off completely. I'm in heat, and the one thing that can soothe me is outside this door.

I sit back and spread my legs again, yearning to touch myself again to relieve the throbbing. But the pain only intensifies as my womb clenches, demanding relief in the form of impregnation.

I try to insert two fingers this time, but all I feel is more anguish. I let out a sob of frustration as my body clenches pathetically around my finger.

I've never been in heat before, and it's worse than I can ever imagine.

"Is everything all right, Lena?" Max calls from the other side, concern lacing his voice.

I freeze, biting my lip anxiously. My body is still throbbing with need for them, but I'm afraid of what they'll do if they see me like this—spread, wet, and ready for the taking.

I don't know if I can take that risk.

Slowly, I pull my finger from myself. It's dripping with slick, and I swallow as I watch it drip onto the floor.

"I'm okay!" I reply slowly. "Everything is f- Oh!"

A sharp, stabbing pain lances through me, and I cry out, overwhelmed by the sensation. I place my hand over my belly, pressing on it to ease the pain.

"Hold on, Lena! We're coming!"

※

The door to the storage room bursts open, and suddenly all three alphas are standing in the doorway, their chests heaving and their pants unzipped- cocks out and angry.

I scramble back and away from them, quickly trying to cover myself with my flimsy dress.

"What are you doing?" Damon growls as he stares at me intensely, his eyes flicking over to my exposed pussy.

"Um, nothing," I squeak.

"You're an omega," he accuses, eyes glowing yellow in the dark room.

*Fuck. He knows.*

"Yes," I admit, breathing hard as we stare at each other for a few moments. The tension in the room is sexually charged.

Max and Gunnar's eyes are zoned in on my pussy, and I shift slightly on the floor, my dress falling open and revealing my most intimate parts to them.

The air is thick with tension, and their scent, combined with mine, makes me want to do depraved things with them. I've never been so horny, and judging by the looks on their faces, they feel the same way.

"You're in heat," grunts out Gunnar.

"Yes," I whimper.

"You need... our knots?" asks Max hopefully.

"Yes, I really..." I start to say, and before I can finish my sentence, I'm flat on my back on the cold storage room floor.

My dress is gone, shredded, and thrown into the corner of the room, and Max's head is between my thighs with lightning speed.

"May I?" he asks, his breath coming in gasps and I nod unable to talk from how horny I was feeling.

He licks in one long swipe from my pussy to my ass and I moan with need.

"Oh god," I gasp.

Damon is naked and kneeling above me, this thick and veiny cock throbbing in front of my face.

"Suck my cock, omega," he growls, grabbing a fistful of my hair and pulling me towards him. I nod, eager to have his cock in my mouth. Even though this feels humiliating, allowing our primal wolf instincts to take over feels so right.

Gunnar slides in behind me and spreads my ass cheeks, and I clench up.

"Relax, little omega," whispers Gunnar, a stranger I met today and now playing with my ass. But now that he knows I'm an omega, it's like we've known each other for years.

Damon's cock is thick and hard in my mouth, and I moan as Max sucks my clit into his mouth, two fingers sliding into my dripping pussy hole. He pushes up against my G-spot, and my hips buck at the pleasure that spikes through me.

Realistically, I know it's crazy to fuck a group of strangers, but I can't stop myself even if I want to.

My omega nature makes me want to please them, but my need to be filled and fucked and rutted is my own, too.

*I don't want them to stop.*

The pleasure from Max's tongue turns into pain, and I pull myself away from Damon's dick to suck in a gasp of air.

"It hurts," I whine, grabbing at my stomach. "Make it stop!"

"She's in heat," Damon barks. "She needs to be knotted. Lena, please answer truthfully. You're an omega, correct? We need to make sure."

I nod feverishly. My whole body feels so hot, like I might burst into flames at any moment.

---

"Yes, but I don't think it's my heat," I cry out, not understanding. I've never gone into heat with my old pack and never reacted as viscerally with them as I am now.

"You're definitely in heat," says Damon. "We're going to rut you. You know what happens if you don't get knotted, right?"

"I'm aware," I gasp, craving all of them to knot me. "Please."

Suddenly, Max pushes my thighs open wider and shoves his thick cock inside me. He's stretching me, filling me to the brim, and it feels so fucking good as he moves inch by inch into me.

"Max will take care of you first, Lena," murmurs Damon as he watches Max enter me.

I cry out in pleasure when he begins to move, thrusting into me hard and fast. I can feel every inch of him, and he continues to thrust over and over, pounding mercilessly into me.

"Does that feel good, baby girl?" Max asks lowly, rubbing my clit with his free hand. "Are you going to cum all over my fat cock?"

"Yes," I keen, sucking in a sharp breath as my pussy clenches around him. I can feel my orgasm building, and I know it's going to be better than anything I could have given myself.

He groans when he feels me tighten around him and then picks up the pace, thrusting into me faster and harder. Gunnar keeps my ass cheeks spread, intensifying my pleasure.

Damon takes the opportunity to put his stiff rod back into my mouth. I choke in surprise, but he grabs my hair again and tilts my face so that he can look me in the eyes while he fucks my mouth.

"There's a good girl," he croons. "Take my dick. It's all for you, my sweet."

I moan around him, loving the way he's throbbing in my mouth. His shaft is thick and veiny, and I run my tongue over it, licking the slit in the head and tasting his precum. He groans in pleasure, the grip on my hair tightening.

My eyes water when he hits the back of my throat, but I keep going, wanting to please him.

Gunnar's finger rubs my asshole gently, and now and then, he slides his finger from my ass to my clit and back again, coating my rosebud with my juices.

"You have such a cute asshole, Lena," Gunnar murmurs, rubbing my sphincter more firmly. "I can't wait to fuck it and stretch it with my cock."

He pushes harder until his finger breaches the tight ring of muscle, and he slips inside, going deeper, making me cry out.

The different sensations from all three alphas pleasuring me become almost too much to bear, and before I know what's happening, a powerful orgasm surges through me.

I scream my release, my pussy clamping down on Max's cock and soaking it with my cum.

"Fuck," Max roars, thrusting into me one final time before he comes, knotting deep inside me.

I can feel his cock pulsing inside me, his hot load coating my insides and soothing the pain of my heat. His cock swells at the base, stretching me wider and wider as his cum spurts into me.

Damon doesn't stop fucking my mouth, and Gunnar's finger stays buried in my ass, gently pleasing me as they wait for Max's knot to subside.

I pull away from Damon to gasp for air, tears streaming down my face.

"This is crazy!" I breathe, unable to stop the shudder that runs through me when Gunnar finally removes his finger. "We shouldn't be doing this. We don't even know each other!"

I know I should feel more panicked, but I only feel boneless as the heat raging inside me dies down to a low simmer.

"Don't worry, darling," Damon soothes, brushing some hair away from my face. "We'll take care of you during your entire heat. We're not going anywhere."

Thirty minutes later, Max's knot has eased off enough for him to slip out of me.

But as soon as his knot plops out of my pussy, the tightening sensation within my pussy rises to my belly all over again.

"Oh god," I groan, clutching my belly, but Gunnar surprises me by flipping me onto my stomach. Some of Max's cum leaks out of my pussy, and my face reddens.

Gunnar smacks my ass and pulls me onto my knees.

"On all fours, baby," he rumbles lowly and proceeds to spread my ass cheeks.

"Stop!" I blurt, realizing what's about to happen. I don't think I'm ready for him to take me anally.

"You need to be knotted."

"I know, but please," I beg. "I don't know if I can take you in my ass. Not yet."

"Are you sure?" he asks, rubbing and squeezing my cheeks. "I promise I'll be gentle."

I shake my head. "No, I'm scared."

"All right. I'll take your pussy instead. But soon enough, I'll knot your ass," he says, chuckling darkly as he strokes my hair.

Without warning, he shoves himself into my pussy, and I scream, struggling to take his thick girth even after Max has stretched me. He groans as he bottoms out against me. "Fuck, baby. You're pussy is thirsty for us. It's like your pussy was made for our pack."

He pulls out slowly and then pushes back in, setting up a punishing rhythm as he pounds into me.

"Oh God," I whine, pushing back against him and meeting him thrust for thrust. "It feels so good. Harder!"

Gunnar shoves every inch of his dick into my pussy as I squeeze my walls around him tighter, and he groans with ecstasy.

"She's so needy. I love it," Max mutters as he fondles my swinging breasts, which heightens my pleasure. "She's desperate for Gunnar's cock."

Damon grins, stroking his cock while he stares at me. "Aren't we lucky to have found such an obliging omega? She's ready to serve her alphas with her sweet cunt."

"Oh," I cry out when Gunnar grips my ass cheeks, slamming harder into me until I feel his muscular hairy thighs rubbing against me.

"Make Gunnar cum inside you, sweetheart. Milk his cock dry with that needy pussy of yours," says Damon.

I feel like I'm on the edge of something explosive, their dirty words only spurring me on. A tingle races down my spine, and when Gunnar sticks his thumb in my ass, I lose control completely.

"Ahhh!" I wail, cumming hard around his dick. My pussy spasms around him, locking him into me, and soon enough, he follows suit, grunting out his ecstasy. I can feel him swell inside me, knotting me and spilling his seed deep inside me.

I slump onto my elbows, exhausted but completely satisfied. My pain has gone, and Gunnar drapes himself over me while knotted to me. The swell of his cock feels so good as I stretch my legs further apart to accommodate his thickness.

*I can't believe I let total strangers fuck me into oblivion.*

"That was incredible. You're pussy...so fucking good," whispers Gunnar into my ear, making me blush like crazy as my pussy twitches around him uncontrollably.

"It was," I whisper back, feeling his hot breath on my neck as he spoons me. "But I feel so weird."

"Why, Lena?"

"We just met."

"It doesn't matter. You're an omega, and I'm an alpha," he says. "If I see you in heat, I go into a rut. That's all there is to it. And well... if all goes well, you'll carry our baby."

"Nope, it isn't possible," I say, shaking my head. In all my years with my old pack, they were never able to impregnate me successfully, so I wasn't worried about that. Zorin deemed me unworthy and useless in his eyes when I never got pregnant.

*But I've never been in heat with them.*

Worry starts to rise within me.

"What makes you say that?" asks Gunnar, pushing himself deeper into me, locking us together even more. "Because I know my cock will make you pregnant."

"I would like to know too," says Damon gruffly as he stretches on my other side, stroking his cock and watching as Max squeezes my breasts. The little storage room is dusty and small, so these massive alphas fill every space surrounding me with their scents.

"I never got pregnant with my old pack," I explain. "That's all."

"You had a pack?"

"I don't want to talk about it," I say quickly, my heartbeat rising.

"Why did you hide your true nature, Lena? Why go to all the trouble of scent blockers and inhibitors?" asks Damon, not letting it go.

I shrug, trying to decide on the best answer to give.

"I wanted to live a peaceful life without the trouble of alphas," I say, hoping this explanation will suffice.

"Why? An omega needs a pack," Max says, frowning. "And I like you already."

"Besides, how on earth do you think you'll survive during your heat?" Gunnar asks. "This is a prime example of why we need each other."

"Yes, but I'm not looking to have a permanent pack right now," I say, looking away from the three shocked alphas.

I don't care that they think I'm a weird omega. *Why can't they understand the concept of a good time without getting attached forever as mates?*

# CHAPTER 7

**Lena**

The next morning, a loud rumble of thunder wakes me from my sleep, and I sit up in the darkness of the storage room.

At first, I'm confused and disorientated at finding myself in the library.

My belly immediately clenches in pain, and I look around wildly, seeing the three alphas sprawled all over the floor around me. They're all naked, and my eyes roam over their gorgeous forms hungrily. The memories of the past night flood through me, making me blush.

I look over at Damon, the pack leader.

I can't help but stare at his muscles, fascinated by how they flex and relax with his breathing. My heart pounds faster, and I stretch out a tentative hand to trace along the contours of his body.

"Do you like what you see?"

I jump at the sound of his voice, looking up to see him watching me through half-lidded eyes, a sleepy smile in place.

"I'm sorry," I whisper. "I didn't mean to wake you."

"Not at all. Come here," he opens his arms for me, and I cuddle into his chest, snuggling closer when more thunder sounds.

"It's just a bit of thunder, darling," he soothes when I flinch against him. "Nothing to worry about. I've got you."

"I don't like storms," I admit quietly. "I never have."

"Well then," Damon says, smoothly rolling out from under me until he's hovering over me. "Maybe we should try and get your mind off of it." He gives me a feral grin, nudging against me so I can feel his cock, already like steel, pressing into my thigh.

"I thought I would have worn you out already," I wince as another sharp stab of pain directly hits my center.

"Maybe the others, yes, but not me. I was denied the opportunity of knotting inside this sweet pussy," he growls lowly. He nudges me again, and, not needing to be asked twice, I open my legs for him to slip between.

"I need your knot, Damon."

"Holy fuck, you're already so wet," he groans as he stretches my pussy wide with his girth.

"Deeper, please," I whimper as slick seeps around his cock and onto the floor. "I need you deeper inside me."

He pushes forward, and his cock presses into my pussy, sliding in easily. He's quite thick, and I hiss as he bottoms out, stretching me to the point of pain. He starts to thrust into me, slowly at first, but then picking up the pace, the sound of our skin slapping together drowning out the thunder rumbling overhead.

Clenching my thighs around his waist, I grip his hairy forearms for balance. My mind and body fully consumed by the alpha in the dark room with me.

Damon leans down, breathing into my neck, kissing me as

he pistons deeply into me. My pussy walls tighten around him as the feeling within me escalates.

"Lena, sweetheart, you're killing me," Damon groans. "I'm going to come too fast if you keep squeezing your little pussy like that."

"Then do it. Cum inside my pussy. Knot me," I beg, and he picks up the pace pushing his cock in and out of me.

Hard and fast. Faster and faster until I'm squirting all over his dick, holding back my screams so as not to wake the others.

"Fuck," he groans, shooting loads of hot semen into my throbbing pussy, combining with my slick. "My god."

He drops his head to my shoulder, trying to catch his breath. Our fast breaths mingle as one while his cock begins to swell inside of me.

I cry out as the sudden stretch of my pussy shocks me.

"God, that feels so good," I moan, kissing his cheek.

"It does, and there's no fucking way I'm letting you go after this," he growls, nipping at my neck, and I nearly have a heart attack thinking that he's about to mark and claim me as his omega.

"And good morning to you, too," Max interrupts, grinning at me from where he's lying on my other side. His cock is erect, a drop of precum already glistening at the tip.

I blush, embarrassed for him to see me knotted already.

"Good morning," I say, looking away shyly.

"Oh, come now, don't be shy. We saw so much more from you last night," Max growls, kneading my left breast. "Much, *much* more."

I can't help it, but his words make my pussy clench harder around Damon's cock.

"Careful, Max, she's going to need your knot right after I'm done," warns Damon, winking at me when he notices my pussy getting wetter around him.

Damon slips out from me and sits up, pulling me with him. Seeing the three alphas surrounding me, my heart aches for something I've been missing for years.

"I wish I had a nest," I blurt out before I can stop myself.

All three alphas are still, then immediately jump up and leave the storage room. Panicking, I follow them to see what the hell they're doing. They're frantically looking around the library.

"What are you guys doing?" I ask, confused.

"We neglected you. You need a nest, and we're looking for any material to use," barks Max, charging to the nearest bookshelf. "There!"

"Stop!" I yell as they start to pull books from the shelves. My heart is in my throat when Gunnar opens the book in his hands, looking ready to tear out the pages. "What the hell are you doing? You can't use library books to build a nest!"

Gunnar shrugs as if it's no big deal. "There's nothing else around here to use."

"We have a lost and found, you great brute," I seethe, annoyed now they wouldn't at least ask first. "There are plenty of blankets and old clothes in there that you can use."

"But what about bedbugs?" Gunnar mutters. I stare at him, wondering if I heard correctly as I clutch my dress against my chest.

"I beg your pardon?"

"Bedbugs. You know, those insects that live in your mattress?"

"Dude, what the fuck," Max laughs. Damon shakes his head incredulously.

"What about them?" I challenge.

"Well, who's to say that there aren't bedbugs living in those old clothes and blankets?"

I raise a skeptical eyebrow. "What kind of place do you think I run, Gunnar?"

He shrugs. "I'm just saying. You never know."

"Okay, you know what, never mind," I say, holding up my hands. "Use the books, but only the damaged pile."

The alphas grin at me before rushing off to get the supplies they need to build my nest.

I watch as they layer on papers all over the ground of the storage room. I start to feel a sense of being safe, protected, and cared for. I can't explain it, and I start to feel warm when I'm around them.

"There you go, honey," says Max, pressing a hand on the small of my back while I admire the nest of book pages and the smell of books in the room. "Let's christen your little nest, shall we?"

And the morning passes in a blur of eating, napping, and knotting.

I'm wired, constantly needing attention since it's been so long since I was last knotted, and the alphas are more than happy to fulfill all of my desires.

---

I'm writhing on top of Damon's cock, riding him, Max and Gunnar watch. They don't mind in the slightest as they stroke themselves while watching me.

"Look at her go. Bouncing her little pussy up and down on our pack leader," whispers Gunnar, and my heart races wildly when I see his eyes zoned in on my pussy.

"Exactly," says Max, groaning as he strokes himself to completion, watching me as I work Damon's cock harder into me wiggling over him.

"Good girl," says Damon, whose hands are on my waist, helping me go up and down since he's a giant of an alpha.

"Ah!" I scream when he slams me down onto his steel of a cock, penetrating me deep into my womb. My pussy spasms around him as slick gushes out, and he smiles in satisfaction when I'm weak. Then, at that moment, he explodes inside of me, his release shooting straight up inside of me.

I collapse onto his chest when his cock swells, finally knotting me to him.

"You look so satisfied, sweet omega," Damon croons as he rubs my hair back while kissing my face and pumping more semen into me. I'm catching my breath while he mutters sweet nothings into my ear while his cock is nice and snug inside of me.

It's one of the hottest things I've ever experienced.

*An omega could get used to this.*

### Damon

I wake from the nest, startled when I don't feel Lena beside me. Gunnar lies not far from me, but it's also empty next to him, and I wonder where our omega could have gone.

"Lena?" I call out as I quickly get up from the nest, tripping over papers as I leave the storage room.

A small whimper catches my attention, and I walk towards the sound. I finally see her with Max. Max is leaning against the wall near the library's front door, with Lena standing before him.

Her eyes are half-closed in ecstasy with his hand between her naked legs.

She's gripping his shoulders while his hand dips between her thighs, gently fingering her pussy. I watch as he pushes his index and middle fingers inside her, then pulls them out and pinches her clit.

Her knees buckle at the sensation, a rush of moisture coating her thighs.

"Oh fuck, Max," she whines, grinding her cunt into his hand when he slips his fingers back inside her.

My cock hardens immediately, so aroused by watching Lena get used and fucked until she can't take it anymore.

I stand and walk over to them, also wanting to be part of the action.

"Mind if I join?" I ask with a grin, coming to stand behind Lena.

"Not at all," she sighs in pleasure.

I dip my head, placing gentle kisses all along her shoulders, down her back, and up again. Her skin is so smooth and soft, and the way she sighs when my lips brush against her makes precum leak from my cock.

An excited grunt from behind me tells me that Gunnar is awake, his hand fisting his shaft as he watches Lena get pleasured by me and Max.

I kiss up her neck and towards her mouth, ready to capture her lips with mine, but she tenses beneath my touch. Her reaction confuses me, but instead of questioning it, I kiss her on the cheek and reverse my path back down to her shoulders.

*She doesn't want me to kiss her on the mouth.*

Part of me wonders what happened to make her react in such a way to a kiss, but I don't linger on it for long when her creamy thighs start to shake, watching her orgasm build from Max fingering her.

"Oh, Max," she cries out as she reaches her climax. She moans and cries, digging her nails into Max's shoulders as she starts to orgasm.

Slick drips from her pussy onto the floor, and Max smiles when her pussy clenches around his fingers. More precum leaks from my cock at the sight, and I wish my fingers were inside her instead. Her intoxicating vanilla scent is so much stronger now, enveloping all of us as we crowd around her shaking form.

Lena slumps against Max briefly to catch her breath.

"That was...," she says at a loss for words. Then she turns to me, looking up at me with big doe eyes, an expression that screams she wants more.

"My cock needs you, honey," I growl, picking her up and sliding her easily onto my aching erection. She feels so fucking good, and it takes all my strength not to blow my load instantly.

From behind, Max spreads her ass cheeks and wiggles two fingers into her tight asshole. She tenses at first, then relaxes, allowing him to finger fuck her more.

"I'm the one who stretched her ass," grunts Gunnar, watching with jealousy as Max starts to push his cock into her asshole.

"I'm sorry, brother, but I'll be the first one to take her ass," grunts Max.

"Oh," she gasps against my chest as he slides into her. She's wiggling around and it's pushing my dick deeper into her. Her wet pussy feels so fucking good, and it's turning me on even more.

"Do you like it when he's inside your ass?" I whisper in her ear. All the air seemed to whoosh out of her lungs the deeper Max went into her.

"I do," she gasps. "I thought it would hurt, but..."

"Your ass was made for us, baby," says Max, and soon enough, we settle into a steady rhythm of fucking her in both holes.

"I'm gonna cum," I grunt, picking up the pace. She whines, rubbing herself against me as I move faster.

"Please," she begs. "I need... Knot... Now."

She's almost incoherent with pleasure, and something

about it tips me over the edge. I climax hard, grunting as I knot deep inside her fertile pussy- even though she claims she's not fertile.

A strange warmth settles over me just then, unlike any feeling I've had before. Something about Lena calls to me, and I want nothing more than to figure out what it is.

# CHAPTER 8

**Lena**

My breathing is erratic after being bounced between Damon and Max.

My heart is racing, and I can't deny how good it feels to be sandwiched between their rigid, muscular bodies. My holes are stretched to the limit with their thick cocks. Every thrust of Max's cock in my ass makes my nipples brush against Damon's chest, and I love how wet the sensation makes me.

Now that Max's cock is in my ass, I don't remember why I was scared to have Gunnar stretch me in the first place. *Every inch of him feels amazing.*

"You feel so good," Max croons from behind me, nuzzling my neck when his cock begins to inflate and knot. "I want to stay like this forever."

"Me too," Damon murmurs, kissing the crown of my head, his cock already thick and knotted inside of me. My legs are wrapped around Damon's waist with Max's cock deep inside my ass as they walk to the storage room, with Damon's arms wrapped protectively around me.

They lay me between them while I wait for their knots to deflate.

"So Lena, tell me why you like to stay so mysterious," murmurs Damon as he plays with my tits while Max rubs my shoulders from behind.

"I'm not mysterious," I say, my mood instantly dropping and my heart racing at his words.

"Don't be upset now," says Damon while Max kisses across my shoulders. "I'm falling for you, that's why. My pack and I are falling for you. Hard."

Worry and fear rise within me. I can't allow this to happen.

*I can't fall for this again.*

"I'm sleepy," I say, yawning and avoiding the subject. Damon chuckles softly as I close my eyes and cuddle into his chest.

"Sleep tight, little omega," whispers Damon, kissing my forehead. Tears come to my eyes at the tenderness of his kiss. With my eyes still closed, I feel him rub his thumb underneath my eyes, wiping away my tears.

---

An hour later, I open my eyes, realizing that Damon's knot has released my pussy and Max's cock has slipped out of me as well. I'm lying in the nest of book pages alone as I hear them talking in the central area of the library.

The papers rustle beneath me as I blink awake, my body a little sore after Max and Damon's double knotting.

I sit up groggily, papers crinkling beneath me.

My head spins slightly, the aftermath of heat hormones still coursing through my system, though dulled now after being satisfied. I suppose being knotted by two alphas in one day would leave any omega light-headed.

I press my palm against my lower belly, feeling a pleasant fullness there, a reminder of what they've left inside me. I smile in the dark, remembering Damon thrusting into my pussy while Max took my ass. My pussy twitches at the memory, slick gathering once again between my thighs.

The pain from my heat is still there, but not as strong.

I gather my discarded dress around my nakedness, wincing slightly as I move. Delicious soreness radiates from between my thighs. I wonder briefly if I should be embarrassed, meeting their eyes after everything we did, but the thought dissipates quickly. I need to explain that this is a one-time thing only and that I'm not their omega.

As I bend to retrieve my underwear, a voice stops me.

"Not so fast, love."

I freeze, my fingers curled around the fabric of my sweater, my heart suddenly hammering against my ribs. I didn't hear him enter. I didn't smell him over the overpowering scents of Max and Damon still clinging to me.

Gunnar materializes from the shadows between tall filing cabinets, his gray eyes gleaming with an almost predatory light.

*How long has he been watching me? Had he been watching me sleep?*

The thought sends a conflicting shiver of fear and arousal through me. He moves with lethal grace, each step deliberate as he emerges into the patch of sunlight where I stand.

Gunnar's powerful frame blocks the path to the door, his broad shoulders and chest tapering to a narrow waist. He wears only jeans and a tight black t-shirt that leaves nothing to the imagination, showing every ridge of muscle beneath.

"I didn't know you were here," I say, my voice breathy as my face reddens under his gaze.

His lips curve into something not quite a smile, revealing the edge of his teeth. His gaze travels over me slowly, lingering on my exposed breasts. "Did you enjoy your time with Damon and Max?"

There's something in his tone I can't quite decipher- not quite anger, but maybe a little jealousy that he was left out. My omega instincts flutter in confused response, unsure whether to submit or flee. I clutch the dress tighter around me, suddenly very aware of my nakedness beneath the thin fabric.

"We're done now," I say, suddenly aware of the pinching pain growing in my belly. It's bearable for now, so maybe it's time to kick the alphas out.

The storm outside is over anyway.

I step toward the door, but Gunnar doesn't move aside.

"I said," he says, voice dropping lower, a rumble I feel in my bones- "not so fast."

My heart races against my ribcage, a trapped bird sensing a predator.

The omega pheromones I've released for hours still hang in the air, mixing with Gunnar's potent alpha scent. Even though two knots have satisfied my heat not so long ago, something about his presence is driving me crazy once again.

"I need to get dressed," I manage, my voice small as I try to pull the dress on.

"Why bother?" he says, taking another step closer as he chuckles darkly. "It'll just come off again. Your heat isn't over, you know."

I swallow hard, feeling a traitorous flicker of heat in my lower belly even as I shake my head.

"Damon and Max already—"

"I know exactly what they did," he cuts me off, his voice rough. "I could smell it from the other side of the building. I could hear you." Something dangerous flickers in his eyes. "I've been waiting patiently. Now it's my turn, love."

My body responds to his words with a fresh rush of slick between my thighs. The betrayal of my biology frustrates me, even as it clouds my judgment.

"I think I've been satisfied enough," I say, but my voice lacks conviction. "I'm not some toy to be used."

Gunnar's eyes darken. "You're unmated, in heat, and we're all drawn to you. What did you expect would happen when you go into heat with three unmated alphas smelling like that?"

His words aren't accusatory—just matter-of-fact.

It's true that I knew the risks of allowing them into the library without being truthful about my designation up front. But I never expected my heat to arrive like this when I've never been in heat before.

We stand in charged silence for a moment, the air between us heavy with pheromones and unspoken desire.

Then, without warning, Gunnar reaches out.

I flinch, expecting him to grab me roughly or tear away my blanket. Instead, his fingers land lightly on my bare arm, just below my shoulder, and trail downward in a feather-light touch.

The unexpected gentleness of the contact makes me giggle involuntarily.

"Stop," I tell him, trying to sound stern but failing as another laugh escapes me.

Gunnar freezes, his expression changing from predatory to intrigued. A dark chuckle rumbles from his chest.

"Well, well. You're ticklish," says Gunnar, his voice taking on an edge now mingled with excitement at his discovery as I groan. "Very ticklish, it seems."

My heart, already racing from our confrontation, speeds up further. Something about the way he's looking at me now

—like he's uncovered a weakness he can exploit—makes me feel even more vulnerable than I did before.

"I'm not," I lie, trying to pull my arm away, but he holds it firmly.

"Liar," he whispers, and his fingers snake up my arm again, reaching the sensitive spot near my armpit. I yelp and try to squirm away.

"Please," I gasp between involuntary laughs, "Stop, please."

But there's no mercy in his eyes, only a predatory delight. His hand chases me, finding the spot again, and this time, I scream with laughter, unable to control my reaction. The dress drops further as I twist away from his touch, exposing one shoulder and the upper curve of my breast.

"Your laugh," he says, his voice dropping an octave. Gunnar's nostrils flare, drinking in my scent. "It does indeed turn me on. Massively."

A prominent bulge strains against his jeans, and my eyes widen at how quickly he's ready to knot me again.

"You look very interested," Gunnar taunts, following my gaze. His fingers creep higher up my arm, and I shiver, caught between wanting to escape his tickling and being transfixed by his obvious arousal.

"I—no—stop tickling me!" My words come out between gasps of laughter as his fingers find my armpit again.

I try to push him away with my free hand, but it's like trying to move a stone wall. His muscled chest doesn't budge an inch under my palm. Instead, he uses my momentum against me, spinning me around so my back is pressed against his front. One strong arm wraps around my waist, holding me in place while his other hand rolls down my side and onto my thigh.

"Such a ticklish little omega," he murmurs against my ear,

his hot breath sending shivers down my neck. "I wonder where else you're sensitive..."

His fingers dance along my thighs and are now tickling my inner thighs. I'm helpless in his grasp, my struggles only serving to rub my ass against his hard cock.

The dress has slipped to my waist now, my upper body exposed to the cool air. My nipples harden in response—or perhaps in response to the alpha pressed against my ass.

"Please," I gasp, tears of laughter streaming down my face. "I can't—breathe—"

But he doesn't stop.

"I'm going to tickle you until you squirt all over this floor," he growls, his fingers once again at my armpit as I buck and kick at the floor, laughing hysterically.

The liquid seeping from my pussy doesn't stop. I try to clench to regain control, but he doesn't stop tickling me. His fingers press harder, and I laugh harder.

He suddenly spreads my thighs apart with his knees while holding me on his lap and my pussy suddenly gushes out with slick spraying all over the place.

"Oh fuck yes," he groans. "Now I need to taste your little wet pussy."

I'm breathless and panting, my face red from squirting like that from all the tickling. He releases me so he can eat me out, and I take the chance to run.

# CHAPTER 9

**Lena**

I wrench my wrists free with a strength born of adrenaline and make a dash for the storage room door. My fingers fumble with the handle for a heart-stopping second before it gives way, and I burst into the main library space.

The sudden transition from the dim storage room to the brighter library momentarily blinds me. I blink rapidly, my naked body feeling doubly exposed in the open space. My eyes adjust quickly enough to spot Damon and Max lounging in leather armchairs near the central reading area, deep in conversation. They look up at my sudden entrance, their expressions shifting from surprise to amused interest.

"Help! He won't stop tickling me," I scream.

Damon's mouth quirks up at one corner, and Max's eyebrows rose with interest. Neither moves to intervene as I hear the storage room door slam open behind me. Gunnar's heavy footfalls give me an estimated three seconds before he'll be upon me.

I dart to the right, weaving between tables stacked with research materials.

My bare feet make a little sound on the polished hardwood floor, but my breathing sounds thunderous in my ears. Behind me, Gunnar's pursuit is unhurried but deliberate—the confident pace of a predator who knows his prey has nowhere to go.

My pussy clenches from my heat, begging me to go back to him and just let him knot me.

This chase is making me even more horny.

"You can run all you want, little omega," his voice calls out, echoing among the high ceilings and book-lined walls. "But we both know where this ends."

I risk a glance back as I round a large reference desk. Gunnar stalks after me, his movements fluid and purposeful. His muscled torso gleamed with a light sheen of sweat. The sight sends a treacherous jolt of desire through me.

My eyes dart to Damon and Max again as I pass near their position. Max is openly grinning now while Damon watches with hooded eyes, an amused smile on his lips.

"Enjoying the show?" I snap at them as I dash past.

"Immensely," Damon replies, his deep voice tinged with humor. "It's not often we see Gunnar work this hard for anything."

"She's making him earn it," Max chuckles. "And she looks so cute running around with cum all over her thighs."

Their casual banter infuriates me, but I don't have time to dwell on it.

Omegas like me are small, and we don't have a chance against an alpha's hunting instinct, but we're fast. I hear Gunnar gaining ground behind me, and I push myself faster, rounding a corner and darting into the maze of tall bookshelves.

I take a left amongst the shelves, then a right, hoping to

lose Gunnar in the labyrinth. My heart hammers against my ribs, my breath coming in sharp gasps that burn my lungs.

The chase should terrify me. It should make me feel hunted and violated. Instead, with each step, I feel a growing, insistent throb between my thighs.

My nipples have hardened to sensitive peaks, and I'm mortifyingly aware of the slick coating of my inner thighs.

I slow my pace, trying to quiet my breathing. Perhaps if I stay still, hidden among the shadows, Gunnar will pass me by. I press my back against a shelf, feeling the cool wood against my heated skin.

The library has gone eerily quiet.

I can no longer hear Gunnar's footsteps or the murmured conversation of Damon and Max in the distance. All I can hear is my heart pounding and the soft rasp of my breathing.

Minutes tick by, or perhaps only seconds. Gradually, I begin to relax, wondering if I've managed to evade Gunnar.

That's when I hear a low, harsh panting behind me.

Not human breathing. Something deeper, more guttural. The sound freezes me mid-step, a chill racing down my spine despite the heat of my skin.

---

The far end of the aisle is shrouded in shadow, but within that darkness, two golden eyes gleam like coins. As my vision adjusts, the outline of a massive wolf takes shape—its shoulders easily reaching the height of my waist, its powerful body blocking the entire width of the aisle.

*Gunnar.*

I've never seen any of the pack members in their wolf forms before. The transformation is both magnificent and terrifying. His fur is a rich, dark blonde, almost bronze, where the dim light catches it. The powerful muscles beneath his fur ripple as he takes a step toward me, then another.

My eyes widen as my gaze travels from his muscular wolf form down to what hangs prominently between his hind legs-his erection, fully extended from its sheath.

It's shockingly large, an angry purple-red against his fur, with a prominent knot at the base that makes my inner walls clench involuntarily at the sight.

He's been wanting to knot my ass. *Fuck. Fuck.*

I back away instinctively, my hands dropping to brace against the shelves on either side of me.

"Oh my god," I whisper as he advances toward me. In wolf form, his presence is even more overwhelming than it was as a man—pure predator, pure alpha. His muzzle parts slightly, revealing sharp teeth as his tongue lolls out, tasting the air thick with my omega scent.

I continue backing up until I feel the solid presence of another bookshelf behind me.

I'm cornered now, trapped between shelves on three sides and a massive, aroused wolf on the fourth. My breathing comes in short, panicked bursts as reality settles over me.

He shifted. He *actually* shifted to chase me.

The primitive display of dominance should repel me, but instead, it speaks to something equally primitive in my omega nature. The fear coursing through me mixes with my intense horniness, my body responding to his cock with another rush of slick between my thighs.

Gunnar's nostrils flare, picking up the scent of my arousal as he growls.

I press myself harder against the bookshelf at my back, feeling the edges of books dig into my skin.

"Gunnar," I whisper, finding my voice at last. "What are you doing?"

The wolf's only response is another step forward, his hot

breath washing over my bare stomach. Even though his eyes are animalistic in shape, his gaze holds human intelligence and alpha desire.

This isn't a mindless beast. Gunnar is fully aware and in control, choosing to approach me in this form.

My legs tremble, partly from the exertion of the chase and partly from the conflicting emotions warring within me.

I should be horrified. I should be screaming for help.

The wolf's tongue darts out, tasting the air again. His eyes travel down my naked body, lingering on my breasts, my stomach, and my pussy, where I know my arousal is seeping like crazy. His erection seems to swell even larger under my gaze, the knot at its base thickening visibly.

"No way," I whisper, more to myself than to him. "This can't be happening."

But it is happening.

The wolf before me is real, and his intentions are clear. I can't deny the answering call of my body, the omega instinct that recognizes and responds to the alpha before me, regardless of his form.

He closes the final distance between us, his massive form now mere inches from my naked body. His fur brushes against my thighs, warm and surprisingly soft against my skin.

A scream tears from my throat as Gunnar lunges forward, his powerful body a blur of motion. Before I can react, his weight knocks me backward.

Books tumble from nearby shelves. I'm lying on my back, breathless and waiting.

※

For a moment, fear is the only thing I can process—primal, instinctive fear of the predator looming over me. Gunnar stands above me, his golden wolf eyes gleaming with triumph, his massive paws planted on either side of my shoulders.

"Gunnar," I gasp, my voice barely audible even to my own ears. "Please—"

Then he shifts his weight and moves backward, repositioning himself over my body. His snout nudges insistently at my knees, pushing them apart with casual strength.

"What are you...?" I gasp when I realize what he's about to do. "Gunnar, no, you can't..."

*But he can, and he does.*

With my legs now splayed open beneath him, he lowers his massive head between my thighs. I feel the first hot brush of his breath against my pussy folds, and my entire body jerks in response. My hands fly down reflexively to push his head away, fingers sinking into the thick fur of his neck.

The first touch of his tongue nearly launches me off the floor.

It's nothing like a normal tongue. This is broader, rougher, and impossibly hot against my sensitive flesh. It drags from my entrance to my clit in one long, deliberate stroke that makes me shiver.

"Oh god!" I cry out breathlessly as my back arches involuntarily. My fingers tighten in his fur when I'm about to push him away.

*I want more. I need more.*

Gunnar makes that pleased rumbling sound again, the vibration of it traveling through his tongue and into my core. Then he laps at me repeatedly. The rough texture of his wolf tongue catches against my sensitive flesh in ways a human tongue never could, stimulating nerve endings I didn't even know existed.

My head falls back against the hard library floor as my eyes roll back.

The sensations are too intense and too overwhelming to

process. Each swipe of his tongue sends fresh jolts of pleasure through my entire pussy. The forbidden aspect of it, of being pleasured by an alpha in his wolf form, flickers briefly through my mind.

He adjusts his position, his massive forelegs now straddling my thighs, keeping me pinned beneath him. I hold my breath as he lowers his head again, licking around pussy as more slick seeps out.

His tongue changes tactics, no longer making broad strokes but focusing on my entrance. I feel it press against me, shockingly large and insistent, then push inside.

I cry out at the stretching sensation, my hands now pulling him closer rather than pushing him away.

"Gunnar," I moan, his name. His name is the only coherent thought I can form as his tongue thrusts in and out of me, stretching me in ways that seem impossible. Each withdrawal drags against my sensitive inner walls, and each penetration pushes deeper than before.

The sounds coming from between my legs are obscene—wet, squelching noises that echo in the quiet library.

My cheeks burn with humiliation even as my hips rise to meet each thrust of his tongue. I'm soaking wet now, slick gushing from me in copious amounts and dripping down to the pool beneath me on the hardwood floor.

Distantly, I wonder if Damon and Max can hear us from their position in the main reading area. The thought should mortify me, but instead sends another thrill of forbidden excitement through my core.

Gunnar's tongue withdraws suddenly, leaving me empty and aching.

Before I can protest the loss, he laps at my clit instead—quick, precise strokes that immediately send me rocketing toward the edge of orgasm. My thighs begin to tremble uncontrollably, my breath coming in short, desperate gasps.

"Yes," I pant as he massages my clit with his tongue. "Yes! There, please don't stop."

He doesn't stop.

His tongue works me relentlessly, each stroke building my pleasure higher and higher. He slows down when I'm so near. It's like he knows exactly how close I am, exactly what I need, and is deliberately withholding it, prolonging my sweet agony for his enjoyment.

"Oh my moons," I gasp, my hands tightening in his fur.

His golden eyes watch me from above his muzzle, alight with intelligence and satisfaction as he observes my complete surrender to his ministrations. There's something incredibly vulnerable about being watched so intently while experiencing such intense pleasure.

*Slurp. Slurp. Slurp.*

His tongue laps at my clit as my pussy walls throb and flutter. I'm so close. I need something inside me. I need to be filled and stretched and claimed.

"Gunnar, please!"

As if he understands exactly what I need, his tongue plunges back inside me, deeper than before, while his nose nudges against my clit. The dual stimulation is my undoing. The orgasm hits me like no tomorrow, my back arching off the floor, a broken cry tearing from my throat as pleasure radiates outward from my core to the very tips of my fingers and toes.

But Gunnar doesn't stop. Even as I convulse around his tongue, he continues lapping at my pussy, drinking every drop of slick as I tremble beneath him.

Through the haze of ecstasy, I become aware of a new sensation—an emptiness, a desperate need to be filled more than his tongue can manage. My heat, which had been partially satisfied by Max and Damon, roars back to life with renewed intensity, demanding more.

*Demanding his knot.*

I catch glimpses of his erection between his hind legs as he shifts position—angry purple-red, glistening at the tip, the knot at its base swollen to an intimidating size. The sight of it sends another rush of slick from my core, my body preparing itself instinctively.

"Your knot," I hear myself say, the words emerging without conscious thought. "I want your knot. I need it so badly."

Gunnar's tongue gives me one final, thorough lick before withdrawing completely. He repositions himself, moving up my body until his massive wolf head is level with mine.

"Please," I whisper, reaching up to touch his muzzle, feeling the wetness of my arousal on his fur. "I need you. All of you."

Instead, he backs away suddenly, creating space between us. I make a sound of protest, my body aching at the loss of his warmth and weight.

I push myself onto my elbows, watching in confusion as Gunnar paces a few steps away.

"Don't leave," I plead.

The air around him seems to suddenly shimmer.

His form blurs, shifts, and changes in a way my eyes can't quite follow. One moment, a wolf stands before me; the next, Gunnar, in his human form, kneels on the library floor, naked and gloriously aroused, his eyes still holding that golden glow from his wolf aspect.

"If you want my knot, little omega," he says, his voice rough with desire, "you'll get it. But not as a wolf." His hand drops to his erection, fingers wrapping around its impressive length. "I want to hear you scream and hold you in my arms when I fill you up."

# CHAPTER 10

### Lena

I remain sprawled on the library floor, with my legs still parted— my body flushed and trembling while he's playing with his cock right in front of me.

My eyes drift away from his penetrating gaze, fixing instead on the floor beside me. Something about his human form makes this feel more real, more consequential than when he was a wolf.

"Look at me," Gunnar growls, his voice carrying that hint of alpha command that speaks directly to my inner omega wolf. "Look at what you do to me."

I swallow hard, slowly raising my eyes to look at him. "Oh my god."

"That's better," he says, his tone softening slightly. "I want to see your eyes when I tell you what I'll do to you."

"You talk too much," I manage to say, a feeble attempt at maintaining some semblance of control over the situation. But Gunnar's lips curve into a dangerous smile.

"Do I?" He drops to his knees before me, close enough

that I can feel the heat radiating from his skin, but not touching me yet. "Would you prefer I show you instead of tell you?"

"I...," My voice falters as he leans closer, his entire body overwhelming me.

"You what?" he prompts, one hand reaching out to trail feather-light fingers along my collarbone, down to the curve of my breast. "Tell me what you want, omega."

The word 'omega' sends another pulse of heat through my core. Coming from him, it sounds less like a biological designation and more like a term of possession.

"I don't know," I whisper.

"Liar," he says softly. His finger circles my nipple without quite touching it, the anticipation nearly as maddening as the touch would be. "Your body is very clear about what it wants. Look how wet your pussy is. It's dripping for me."

I glance down involuntarily, seeing the evidence of my arousal glistening on my inner thighs. My cheeks burn with embarrassment.

"It's because of my heat," I mutter, a weak defense.

"Is it? Then why did you respond so beautifully while I was in wolf form? That's not just any omega's reaction. You dripping for me is something special," he chuckles as he runs his finger between my pussy lips. "Something between you and me specifically."

"You're imagining things," I say, but there's no conviction in my voice.

"Am I?" he challenges, his hand sliding down my stomach, tracing patterns on my skin, leaving goosebumps in their wake. "Open your legs wider for me."

My body betrays me, thighs parting further of their own accord, offering him an unobstructed view of my very wet pussy.

"Good girl," he murmurs, and the praise sends a thrill

through me. His hand hovers just above my pussy, not quite touching. "Tell me you want me."

"Oh my god, Gunnar, please," I say, pushing my hair back with a shaky hand.

"Please, what?" he interrupts, his voice dropping lower. "Be specific, omega. I want to hear you say it."

The challenge in his eyes is unmistakable. It's humiliating and arousing in equal measure.

"Please," I repeat, my voice barely audible even to my own ears.

"Not good enough." His fingers brush tantalizingly close to my clitoris. "Tell me exactly what you want me to do to you, Lena."

"I want..." I swallow hard, gathering my courage. "I want you to fuck me. With your cock. I want your knot."

The crude words feel foreign on my tongue, but saying them aloud sends another rush of slick between my thighs.

"Look at me and say it again," he commands, his hand resuming its slow strokes along his length. "I want to see your face when you beg for my cock."

"Why should I beg? You want this as much as I do."

His hand suddenly grips my chin, not painfully but firmly enough to hold me in place.

"Because I said so," he states simply. "You're an omega in heat, and I'm the alpha who's going to satisfy you. And because—" his voice drops to a whisper, "—deep down, you want to beg for it. You want to surrender completely."

The truth of his words resonates through me, striking a chord deep down.

I meet his gaze directly, no longer hiding.

"Please," I say, my voice stronger now. "I want your cock inside me. I want you to fuck me until I can't remember my name. I want your knot stretching me open, filling me. Please, Gunnar."

A shudder runs through his powerful frame, his control visibly fraying at the edges. His hand tightens around his shaft, a bead of moisture forming at the tip.

"Again," he growls. "Say it again."

"Please fuck me," I repeat, each word easier than the last. "I need your cock. I need your knot. Please, Gunnar, I'm begging you."

Something snaps in his expression—the last thread of restraint giving way. His fingers tangle in my hair as he pulls me towards him. He presses his nose to my neck, inhaling my scent deeply.

When he breaks away, we're both breathing hard.

"Turn around," he commands, his voice rough with need. "Get on your knees. I'm going to rut you so good you'll forget those other two even touched you."

Oh wow, he's being possessive tonight.

I turn over with clumsy urgency, my limbs heavy with desire. Behind me, I hear Gunnar's sharp intake of breath.

"That's it," he murmurs, his voice rough with need. "Just like that."

His hand traces the curve of my spine. When he reaches the small of my back, his palm flattens, pressing me down slightly so my ass rises higher. The adjustment makes me feel even more exposed, more presented for his pleasure.

"What a good omega you are," Gunnar praises, his thumbs spreading my pussy lips open, exposing me to his gaze. "So ready for me. So eager."

The praise sends a fresh wave of slick flowing from my center. I can feel it sliding down my inner thighs, embarrassingly abundant. Gunnar notices, and a low growl of approval rumbles from his chest.

"Look how wet you are," he murmurs, one finger tracing through the evidence of my arousal. "All this for me? I feel very special."

"Yes," I admit, pushing back against his exploring finger. "Please, Gunnar. I need you."

He shifts behind me, his thighs pressing against the back of mine as he positions himself. I feel the blunt head of his cock nudge against my entrance, hot and impossibly large.

"Spread your legs wider," he commands, his hands gripping my hips firmly as I start to freak out a little that he might be too big.

I comply immediately, widening my stance on the hardwood floor. The position makes me feel even more exposed, vulnerable, and ready. My forearms lower to the floor, my cheek pressing against the cool wood as my ass rises higher in the air.

"Perfect," Gunnar murmurs. "You were made for this omega. Made for me to breed."

The pressure increases as he begins to push forward, the broad head of his cock stretching me open. Despite the abundant slick easing his way, the intrusion burns—a delicious, overwhelming stretch that walks the line between pleasure and pain.

"Oh," I cry out, biting my lip.

"So tight," he grunts, his fingers digging into my hips hard enough to leave bruises. "So tight for me even after your double knotting, like the little slut that you are, aren't you? You liked bouncing between two grown alphas, did you?"

"Yes," I moan when he pushes the last few inches of himself into me. "You're so big."

"And you're taking me so well," he praises, his voice strained with the effort of restraint. "Just a little more, omega. Take all of me."

With a final thrust that seems to reshape my insides, he seats himself fully within me. I feel impossibly full, stretched beyond what I thought possible.

His hips press flush against my ass, his cock so deep I

swear I can feel him in my stomach. For a moment, neither of us moves—frozen in place as my body adjusts to his invasion.

Then, without warning, he pulls back, withdrawing almost before slamming forward again in one intense thrust.

I scream in pleasure as the sudden fullness of him rubs against every sensitive spot inside of me. Gunnar pauses, his hand sliding up my spine to tangle in my hair. He pulls just hard enough to arch my neck backward.

"Too much?" he asks, his voice tight with restraint.

"No," I gasp, loving every second of this. "More. Please, more."

He releases my hair, hands returning to my hips as he establishes a rhythm—slow, deep thrusts that allow me to feel every inch of him dragging against my inner walls.

"You feel incredible," Gunnar groans, his pace increasing gradually. "So hot. So wet. Made to take my knot."

His crude words send another flood of wetness from my core, making his thrusts even smoother and deeper.

The initial discomfort has given way to pure pleasure now, each stroke hitting places inside me that I didn't know could feel so good. My earlier orgasms from his tongue seem like mere preludes to what's building within me now—something bigger, more intense, more all-consuming.

"Yes," I moan, pushing back to meet his thrusts. "Yes, like that. Don't stop."

"Wasn't planning to stop," he grunts, his rhythm faltering slightly before resuming with even greater force. "Not until you're screaming my name. Not until you're coming on my knot."

His thrusts become harder, faster, more erratic—the controlled rhythm giving way to something more primal, more desperate.

I feel the beginnings of his knot now, the base of his cock

swelling as it catches slightly on my entrance with each thrust.

The sensation is indescribable—pressure and fullness beyond anything I've experienced. Each time the growing bulb of his knot pushes into me, then pulls back, a new wave of pleasure crashes through my system.

"That's it," he growls in my ear, his chest pressing against my back as he covers me completely with his body. "Take it. Take all of me."

The change in angle drives him impossibly deeper, his cock hitting the spot inside me that makes stars explode behind my eyelids.

"Oh!"

"Scream for me again," Gunnar demands, his voice a ragged command against my ear. He punctuates his words with an intense thrust that steals my breath. "Let everyone hear how good I'm making you feel."

His hand slides beneath me to cup my breast, fingers pinching my nipple with just enough pressure to border on pain.

"More Gunnar!" I scream breathlessly. The dual sensation —his cock stretching me from behind, his fingers on my clit —draws another cry from my throat, exactly as he wanted.

The wet sounds of our coupling fill the air around us, loud squelching noises as his cock drives into my soaked hole again and again.

My face burns with embarrassment at how audible my arousal is.

"Listen to how wet you are for me," Gunnar says as if reading my thoughts. "Your pussy is dripping for my cock, isn't it? Making those pretty sounds just for me."

His words send another flood of wetness from my core, making our joining even more audible. I moan into the crook of my arm, trying to muffle the sound.

"No," he snaps, his hand finding my hair again and pulling my head back. "I want to hear you. Every sound, every word. Tell me how it feels."

"It feels—" I gasp as he hits a particularly sensitive spot. "It feels so good. So full. You're so deep—"

"Deeper than the others?" he asks, his voice rough with exertion.

"Yes."

A pleased rumble vibrates through his chest, pressed against my back as he covers me completely.

"And who do you belong to right now?" he demands, his thrusts becoming harder, more insistent. "Whose omega are you in this moment?"

"Yours," I pant, the word dragged from some primal place inside me, even though I didn't mean it. I would tell him that later, but all I wanted right now was his knot to relieve my heat. "I'm yours, Gunnar."

His responding growl is more animal than human. This sound reverberates through his chest and into mine, where our bodies press together.

His hand releases my hair to slide beneath me again, this time traveling down my stomach to the center of my thighs. His fingers find my clit with expert accuracy, circling the sensitive bundle of nerves in time with his thrusts.

"Oh god," I moan, shaking. "I'm going to..."

"Not yet," he says sharply, his fingers stilling on my clit. "Not until I say so."

I whimper in protest, my body tensed on the edge of release. "I can't hold back anymore!"

"Patience, little omega," he murmurs, his voice softening slightly. "We're not done yet. I want to hear more from you first. Tell me what you want."

"I want to come," I plead, trying to push back against him, to force his fingers to rub against my clit.

"And what else?" His teeth grazed my neck while his cock pulsed deep inside of me. "Tell me what else you want from me."

"Your knot," I gasp, beyond shame now. "I want your knot. I want you to fill me up. Please, Gunnar—"

"Who makes you feel this good?" Gunnar demands, his thrusts becoming more erratic, a sign that his control is slipping. "Say my name."

"Gunnar," I moan, the word catching on a gasp as his cock hits that perfect spot inside me. "Oh!"

His responding thrust is so powerful that it drives me forward on the hardwood floor, my knees sliding slightly. His arm wraps around my waist, lifting me back into position and keeping me exactly where he wants me to be.

"Mine," he agrees, the word a feral growl against my ear. "All mine. This pussy. These sounds. These screams. All for me."

Each thrust drives me higher. Each circle of his fingers around my clit brings me closer to the edge. His knot continues to swell, the stretch becoming more intense, more overwhelming with each penetration.

"Are you ready?" he asks, his voice tight with restraint. "Ready to come on my knot? Ready to take every drop I give you?"

"Yes!" I cry out.

His fingers press harder against my clit, moving in tight, fast circles that make my vision blur at the edges. His cock drives into me with renewed purpose, his knot now so swollen it takes real effort to push it inside me with each thrust.

"Then come for me," he commands, his voice a rough whisper against my ear. "Come now, omega. Let me feel you squeeze my cock."

My belly tenses as the orgasm crashes over me, and my

pussy clamps tighter around him. Oh my god. My throat is sore from screaming his name while I'm trembling in his arms.

"That's it," he praises, his voice thick with his approaching climax. "Just like that. So perfect. My perfect omega."

The pressure at my entrance is intense—his knot now fully swollen, stretching me beyond what I thought possible.

The sensation of being so filled, so thoroughly stretched and claimed, triggers another orgasm, rolling seamlessly from the first. I sob with the intensity of it, my body shaking uncontrollably beneath him as pleasure borders on something almost like pain—too much to process, too overwhelming to comprehend.

We remain locked together, our bodies joined as his release continues into my womb.

"So good," Gunnar murmurs gently. He strokes my back as he spoons me from behind, still knotted into me. "You take my knot so perfectly. Did you enjoy it, beautiful Lena?"

"It was...different," I whisper, blushing even though he can't see my face right now.

His arm tightens around my waist. "Good, different?"

"Very good different," I admit, still blown away by the way he thoroughly fucked me like it was no one's business. I feel him smile against my shoulder, and I smile to myself for making enormous alpha wolf cum.

We lapse into comfortable silence, and then our bodies gradually cool, and our breathing slows to normal. His knot remains firmly lodged inside me, though I can feel it beginning to subside ever so slightly.

I suddenly feel his teeth scrape against the sensitive spot on my neck, the traditional location for an alpha's claiming bite.

The alarm cuts through my post-coital haze, sharp and immediate.

"Don't," I gasp, my entire body tensing. "Don't mark me."

The teeth at my neck pause but don't withdraw completely. I feel Gunnar's hot breath against my skin, his hesitation palpable.

A marking bite isn't just a casual gesture between lovers. It's permanent, irrevocable—a biological bonding that would tie me to Gunnar for life. The tradition is ancient, primal, and not something to be decided in the heat of the moment.

My heart stops thinking he's going to ignore me. His knot still holds me to him, and I can't escape if I want to.

Then, mercifully, his teeth withdraw. Instead, his lips press against the spot in a gentle kiss.

"Relax," he murmurs against my skin. "I'm not going to mark you. Not without your permission."

"Thank you," I say gratefully as the tension leaves my body. He nuzzles the spot where his teeth have grazed, his stubble creating a pleasant friction against my sensitive skin.

"Though I have to admit," he says, his voice a low rumble, "the thought is tempting. Very tempting."

His admission makes butterflies flutter in my stomach and worries me. My inner omega wolf is literally rejoicing at the thought of being claimed by this powerful alpha and his pack.

The biological need is strong and hardwired into my DNA over countless generations of evolution.

"It's the pack leader's choice," I say finally. "Who joins the pack, and who becomes the pack omega. That's Damon's decision, not yours."

Gunnar's chuckle vibrates his thick knot holding us together, making me aware of how intimately we're still connected.

"Damon wouldn't be offended if I made that decision here and now," he says, a note of amusement in his voice. "In fact, I think he would approve."

"And Max?" I ask, unable to help myself. "Would he approve, too?"

"Max likes you," Gunnar says as his hand rests on my lower belly and over the bulge of his huge cock. "He's just as obsessed with you as we are."

Panic flutters in my chest. He and the pack have their sights set on me.

This isn't going to be a one-time fling for them.

---

"Mhm, this is so good," I sigh as Max feeds me another bite of butter chicken after Gunnar knotted me so well an hour earlier.

The storm eased up enough for Damon to leave the library in search of food. After insisting on knowing my favorite food, Damon went out to get lunch for everyone.

"What's good? The food or the fact that you're sitting on my cock?" Damon teases, shifting his hips a little so that his knot sits deeper inside me.

"Both," I moan.

Eating good food while Damon's thick cock throbs inside me is a different type of pleasure than any I've experienced so far.

My heat is still ongoing, and to make sure I don't feel any pain, the guys are determined to keep me knotted at all times. After chasing me all over the place, Gunnar is devouring his bowl of food, probably hungry as hell from his naughty games with me.

"There's something about you," Max says slowly, wiping

the corner of my mouth with his thumb. "You look so familiar to me. I've been racking my brain trying to figure out how I know you."

I freeze, memories of that night flooding back. He was definitely the red-headed alpha who was kind to me. He saw me getting dragged away by my ex. Ice-cold dread settles into my stomach.

I'm scared of them finding out who I am. Alphas are unpredictable, and there is a risk of them going after my old pack, especially after I spent years trying to hide from my exes.

"Maybe," I say, then trying to change the subject. "Have you had an omega before? Like in your pack, I mean."

"Yes," he says after a long pause, making me curious.

I wait, giving him space to elaborate if he chooses. When he doesn't, I venture another careful question. "What happened to her?"

His exhale is heavy, somewhere between a sigh and a controlled release of tension. "It ended."

"Sorry, I wasn't trying to pry," I say. "I was just curious about your pack."

"She ran away," Damon says. "Good thing I didn't mark her."

I swallow the next spoonful of rice, my heart beating hard. I wonder what made her run away, but the mention of her is causing all the alphas to tense up. Even Gunnar pauses eating for a second.

"Stop thinking so hard," Damon murmurs, kissing my shoulder gently. "I can practically hear the gears turning in your head."

"Hard not to think," I reply with a small smile he can't see. "Being knotted to someone doesn't turn my brain off, you know."

"I must not have done it right, then."

The tension eases as I laugh at his joke. Gunnar and Max join in, and Damon's laughter is a warm rumble against my back. It's a strange moment of normalcy in an utterly abnormal situation.

# CHAPTER 11

### Lena

The rest of the weekend is a whirlwind of pain and knotting.

My heat is shorter than I expected, but no less intense. Taking heat suppressant pills religiously for four years did nothing to quell the relentless appetite I've had for these alphas. I can't deny that I've missed having sex.

I wake early on Monday morning, nestled between the alphas.

Damon is on my right, his arm draped across my middle. Max is on my left, one hand cupping my breast, and Gunnar is below me, his head resting between my thighs. I'm warm and comfortable, and I can hardly believe that my nest made of old books is so cozy. My pussy tingles at the thought and care my alphas put into making this nest for me, but my blood cools at the label I've assigned to them in my head.

*My alphas.*

They're not mine. I barely even know them.

Sure, I had the best sex of my life this weekend, but it was with strangers. Embarrassment crawls up my chest, and my face suddenly heats.

*What have I done?* This isn't who I am at all.

I don't have sex with random alphas, and I certainly don't have sex with a pack that isn't mine. Three hot alphas walking into my library isn't an excuse for me to throw away the carefully crafted life I've built for myself here.

I don't want another pack. I don't need one.

Damon stirs next to me, and I flinch away when he tries to nuzzle into my neck.

"Lena?" he mumbles, still half asleep.

I hate how utterly captivating he looks just waking up. It's so different from the cool, calm, and collected alpha he usually presents. Gunnar sits up and stretches, his abs glistening in the sunlight. Max yawns, running a hand through his luscious hair.

*No, Lena!* I chastise myself. *They're not yours.*

"What's wrong?" Damon asks, sitting up and hugging me, but I extract myself from his embrace.

I shuffle toward the edge of the nest.

It's cold being away from them, and my heart aches at the confusion on their faces, but I know I have to be strong. I have to do this for my future, even though I hate it.

"Thank you for the weekend," I say, clearing my throat. They start to tense, knowing there's a 'but' coming. "But this, whatever it was, is over. I had a lot of fun, but nothing else can happen between us. I appreciate you for helping me through my heat."

At first, they're silent, just staring at me, and then they all start talking at once.

"Lena, honey..."

"Are you serious right now?"

"Baby, you can't say things like that! You're part of our pack."

"I'm serious, guys," I say, shivering as I cross my arms over my chest. "I know you're disappointed, but it's for the best. It's what I want."

"No way," Max says vehemently, shaking his head and looking hurt. "I don't believe you. What the four of us shared was incredible. I don't understand why you want to throw it all away. We're fated to be together. Don't you feel the bond between us? I know you feel it too, Lena."

Damon remains quiet, watching me intensely, which makes me shrink, but I have to stand my ground.

Max is right. I do feel the attraction between us, but I can't allow myself to think about what that means.

*Alphas are dangerous.* They're trying to trap me.

"Max, I understand what you're saying, but—"

"Lena," Gunnar cuts in. "It could be that you didn't feel the attraction right away. Sometimes that happens. If that's the case, maybe you should spend more time with us and give it a chance. Give us a chance to bond."

My heart starts to race with panic.

"No!" I say sharply, barely stopping myself from shouting. I don't want to make them suspicious, but the panic I feel at the mention of bonding makes me feel physically ill.

I can't do it.

"We won't force you to do anything you don't want," Damon says in a low voice. The three alphas look at me as if I am their whole world, and now I'm disappointing them.

My heart aches, and it practically hurts right now. Glancing at the clock on the wall near the front door, I jump up when I see the time.

It's almost eight o'clock, and Annabelle and Paige will be here soon to get the library ready to open at nine.

"I think you should leave now," I say, backing away from them. "My co-workers will be here any minute, and I don't want them to see the mess we've made."

"Will we ever see you again?" Damon asks. He's been quiet, his expression carefully neutral, but I can see the hurt in his eyes. "Can we at least help you get this place cleaned up?"

I shake my head quickly.

"No. I don't think that's a good idea," I say, rechecking the time. My panic rises when I see how little time I have left to get the library in order.

Gunnar looks upset that Damon isn't forcing me to be their omega.

"Lena," Gunnar starts.

"Please, I need you to leave," I beg, pointing a shaking hand at the door. "I don't have much time."

Max and Gunnar start to protest, but Damon holds up a hand, silencing their objections.

"Enough," he says sternly, and the other two fall silent. "We will respect Lena and her wishes. If she wants us to leave, then we will."

He stands, and Max and Gunnar follow suit. The silence is unbearable as they begin to pick up their things, which are scattered haphazardly all over the floor.

Once they've dressed, Damon turns to me and nods before walking to the front door and pulling it open.

"Goodbye, Lena," says Max, hugging me one last time.

"Bye," I say without looking at him, not wanting to change my mind. The three alphas walk resolutely into the weak sunshine outside, shutting the door behind them.

The silence in the library after the door has closed is suffocating, made worse by the realization that I now have to clean up.

I look at the mess on the floor, my stomach sinking.

The carpet is strewn with torn books and papers covered in a mixture of our cum and sweat. Somehow, a couple of blankets from the lost and found also made their way into our nest.

Glancing at the clock, I run to the break room to grab a black plastic bag. I work quickly, shoving papers and ruined books into the bag, ensuring nothing is left behind. The storage room also contains some cleaning supplies. After tidying up there, I move swiftly around the library, making sure to eliminate any evidence of my heat and knotting.

Frantically, I spray air freshener throughout the library, hoping to mask the scent until I can open the front door and a few windows.

My human co-workers probably won't notice the smell, but I want to ensure all traces of my weekend heat are gone.

The books that survived Damon, Max, and Gunnar's onslaughts are stacked into piles and returned to the storeroom, where I find my blue dress stained and slightly torn. Thankfully, I keep a spare hoodie in the break room, which I quickly slip on over my clothes, hoping it will conceal the stains.

I should throw away my dress and eliminate any reminders of the alphas. But their scent lingers only on this dress, and I'm reluctant to part with the one piece that encapsulates the most exciting weekend I've ever had.

After the library is clean and I'm satisfied that I haven't left any incriminating evidence, I open the front door and head to my car.

I've barely taken two steps when I spot Annabelle coming down the street. I freeze, hoping she hasn't seen me.

Fortunately, she seems lost in her own world as she glances down at her phone, so I rush back inside and decide to use the back door instead. My car is parked in front of the library, but I can't get to it without running into Annabelle, so I will have to wait until she enters the library.

After a few minutes, the coast is finally clear, and I sneak around the side of the building toward the front.

My car is parked in the lot, and I quickly check my surroundings before hurrying forward.

A black sedan I hadn't noticed starts to drive toward me as I get closer to my car, prompting me to quicken my steps, determined to get inside and away from whoever is in the other vehicle.

The sedan stops, and Damon gets out from the driver's side, standing by the door of my car. Part of me is relieved that he hasn't left, but a larger part is panicked that he has stuck around to see me off.

"What are you doing?" I ask, clutching my keys tightly. "I thought I told you to leave!"

"I want to know why you don't want to see us again," he replies bluntly. "Max and Gunnar are right. We know you felt the attraction between all of us."

I stay silent, unsure how to answer without exposing myself. I don't want to reveal my true feelings because it might make him try harder.

I don't know if I can trust him.

"Come on, Lena," he urges. "How can you shut me out after everything we shared this weekend? I want to see you again, and I know the others do, too. We're fated to be together."

He steps out of his car, and my heart flutters wildly. Then he cups my chin in his hand.

Electricity sizzles beneath my skin at his touch, making my heart skip a beat.

I can feel the fire burning between us, waiting to become a raging inferno given half the chance. The wild and reckless part of me wants nothing more than to dance in the flames, but my cautious side, the one that's been burned before, is reluctant to get too close.

Reluctantly, I pull away from his grasp and step back, wanting distance between us.

"I guess you're just not my type," I finally say, knowing it's a bald-faced lie. Damon's eyes darken, and a low growl escapes his lips. "Please leave me alone, Damon. I don't want to see you or your pack ever again."

It feels like I've chipped pieces of my heart away with my words. My chest aches, and tears sting my eyes.

I don't understand what's happening to me. After my ex-pack dumped me and left me for dead, it hurt, but it didn't feel like this. This feels like I've clawed my own heart out and shoved it through a meat grinder. I take a deep breath, willing the tears not to fall.

*I need to be strong.*

Damon stares at me, probably wondering if I'm lying. His face darkens, and the pain in my heart intensifies at the hurt that crosses his eyes.

"Alright," he says after a beat. He steps aside, allowing me to open my car door. "I respect your decision, then, Lena. Can I give you my number in case you change your mind?"

"Sure," I reply before getting into the car. I pulled out my phone and quickly typed in his number.

"Call me if you need anything at all," he says firmly, and I nod before closing the car door.

Slamming the door shut, I stare straight ahead, not turning around when he walks away. I don't look back when I hear his car start up again.

He drives out of the parking lot, taking my heart with him. Breathing hard, I lay my forehead on the steering wheel, finally allowing my tears to fall.

# CHAPTER 12

**Max**

It's quiet in the office, interrupted only by the occasional mouse click and the tapping of keyboards. Damon, Gunnar, and I sit at our desks, working on our laptops.

We're supposed to be searching police and security databases for criminals and trying to locate their whereabouts, but I can't concentrate.

My thoughts are consumed with Lena—the way she smells, the way she tastes, and, most importantly, what she's doing right now. It's been three weeks since our encounter at the library, but she's been on my mind nearly every day since.

It's almost bordering on obsession.

"I wonder what Lena is like outside of work," I muse aloud, picturing her sweet face and those sparkling blue and green eyes. The sound of Gunnar's keyboard stops, and he raises his head to look at me. Damon remains focused on his work, but I know he's listening. He's always listening whenever Gunnar or I bring her up. "Do you think she has any hobbies besides reading?"

Gunnar snorts. "She's got personality."

"I never said she didn't," I snap, irritated by his barb. "That's why I'm curious about what she likes to do for fun outside of work."

He opens his mouth to retort, but Damon cuts in.

"Enough," he says firmly, and Gunnar turns back to his laptop. "You two need to stop fixating on her and wondering what she's doing. It's a waste of time. She's out of our lives now and not coming back."

"No, she's not," Gunnar protests. "Stop pretending our bond with her doesn't exist."

"I felt our connection at the library. She's our omega," I add.

"It's her scent that got us all," Damon growls. He closes his eyes and sighs, pinching the bridge of his nose with his fingers. "But that doesn't mean anything. She rejected us and didn't give a good reason why. She clearly said we weren't her type, so obviously, there's a mismatch in our scents."

"Has it ever occurred to you that maybe she went through something with an old pack?" I ask, annoyed that Damon would jump to conclusions so quickly.

"Yeah? Like what?" Damon challenges, glaring at me from across the room. "From the start, she was cagey, never answering questions honestly. For fuck's sake, she was hiding her omega designation. She clammed up when we asked why she didn't have a pack."

"It doesn't mean we should deny our connection to her," I say, taking my opportunity since he's been shutting Gunnar and me down. "She misses us."

"That's bullshit, and you know it, Max. There's something off about her, and I think we should keep our distance. She might be trouble."

"I think we should try to reach out to her," I say hopefully, knowing that Damon is still listening. "We probably came on a little strong at the library, so maybe we need to soften things. How about sending her some flowers?"

"Hmm, flowers might work on her," Gunnar says. "She's the sweetest and purest omega I've ever had the pleasure to knot."

"It's worth a shot," I say, grinning despite myself. "She might love them and finally give us a call."

"Or she'll simply throw them away," Damon mutters, still staring blankly at his computer screen. He's pretending to be interested in profiling a random creep, someone we could potentially target as our next mark, but I know he's barely paying attention.

"At the very least, we could stay friends with her," I say, ignoring Damon. I won't let him downplay this when I know he also felt the connection with Lena.

"And what if she throws them out?" Gunnar asks me.

"Then we keep trying," I reply, deciding to let the conversation rest for now and focusing instead on what I can scrounge up about Lena online.

I type her name and '*Willowstone Library*' into my search engine, but nothing comes up except that she works there. The library has a small website, but staff are only listed by their first names and job titles, yielding little to no results.

I'm intrigued by the lack of online information about our mysterious omega, but I know I won't let that stop me from finding out more about her.

# CHAPTER 13

**Lena**

I stare at my plate, twirling my fork mindlessly through my spaghetti bolognese.

It's another lonely night, as usual. My appetite has disappeared over the last couple of weeks after my heat with Damon and his pack.

Even though it's been weeks, I can't get them off my mind. Damon's smoldering gaze, Max's flirty smile, and Gunner's dominant touch all linger in my thoughts, and I can't seem to shake them.

I force a forkful of spaghetti into my mouth, but chewing feels like a chore, the food resembling wet yarn in my mouth.

To make matters worse, I've been experiencing a strange sensation for the past few weeks—like I'm being watched. I get the distinct impression that someone is observing me. The alphas weren't too happy after I turned them down and told them I didn't want to be their omega.

I hope they're not following me.

Even going to work, I'm extra cautious and wary of the

possibility that any of the alphas might be waiting in the parking lot or could show up at the library again.

If they are following me, I don't understand why they would be interested in me.

There's nothing I can offer them that they wouldn't find in another omega. It's not easy to erase the trauma I feel from my old pack. They abused me and shattered my self-esteem for years, resulting in me not feeling worthy enough to seek love and acceptance from a new pack.

Being out of the home intensifies the feeling of being watched.

Every time I go for a walk or head to the store to grab a few things for the apartment, the hairs on the back of my neck stand on end. My senses are already heightened, but not being able to pinpoint what's causing this unease makes me even more anxious.

My doorbell rings, jolting me out of my thoughts.

It rings again, and I freeze, my anxiety spiking. I'm not expecting any guests. If it were one of my neighbors, they would have just knocked. I push my cold food away, get up from the table, and head to the front door. Pressing the speaker button on my intercom system, I want to check who it is before letting them in.

"Hello?"

"Hi there," a female voice replies. "I have a delivery for a Miss Lena."

"Oh, of course," I say with a relieved sigh, buzzing her in. I really need to calm down and stop freaking out over nothing.

Moments later, I open the door to find the smiling face of a petite woman.

"These are for you," she says, handing me a bouquet, a box of chocolates, a bottle of perfume, and a small box tied with a ribbon.

"Oh!" I exclaim in surprise, taking in all the gifts. "Thank you!"

"You are one lucky girl," she says, gazing dreamily at the presents.

I sign for the delivery and close the door, overwhelmed by the gifts now cluttering my dining room table. But I quickly feel suspicious.

There's a card attached to the flowers, and I open it: *Thinking of you, beautiful Lena.*

Part of me is touched that they knew where to find me and went to such trouble to send me something, even though I ultimately rejected them.

I don't want any ties to them, so I swiftly walk across the kitchen floor and toss the flowers into the trash. I don't want them in my house. And if the alphas are watching me, I don't want them to get the wrong idea when they see flowers in a vase on my coffee table.

I walk back across the kitchen to grab the box of chocolates to throw away, but I hesitate when I pick them up. They're Belgian chocolates with a truffle center—delicious, no doubt—so I set them back down on the table, deciding to keep them as a treat for myself. I glance guiltily at my bowl of uneaten spaghetti.

Inside the box with the ribbon is a pair of earrings and a necklace. The earrings look like they could be diamonds, but I'm not sure. They look expensive, so I can't bear to throw away something so beautiful. I set the box aside with the perfume.

Seeing all these gifts sends a pang of loneliness through my heart. I hope the alphas will move on.

Despite my best efforts, I can't stop thinking about them, and by the looks of things, they haven't stopped thinking about me either. I should want them to move on, but a tiny, desperate part of me feels warm and fuzzy.

The rest of the afternoon passes slowly as I putter about my apartment, washing dishes and vacuuming. I treat myself to a few chocolates for dessert.

After a long, luxurious bath to wind down for the evening, I head into my room and drop the towel after drying myself. The box of jewelry catches my eye, and curiosity overcomes me. The diamond necklace looks big and magnificent as I clasp it around my neck. Admiring it in the mirror, I don't want to take it off just yet as the gem settles between my naked breasts. Feeling like a million bucks, I put on the earrings, admiring how they look as I preen in front of the mirror.

As I blow-dry my long auburn hair, I stare at the jewelry, thinking of Damon's last words to me and the intensity in his eyes: *"I just know we're fated to be together."*

### Gunnar

Lena looks so beautiful as I watch her from outside her bedroom window. Seeing her prance around her room in nothing but the jewelry I gave her turns me on, even though my mission is to keep a close eye on our omega.

Even though Damon is against this, I can't look the other way and pretend she isn't ours.

I know in my heart that she'll be my omega soon, and I can't bear to keep her out of my sight. Her safety is too important to me.

I've been standing outside her apartment all day, hiding in the shadows of the building and the nearby trees, watching her putter about the kitchen and the living room.

Seeing her angrily throw away the flowers surprised me; I wasn't sure whether to laugh or be offended. But watching her petite figure stand in front of the mirror, wearing nothing but the diamonds I bought her, makes me forgive her instantly.

The curvature of her breasts and hips nearly drove me wild. She looks stunning, and I watch her greedily as she bends over her nightstand to take a couple of pills while still adorned in the jewelry.

"Fuck," I whisper, watching her sweet ass bounce as she plops onto the bed. She doesn't turn off the light yet, and I'm glad because I want to keep watching.

She lay back on the bed, absentmindedly massaging her thigh with one hand while looking at her phone with the other. I watched eagerly as her thighs gradually separated, revealing her tiny pussy.

The same pussy I had ravaged weeks ago.

My cock hardens as I listen to her humming through the window and jiggling one of her legs, giving me a clearer view of her pussy. A stream of clear liquid ran down from her little hole to her ass.

*I need to taste her slick. I need her.*

After an hour of watching and waiting, Lena finally falls asleep, leaving the bedside lamp on. Knowing this is my chance, I creep toward the building, slowly opening the bedroom window, carefully sneaking in, and shutting it softly behind me.

She looks so peaceful lying on the bed.

I slowly climb onto the bed with her. Lena's deep asleep, her mouth slightly open, and her hair fanned across the pillow. Her thick diamond necklace sparkling around her slim neck.

*Fuck.*

My cock is rock hard from the scent of her secretions wafting from between her legs. The soft smell of vanilla drives my wolf crazy as I dip my head between her legs.

Hesitantly, I stick my tongue out to taste her, hoping not to wake her. I lightly touched the tip of my tongue to the center of her pussy, allowing her juices to flow delicately onto my taste buds. I want to groan with delight when the first drop falls onto my tongue.

I growl ferally against her pussy and freeze when she adjusts herself, spreading her legs wider for me.

I need to be more careful. But damn, I can't help it.

My cock jumps in my jeans as I kneel between her legs. Unzipping my fly, I grip myself as I dip my head between her legs once again after she starts to snore again.

She tastes phenomenal, so sweet on my tongue, and as I lick all around her folds, making sure to get every last drop. She moans in her sleep, and I push my tongue into her tight hole.

I push her thighs farther apart with both hands and stick my tongue inside her, drinking her sweet nectar up as my cock throbs.

"Gunnar?" Lena mumbles sleepily, her hand reaching my head, and I freeze. She curls her fingers into my hair, gripping me closer to her pussy.

I panic, thinking she's awake, but her eyes are still closed.

"Shh, Lena, it's just me," I whisper, kissing her inner thigh. "Relax, baby, enjoy your sleep. I only want to taste you. You taste like honey. I can't get enough."

"You're not supposed to be here," she mumbles sleepily with a small smile, opening her thighs wider to give me better access.

"I know, baby, but I can't stay away. Not when you taste this good. Let me make you feel good. I want to taste your cum on my tongue."

"Mmm, oh!" she whimpers when I start to lick her.

Her grip on my hair tightens as she grinds my face with her pussy. I'm more than happy to be there, licking around her opening and sucking her hard little clit into my mouth.

I'm beyond horny, aching to shove my raging cock into her tight hole and fuck her senseless, but I hold back, instead jerking myself off while I eat her out. I used the precum leaking from my cock as lube while I strok myself- Lena's sleepy whimpers and moans spurring me higher.

Sucking on her pussy is a delight. I need her to release all over my face as slick pours relentlessly from her hole. I turn my attention to her clit, which is peeking out now, swirling my wide tongue around and around her nub.

Her breathing hitches as I suck on her clit and push a finger into her pussy at the same time. I suck harder onto her clit, and she finally cums, shuddering beneath my tongue and releasing more slick into my mouth with a quiet squirt.

I moan at the taste of her and sit up, jerking off forcefully as I near my release. With a grunt, I orgasm, aiming directly at her pussy.

There's something so gratifying seeing my white hot seed splash onto her naked pussy, and she sighs when she feels it coat her skin as if she can't get enough of the feeling.

I smile, satisfied with the sick pleasure that seeing her covered in my cum gives me. Using my fingers, I push my cum into her still-drenched pussy. If I can't have her cum on my cock and knot her that way, I'm going to make damn sure she still takes my load.

"Oh yes, good girl," I purr quietly in the dark.

I want her pregnant, and the thought of seeing her belly round with my child makes me want to knot her.

Lena has fallen asleep again.

Satisfied with my work, I tuck the blanket around her and

kiss her forehead. I make my way to the window while shoving my cock back into my pants.

I was fucking lucky tonight, but I know that if Damon found out, he would be furious. I shrug as I close the window behind me and make my way back to my watch post. What he doesn't know won't hurt him.

# CHAPTER 14

**Damon**

"*Oh, Damon!" Lena cries, arching her back as I thrust into her. I'm fucking her hard, spreading her ass cheeks wide so she can take every inch of my thick cock in her tight pussy. She feels incredible, and the way she moans and cries with each thrust makes my length swell inside her, ready to knot her.*

*"You take my cock like such a good girl," I growl, pulling her head back by her hair. "Come for me, Lena. I want to feel you tighten around my shaft."*

*Her orgasm hits her hard, and she screams, her pussy clenching tightly around me. It feels too good, and my own orgasm races down until I erupt, knotting deep inside her and spilling my load. I tilt her head back again and sink my canines into her pale neck, marking her. She climaxes again at the sensation, hot tears spilling down her cheeks as she cries.*

I wake with a start, sitting upright in bed with my heart pounding and my chest heaving. Drenched in sweat, I realize I have the most potent erection I've ever woken up to, and it's almost painful.

Every night, these vivid dreams of Lena tease me and remind me of her. And each time I wake up, I'm left with an empty bed, a hard-on, and a longing for an omega who doesn't want me. I've never been this affected by an omega before.

The dreams, as much as they turn me on, worry me.

They could mean many things, but I know there's only one very real possibility.

*Lena is my fated mate.*

There's no denying it anymore. And now I'm hell-bent on changing her mind. I glance at the clock on my nightstand and see that it's just after one a.m.

Knowing it's useless to try and get back to sleep now, I throw the covers back and get out of bed. The bathroom light is bright against my eyes, but I squint through it and wash my face, trying to wake myself up further. I'm restless and on edge, and I know that the only way to wind down after that dream is to see Lena.

I need to check on her and make sure she's all right.

Max, our go-to tech guy, had done some sleuthing and figured out where she lives. It's a cute building in a good neighborhood, and any anxiety about her safety eased when Max showed me what he found.

The roads are quiet as I drive toward the part of town where Lena stays.

The moon is hidden behind clouds, and dappled half-light peeks out now and then as the clouds shift across the sky. This time of night is my favorite, so I don't rush, enjoying the smooth drive of my sedan on the open road.

Lena lives about thirty minutes from the city. When I approach her apartment building, I park about a block away so she doesn't recognize my vehicle. As I leave the car, I notice the night is calm, and the air is crisp, with a slight chill.

I stop across the street from her building and hide in the

shadow of a nearby tree. Looking up to where her apartment is, I see the light on. It's late, and I figured she would have gone to bed by now.

I wonder if I should go up and see her, thinking she might like the company, but movement out of the corner of my eye catches my attention and derails my train of thought. There, creeping out of what I suspect is Lena's bedroom window, is Gunnar.

He's in wolf form, jumping nimbly off her balcony and onto the grass below. I squint when I see that his dick is out, the purple head leaking with cum.

*What the fuck?!* I shake my head. Unbelievable.

I know I'm not in the right either, having come this far to check on her, but I'm going to have a seriously stern talk with my pack. We did not agree to sneak into her bedroom in the middle of the night and take advantage of her. I want her to come to us naturally, not because we break into her house. Part of me can't blame Gunnar for his actions, Lena is a delectable little snack, but I'm also annoyed that I wasn't the one to be in her bedroom.

Gunnar slinks away into the trees, and I turn to watch him go, but standing just a few feet from where he disappeared is another person.

Alarm goes through me when I see this second person.

This strange figure is tall, dressed in all black, and wearing a long jacket. They are also watching Lena's window the way I am.

*Could it be Max?* I shake my head. No, the height and build of this stranger don't match Max's. Not to mention, he wouldn't be hiding under dark clothes and a long jacket.

I don't recognize this person, and unease sinks into my stomach as I duck behind the nearest tree to avoid being seen. The stranger continues to watch her window as if they are looking for movement inside. They stay that way for quite some time, barely moving as they keep watch.

Pulling out my cell phone, I quickly take a picture of this person. *Could they be someone from Lena's old life, perhaps a member of her old pack?* Or could they be some kind of stalker, someone who saw her at the library or the store and followed her home? I don't like either option, but I hide behind the tree again, wary of giving my position away.

I peek from behind the tree again, hoping the stranger has left. Instead, I see they have turned away from watching Lena's window and now seem to be looking my way. I stiffen, wondering if I made any noise that caught their attention. I keep still, ready to kill if he comes my way.

Their unnatural stillness and focus make me wonder if this person is another werewolf, lending credibility to my theory that they could be one of Lena's old pack.

Eventually, after what seems like an eternity, the figure turns away from me and walks down the street, avoiding streetlights and sticking close to the shadows of the trees. I leave my hiding place and watch as they walk away, worry churning in my gut.

*Who the fuck are they, and why were they watching Lena's apartment? Were they waiting for someone else? Or were they waiting for Lena?*

Either way, I believe Lena is in danger. A low growl rips from my chest at the thought.

No one will harm her. If they do, I'll kill them.

I settle in across the street for the rest of the night, determined to keep watch so that I know she's safe. The night is long, but Lena's safety is my utmost priority, and I will make sure no harm comes to her.

# CHAPTER 15

### Lena

I stretch, waking up to a bright morning, but I suddenly notice that my inner thighs are sticky.

"What the hell?" I mutter as I push the blanket off my body to investigate. Spreading my legs apart, I see that my pussy is also covered in something, and I feel a pleasant soreness in my vagina.

Panicking, I stand up from the bed and notice stains on the mattress. My head feels foggy, and I reach up to touch the diamond necklace still around my neck.

I must have passed out hard last night not to have taken it off before sleeping.

There's a particular smell in the air, like sandalwood, and suddenly, a memory of my dream emerges. Gunnar sneaking into my bedroom last night comes to mind, and I blush, thinking of his wide tongue and the way he licked me clean after making me orgasm.

My pussy starts to throb, and my heart rate speeds up.

*Wait, was that real? Or just a dream?*

I glance over at my bedroom window, noticing it's slightly ajar, and my heart races as I quickly close it.

Gunnar was here last night. *It wasn't a dream.*

Now that I know for sure, I realize it must have been him and his pack following me around town this entire time. I need to move out of this state to escape because alphas never like to be rejected.

Hopping into the shower, I feel a little sad to wash off all the sticky residue from my legs and private parts. The memory of Gunnar eating me out last night makes me happy for some reason, even though I rejected him and his pack.

*I want him, but I don't at the same time.*

---

Today has been a busy day of running errands.

The last chore was grocery shopping, especially since I needed to stock up on essential items like toiletries and cleaning supplies. Now that I'm back home, I'm exhausted and looking forward to putting my feet up on the couch with a good book once everything has been put away.

I unlock my apartment door and push it open with my shoulder, propping it open with the doorstop as I bend down to grab a few grocery bags.

The bags are heavy, and I set them down in the hallway when I notice that the glass door leading to my balcony is open.

Confusion washes over me as I stare at it. I don't remember ever opening the balcony door.

Suddenly, I feel on edge, wondering if Gunnar or any of his packmates are back for me. An eerie sensation takes over, and I glance down at the scar on my arm, nervously running a finger along the puckered skin. The scar tissue occasionally tingles, as if my skin remembers how I got it, but this feels different.

It feels more visceral as if reacting to the air around me. I try to shrug it off.

I step toward the front door again to retrieve the rest of my groceries when a bang in the kitchen stops me in my tracks. I freeze, wondering what the noise could be. My heart races when I hear more noise coming from the kitchen.

*There's someone here.*

I turn toward the kitchen and tiptoe in that direction, trying to stay as quiet as possible. At the doorway, I peek inside and see a tall figure wearing a dark trench coat rifling through my pantry. His back is turned to me.

I can't see his face, but something about him causes my heart rate to spike. Suddenly, I turn and run out the front door, leaving my groceries strewn across the floor.

I don't care about anything except getting away. I fly down the stairs, my heart pumping and breaths coming fast in panic.

My only goal is to get as far away from the building as possible.

I hear someone running behind me, but I don't look back as I wrench open the main entrance door and dash into the daylight. In my haste, I forget about the two stairs leading up to the door and trip over my feet, tumbling down them and landing in a heap at the bottom.

"Ow!" I cry out, feeling pain shoot up my ankle as I land awkwardly on it. Tears prick my eyes when I try to stand, but it hurts too much to do more than balance precariously. I know it's twisted, but the joint is already starting to swell and turn red.

I slump down again, ready to call for help or crawl away

from the building. But when I look up to do just that, I see Damon standing over me, his face a picture of concern.

"Damon?" I ask tearfully, wondering what he's doing here.

"Lena, darling, what have you done to yourself?" he asks, reaching down to help me.

I wave him away and try to stand up again. I can't let him help me. I don't even want him here.

"It's nothing," I say, struggling to my feet. "I just slipped, but I'm fine."

My ankle gives out from underneath me, but before I can hit the ground again, Damon catches me in his arms, the scent of him reminding me of that fateful night.

*The strange alpha who carried me in the rain. The alpha who took me to the hospital that night.*

"You're not fine," he points out. "That ankle looks twisted."

"It's probably just a sprain," I say breathlessly as I watch him examine my ankle. Damon prods my ankle gently, and I hiss in pain.

"We should get you to a hospital. Right away."

"Damon, I'm fine— Oh!" I squeak in surprise when he scoops me into his arms and carries me to his car parked across the street.

I look back at my apartment building one last time before he places me gently inside the car, but I don't see the mysterious figure again.

My heart is still racing, but I feel calmer knowing Damon is with me. He rounds the front of the car, gets into the driver's seat, and starts the engine.

"What were you doing out there?" he asks as we pull away. Willowstone Hospital is about twenty-five minutes from where I stay, and I know he won't stop asking questions until I give him an answer.

"I live there. I was bringing in groceries," I reply, turning to look out the window. "You shouldn't even know where I live!"

"Why were you running down the stairs like a ghost was chasing you?"

"So you weren't the one in my kitchen?" I ask slowly.

He glances at me, a frown creasing his brows. "What do you mean?"

"There was someone in my apartment," I whisper, anxiety clawing at my throat. "I was running away when I tripped and fell down the stairs in front of the building. I thought it was you."

"Who do you think was in your apartment?" Damon asks, his voice turning serious as he focuses on the road.

Either he's telling the truth or is a very good liar. But he is dressed differently from the person in my kitchen. Damon's in a sharp suit while the person in my kitchen looked worse for wear.

"I have no idea," I reply lightly. This is delicate territory. If Zorin found me, I'd have to sleep with one eye open.

"Well, it wasn't me in your apartment," he growls. "I've never been inside. Don't worry. I'll track him down and take care of it."

"Wait, then, what were you doing outside my home?" I ask suspiciously, wincing from the pain. Being near him again sends my body into a frenzy.

Deep down, I'm longing for him to hug me and comfort me despite the throbbing in my ankle.

"To protect you."

Warmth spreads through me at the thought of being shielded by this imposing alpha with a fierce expression.

My body tingles, but the pain in my ankle cuts through the moment, forcing me to focus on it and not fall in love right here and now.

"I don't need your help finding whoever was in my apartment," I say stubbornly.

A part of me still suspects it was *him* in my kitchen and that he jumped off the balcony to cut me off at the entrance to my building, throwing off his trench coat. It feels almost too convenient that he showed up at that moment, which makes me suspicious.

"Lena," Damon growls, "I'm not taking no for an answer. Whoever was inside your home could be dangerous. You need protection, and my pack and I are the best for the job. I don't care if you don't want to be with us— we will keep you safe."

"I'm not your omega, so I'm not your responsibility."

"Yes, you are," he replies, refusing to budge.

"Fine, wear yourself out," I huff, crossing my arms over my chest and turning back to the window. I don't like it, but I'll let it slide. If he wants to waste his time caring for me, that's on him.

---

Twenty minutes later, we finally arrive at the hospital.

"Stay inside the car. I'll help you," Damon barks when I reach for the car door handle. I watch him walk around the car, clearly wary of my next move.

He opens the door, and I take his offered hand.

Once I'm out of the car, Damon scoops me up in his arms and carries me straight into the emergency room. In his arms, I can't help but feel safe. His warmth seeps into my soul, invigorating me in a way I've never felt with my ex-alphas.

The waiting room is thankfully empty, and a nurse quickly triages me. I'm relieved because the pain in my ankle is worsening and has turned an ugly purple color.

"Miss Lena?" the nurse calls a few moments later, checking her clipboard before scanning the waiting room.

Damon stands while holding me, and she smiles kindly when she spots us. "Doctor Roman will see you now."

She wheels a wheelchair toward me, and Damon gently places me in it. The nurse pushes the wheelchair, and I have no idea if Damon is following behind us.

But as soon as we enter the room, Damon is there. He helps me onto the bed and settles into the chair in the corner. His knees are spread dominantly as if declaring that I'm his.

*But I'm not his.*

The nurse leaves after taking my vitals, and I turn to him.

"What are you doing?" I ask, panicking as he makes himself comfortable, leaning back in his chair with his arms crossed.

"I'm staying with you," he replies as if it's obvious.

I shake my head. "That's not necessary. You've done enough just getting me here."

"Lena—"

"Please," I beg. I'm embarrassed to be in this situation, and the fact that he won't leave my side is making it worse. "I just really want some privacy. Today has been a lot. Thank you for all your help, but I'd prefer it if you left."

He sighs and stands again, running a hand through his hair.

"All right," he concedes, walking over to me and giving me a peck on the forehead. "I'll be in the waiting room, but if you need anything, just call."

I breathe a sigh of relief. Damon makes it hard to think whenever he's around. I can barely clear my head from everything that's happening. Why was Damon at my apartment? And who the hell was that person in my kitchen?

I'm alone with my thoughts for only a moment when the doctor walks in shortly after Damon leaves.

"Hello, I'm Doctor Roman," he says with a kind smile. He

has a short grey beard and gentle brown eyes. "What can I do for you, Lena?"

I gesture toward my ankle sheepishly. "I think I've sprained my ankle. I was running and tripped down the stairs."

"Hmm," he hums, examining my ankle and gently pressing the swollen spot. "So it would seem. Before prescribing any medication, I need to take your urine sample."

He helps me off the bed and into the en-suite bathroom, handing me a small cup before closing the door.

Hobbling to the toilet, I fill the cup, wash my hands, and then open the bathroom door, where Doctor Roman is waiting to help me back onto the exam bed.

"Thanks," I say, grateful for his help.

"I'll be right back," he says with a smile before leaving the room.

My ankle throbs dully as I wait.

The only sounds in the emergency room are the steady rhythm of my heartbeat and the slight drip of the sink faucet in the bathroom. I clutch my ankle tightly, hoping it will help ease the pain.

Doctor Roman returns a few minutes later with some wrapping for my ankle.

"The lab tells me that you're pregnant," he says, and I freeze. "Are you aware of that fact?"

The world around me narrows until the only thing I see is the doctor with a smile on his face.

"I'm...what?" I ask in shock.

"You're pregnant," he replies cheerfully as he wraps my ankle. "I had to run a quick pregnancy test before I could prescribe painkillers. You only have a mild sprain, so an ACE bandage should do the trick. I recommend taking the pain medicine three times a day with meals. Be sure to keep your ankle elevated and apply ice to reduce swelling. Come see me if you still have issues in a few days."

I'm barely listening to a word he's saying as I contemplate the possibility of a baby.

*What the hell does this mean for me?*

I never intended to get pregnant, although after all the sex I've been having, it doesn't come as a complete surprise. I place a hand over my belly and think of Damon.

*What do I say to him? How will he react?*

# CHAPTER 16

**Damon**

I'm sitting in the waiting room as Lena is getting looked at by the doctor. People are being rushed in by ambulance, but all I can think about is my sweet omega. She *will* be mine even though she doesn't know it.

If the stranger hadn't been in her home, she would never have run down the stairs and hurt herself. A low growl rumbles in my chest at the thought of that stranger taking advantage of Lena.

*If he ever hurts her, I'll kill him.*

I find it strange that someone else was watching her besides Gunnar, Max, and me. With how much Lena keeps to herself, it strikes me as odd that anyone would have her on their radar.

A door down the hall opens, and the doctor is rolling her out in a wheelchair.

He brings her to where I'm sitting. Something is wrong. She looks both stunned and sheepish, avoiding eye contact with me when she comes to a stop in front of me. Now I'm on high alert.

"You must be the father—congratulations!" says the overly enthusiastic doctor.

I stare at him, not understanding what he's telling me. I glance at Lena, who has gone bright red, expressing absolute mortification.

"Damon, we should get going," she mumbles, her face aflame. She struggles to her feet and grabs my arm, trying to tug me toward the exit doors. I stand my ground, unwilling to leave until I get clarity from the doctor.

It's almost comical how Lena is trying to drag me away with her tiny hand on my arm, but I don't laugh, needing to get to the bottom of this.

"I don't understand, Doctor," I say, speaking to him while holding her to me so she won't fall. "What do you mean?"

He glances at Lena and frowns, clearly confused by her reaction to me. He clears his throat and straightens his spine.

"I'm sorry," he says, "but I'm needed elsewhere. Lena, please call me anytime if you experience any pain or if your symptoms worsen. I'll see you soon." He gives her a tight smile and hurries off.

"What did the doctor mean?" I ask once he's gone, my curiosity piqued. Several people in the waiting room are now eagerly listening to us, but this can't wait.

"Mean what?"

"By 'you must be the father,'" I clarify. She knows exactly what's happening, as my chest pumps with adrenaline. "Are you pregnant?"

"I have no idea what he's talking about," Lena says, shrugging and trying to appear nonchalant, but I can read in her eyes that she's clearly lying. "Maybe you misunderstood him."

"Oh, I heard him well enough."

"Damon, can we please go?" Lena begs quietly, glancing around the waiting room. "My ankle is killing me."

She gestures down at her bandaged ankle, but I don't budge. I need answers to what I'm starting to suspect may be true.

"We're not going anywhere until you tell me what the doctor meant."

"Oh my god, everyone's watching us," she whispers harshly, looking away.

"Lena, look at me," I growl, and she finally meets my gaze, her face bright pink.

"Fine, I'm pregnant," she whispers, embarrassment clear on her face. "Doctor Roman confirmed it with a pregnancy test."

"Oh fuck," I say, my heart racing as I struggle not to howl for joy. I want to embrace Lena and kiss her senselessly, but I calm myself, seeing that she still looks flustered by the news.

I immediately pick her up and carry her out of the emergency room, away from curious eyes.

"What are you thinking?" she asks worriedly.

"You are the most amazing thing that has ever happened to me," I say, my heart soaring at the thought of a little one stumbling around my home, learning to walk. "My omega."

"No, I'm not your omega," she says as I gently place her in the passenger seat of my car. My excitement dwindles at the realization that her safety is now paramount.

I can't let anything happen to her or our pup. If I wasn't sure about my decision to watch over her before, I am sure as hell now.

"Alright, if that's the case, you'll need to stay with us during the pregnancy at least," I say firmly. Maybe she'll eventually fall in love with us and get comfortable.

"Why?" she asks in protest, her eyes widening.

I cup her jaw, stroking her cheek tenderly with my thumb. "I want you to be safe, and you're always safest with a pack of alphas."

When I enter the driver's seat and drive toward the pack loft, she looks deep in thought. For the entire ride, she remains silent, and it worries me.

"Please don't tell your pack," Lena says softly.

"About?"

"The baby."

"Why?" I ask, flabbergasted. This was our baby, and they should know the good news right away.

"I want them to know eventually, but I just need a moment to soak it all in," she says simply, and I nod as I turn left.

"I can accept that," I say, and she lets out a long sigh, leaning back against her seat. I'm confused by her, but I'll play by her rules for now.

---

Max and Gunnar are waiting outside our home when we arrive, and I can tell that Lena is surprised to see them.

Max rushes to open her door and helps her out as she leans against his arm.

"This is a surprise," she says, breathless, but I can tell she's excited to see him again from the way her scent turns muskier and sweeter. She's aroused to see my pack again, which is a good sign.

*A really good sign.* Because I'm hard as fuck for her, especially knowing that she's pregnant with my pack's baby.

"Damon called us while you were at the emergency room," Gunnar says. "How's your ankle feeling?"

"It doesn't hurt as much anymore. I took a pill on the way here," Lena replies. "But I'd like to go home now, please."

Alarm spikes through me at her rebellious nature.

"I already said you're coming home with us," I say.

"I don't want to go home with you!" she exclaims, pulling away from Max and leaning against the car instead.

"There's someone out there following you. I know you may hate me, Lena, but your safety is important to us."

"I don't hate you," she mumbles, breaking eye contact. "I'm just not ready to be part of a pack. I'm perfectly safe as I am. I can take care of myself."

"But what happened?" Max asks urgently.

She bites her lower lip, nibbling on it for a moment before taking a deep breath and steeling herself.

"When I told you that I thought someone was in my apartment, I actually saw them. They were standing in my kitchen, going through the kitchen cabinets. I got scared, so I ran," she confesses, tears sparkling in her eyes.

"Gunnar," I bark, and he stands at attention, his gaze hardening. "Go check Lena's apartment. Search everywhere. If you find anyone, you know what to do."

He nods and turns to leave, but Max interjects.

"I'll go," he offers instead. "Gunnar can stay with Lena."

"I don't care who goes. I just want to get Lena to safety and inside the penthouse," I snap. "We need to keep our omega safe. Is that clear?"

Max and Gunnar nod, and with a shared look, Max gets back into his car and races out of the parking lot.

"Come," I say, walking toward my home. Gunnar takes Lena's hands, preparing to lift her in his arms if she doesn't comply.

"Damon, please," she whines. "This isn't necessary. I don't need to live with you. All my things are at home; you can take me there. I'll be fine."

"Max will get everything you need from your apartment,

love," I say calmly, unlocking the door to our penthouse with a code. "I promise he won't leave anything behind."

"Please let me go. I just want to go home. I promise I'll be okay," her voice high, like she's about to go into hysterics.

"Let me show you around," says Gunnar. "You can tell me where you want to build your nest."

"No!" she yells, pulling her hand out of Gunnar's grip. "I'm not staying here! Why can't you all leave me alone?!"

"Lena, baby—"

"Leave. Me. ALONE!" Lena screams, stumbling backward. Gunnar's eyes widen in surprise at her forcefulness, and I'm also shocked. "I don't understand why you're all so obsessed with being with me! Just let me go!"

She turns and tries to push past me at the doorway. Damn it, she's putting up one hell of a fight despite her aroused scent filling the air.

Lena pushes against my chest with all her strength, trying to get me to move. I calmly wrap my hands around her upper arms, alarmed by her desire to escape us.

"What are you made of, bricks?" she hisses when I don't move an inch. She tries to push me again but almost topples over, grabbing my muscular forearm to steady herself.

My arousal heightens from her touch and her enticing scent, but I try to calm my erection, not wanting to agitate her further.

"Lena, you're stressing yourself out for no reason," I say, looking into her tearful eyes. "You don't need to worry—we won't force you to be our omega. You know that deep down, honey."

I feel my arousal intensify when her grip on me tightens.

She glances down, her eyes widening at the sight, and I groan, realizing that my erection might have crossed a line that she's not quite ready for.

To my surprise, she licks her lips and starts to breathe heavily, her breasts heaving with every breath.

*God, I want* her.

The intoxicating scent of wild honey and vanilla fills the air, and I know Lena feels the same way I do. I glance down and see a wet spot on the front of her white leggings. She is soaked, ripe, and ready for me.

She follows my gaze and blushes when she sees the evidence of her arousal on her leggings.

"Are you sure you want to leave?" I growl lowly, placing my hands on her hips. She blushes and shakes her head quietly.

I caress her back, pleased with her answer, loving how her breathing hitches with my touch. She turns away from me to face Gunnar, freezing in shock to find him already naked, his erection proudly jutting out.

She lets out a little gasp of surprise, and he grins, his smile feral.

"Don't be shy, baby," he croons, taking a step toward her. "It's nothing you haven't seen before."

"What makes you think I even want you guys?" Lena says breathlessly, but this time without the venom in her voice.

"Right here," I say, reaching around to cup her pussy, rubbing the wet spot on her leggings. "This shows me that you want it. You want us to knot you, don't you, honey?"

Although I know she won't admit it, Lena is turned on too. Her scent lingers in the air, and the wet patch on the front of her leggings grows more saturated at the sight of Gunnar's angry cock on display.

"No, I don't," she says, taking a step back, but she crashes into my chest. Lena may claim she wants to leave, but her actions suggest otherwise. Her defiance turns me on and makes me even more desperate to pin her down and fuck her.

"Where do you think you're going, hmm?" I ask, pulling

her toward me. I bend down and kiss her neck, inhaling her intoxicating scent.

"Oh god," she mumbles, her head lolling back against my chest while I kiss along her shoulder. I press my hard-on into her back, making her aware of the effect she has on me.

Lena groans and pushes back, rubbing her ass against me wantonly while her eyes remain locked on Gunnar. She may have wanted to leave, but she's not going anywhere now.

# CHAPTER 17

### Lena

I tried. I really tried.

But the feeling of Damon's hot alpha body pressing against my ass is turning me on.

He's huge and hard, and my pussy clenches at the memory of him inside me, stretching me to my limit. My mouth waters as I glance at Gunnar- I can tell from the look on his face that he's going to knot my ass.

My asshole tingles in sync with my pussy, and I can't help but rub myself harder against Damon.

*I want them both inside me.*

I always feel hypersexual around the alphas, but this time, it feels different. My mind is fuzzy, and I know the pain medication I took at the hospital has weakened my inhibitions.

I'm desperate to have two thick cocks filling me this moment. I can sense their desperation, too, because of how hard they are.

Damon wraps an arm around my waist, pulling me tightly

against him while using his other hand to rub my pussy over the front of my leggings.

It feels so good, and I whine in pleasure as I rock my hips in sync with his movements. He chuckles darkly in my ear, nipping my earlobe with his teeth.

"You're such a needy thing, aren't you?" he rumbles, his chest vibrating against my back. "Your sweet pussy is dripping for us."

Gunnar approaches slowly, a wild look in his eyes as he rakes his gaze down my body, stopping at the wet patch between my legs.

"Mm, you look so juicy, baby," he groans. "So ripe and ready to be eaten."

I feel Damon nod behind me. "Go ahead, Gunnar," he says. "You do the honors."

Gunnar grins, winking at me before shifting into his wolf form.

My breath catches in my throat when he approaches and rips my leggings down my legs with his teeth. The sound of fabric ripping echoes through the giant penthouse, making my pussy throb.

I bite my lower lip as Gunnar gives me a wolfish smirk before grabbing my panties in his teeth and tearing them off as well. I'm horny for him, and my pussy clenches immediately when the cool air hits me. Drool drips from the corners of his mouth as he tastes the slick from my panties, and I blush.

"Spread your legs for him, sweetheart," Damon says, gently prying my legs apart with one foot. He's careful with my ankle, ensuring I keep all my weight on him while I stand in front of him, legs wide open, with my pussy on full display for Gunnar.

I know I should feel embarrassed or ashamed to be in this situation with them, but all I feel is an overwhelming horniness that makes it hard to think straight. Damon is a solid wall of muscle behind me, keeping me in place, while Gunnar looks at me and licks his lips as if I'm his last meal.

I grip Damon's forearms for balance as Gunnar shoves his nose between my legs. He sniffs, growling deeply, and then licks my pussy in one long swipe with his massive werewolf tongue.

I cry out from the sensation. His tongue is rough and firm, licking from my asshole to my clit. I've never felt anything like this before, but the strangeness doesn't stop me from shuddering under his tongue, desperate to come on his face.

"Oh god," I groan as he tastes my pussy.

"Such a good girl," Damon murmurs, spreading my ass cheeks. "Does it feel good to have Gunnar licking your pussy like this?"

I nod, sucking in a sharp breath when I feel Damon's finger at my anus.

"Oh!"

"Relax, baby," he says, coating my asshole with my juices. "Just relax and let go."

He squeezes my ass, and just then, Gunnar shoves his tongue deep into my pussy. I scream, pleasure pulsing through me, and he shifts back into human form, his head still between my legs. I stare down at him, my heart racing, and his steel-gray eyes look back at me with pure lust.

---

Damon pulls my shirt up and over my bra, then tugs it down until my breasts spill out of the cups. My nipples are hard, and he groans at the sight, taking one between his fingers and pinching it.

I moan, the sting of pain shooting straight to my clit.

"I fucking love your tits, baby," he says, wetting a finger in his mouth before rubbing it around the hard nub. "Your tits are so perfect that I want to shove my cock between them and fuck them."

My pussy clenches at his words. The thought of him fucking me in that way makes me even wetter and more excited.

"Our sweet omega likes it when we talk dirty to her," says Gunnar, coming up for air, his lips shiny from my juices. "Look how fucking soaked it makes her pretty cunt."

He dips his head again and licks along my pussy folds, making me moan.

"Oh, Gunnar," I shout when he swirls my clit around and around with his tongue.

"Let me clean this up for you," he mumbles against my swollen clit. "I want you to make a mess all over my face."

I gasp when he lifts my leg with the sprained ankle over his shoulder, giving him better access to my pussy.

"Hmm, the doctor did say to keep your leg elevated," Damon chuckles when he sees what Gunnar is doing.

My giggle turns into a moan when he starts playing with my nipples again, pinching and pulling them away from my body, making them even harder.

Between the two alphas, I feel an orgasm building from deep within my core.

With one hard suck on my clit and a well-timed tug on my now-oversensitive nipples, my orgasm crashes into me, and I scream out my pleasure, soaking Gunnar's face in my slick.

My legs start to shake, but he continues to lick me, only pulling away when I beg him to stop.

"I love your juices, baby," Gunnar says. "I can't get enough of your taste, sweet thing."

I feel weak after my intense orgasm, but Damon doesn't

allow me to rest for long when he turns me around to face him.

In one swift move, he picks me up, strides over to the nearest couch, and sits down, straddling me across his thighs.

"I want you to ride me, baby," he says, lifting me so that I'm hovering over his cock. He aligns himself with my entrance. "Is your ankle okay like this?"

I nod, adjusting myself for comfort.

"I'm perfectly fine," I say as he positions me over his cock. I'm nearly drooling, wanting him inside me as soon as possible.

"Good," he replies, and without warning, he slams me down onto his stiff length, my mouth popping open in surprise.

"Oh god!" I scream, feeling his length moving inside of me. No matter how wet and ready I am, Damon's cock always fills me to the brim, pleasuring me to the point of pain. He groans as he feels my tight heat sink down on him, his eyes smoldering as he gazes at my bouncing breasts.

"You're so fucking tight," grunts Damon, shoving more of himself into my pussy.

Suddenly, I feel my ass cheeks being spread and look back to see Gunnar behind me, a look of total concentration on his face as he rubs his finger around my asshole.

"I'm going to fuck this delicious little rosebud," he growls, spitting onto my sphincter to lube the area.

My heart races with anticipation as I feel slick slowly seeping out from my ass, the hornier I become.

Damon fucks me leisurely, slowly thrusting in and out of my pussy while Gunnar teases my back entrance, finally pushing a finger into my ass when he's gotten it nice and wet.

"Oh fuck," I moan, my pussy clenching involuntarily around Damon's cock. My fingers tighten around his forearms, and I lean forward, allowing Gunnar to have better access to my ass.

"Do you like what he's doing to your ass?" Damon growls, his dark eyes intense as he lifts me up and back down onto his giant cock.

"Uh-huh," I whimper, rocking my hips so that I can feel him deeper inside me.

"Greedy girl," Gunnar snarls, slapping my ass. It stings, but I enjoy the sensation and release another gush of wetness from my pussy and ass. I'm so fucking horny that I can feel the slick dripping from my anus and probably onto their beautiful couch.

"Your couch is going to be messed up," I say worriedly as Damon takes my breath away, shoving me onto his cock again.

"That can be replaced," growls Damon, pushing his mouth against my hair. "But you can never be replaced."

Never in my wildest dreams did I ever think I would find myself here again, but I can't imagine being anywhere else but between these two gorgeous alphas.

Gunnar groans when he sees the mess I'm making on Damon's cock and the couch as I squirt everywhere.

"I think our sweet girl is ready for a big fat cock in her ass," he says hungrily. "Isn't that right, baby?"

"Oh God, please," I beg, squirming on Damon's lap.

He stops fucking me for a moment and spreads my ass again, giving Gunnar the all-clear.

"Go ahead, Gunnar. Stuff her tight little hole. I want her to feel the two of us pumping her together."

Gunnar slowly slides his cock into my asshole, nudging the tip inside first, making me moan in pleasure. I stiffen a little when he pushes more of him inside me.

"Relax for me, Lena," he commands. "Your asshole is a

little tense. There's plenty of slick seeping out, so I know you're not in pain."

"It's not painful. I'm just not used to it," I say, squirming from the uncomfortable sensation of him penetrating me from behind. "Oh!"

He pushes the rest of his huge cock inside of me with a low growl while biting my ear.

"So good," Gunnar groans, and I'm overcome with a wave of pleasure, feeling both alphas stuffed inside of me. "Such a greedy little omega, aren't you? You're clenching so tight, not wanting to let us go."

It was true. A part of me has craved to be sandwiched between the two of them, letting them fuck and knot me senseless.

Damon lifts me by the hips using his alpha strength, picking me up and shoving me onto their waiting cocks. Then they start to move in tandem, thrusting into me with rhythm as I grip Damon's forearms, his white shirt drenched in sweat.

"I want to see your muscles," I say to Damon, and he immediately rips off his shirt with a growl, making me smile.

My holes are stretched to the brim, and I can only writhe against Damon's chest as they wring every inch of pleasure from my body.

They can do whatever they want to me at this moment. I want it.

"Beautiful," says Damon, staring at my face as I moan from the intensity of them stretching me. I want to feel their knots soon so I can be stretched even more. "It's like your body was made just for us."

"Such a good girl," mutters Gunnar. "I'm going to knot in your ass and watch my cum drip down into your pussy tonight. Imagine if you lived with us- you'll get this every moment of every day."

Their dirty words of pleasure spur me higher, and just when I think I can't take it anymore, I orgasm for the second time, crying out my release as I clench tightly around their cocks.

Gunnar speeds up his pace, slamming into me until he stills, grunting his pleasure into my ear. Damon follows not long after, filling me with so much cum that I feel some of it leak out and drip down onto Damon's thighs.

I slump onto Damon's chest, languid and wrung out.

"Your poor couch," I mumble, and his chest rumbles with laughter beneath me.

"It's okay. It's nothing that can't be cleaned."

---

Thirty minutes later, a companionable silence falls over us, and I can feel I'm on the verge of falling asleep when a strange noise sounds from the front door.

"Is that Max?" I ask, sitting up between Damon and Gunnar. Damon quickly pauses the movie we were watching on low volume.

Damon and Gunnar glance at each other, making me nervous.

The noise sounds again, and Damon puts a finger over his lips, indicating to keep quiet. It sounds like someone was trying to turn the knob to the front door, but I saw an access pad on the way inside and assumed it locked automatically when the door closed behind us.

"I'm going to check it out," Damon says quietly. He stands and dresses again, checking the living room windows before heading outside.

"It's not Max," says Gunnar in reply to my question, his body stiff with alarm. "Can't scent him."

Damon returns after a few minutes, looking confused but not all that alarmed.

"There wasn't anything," he still looking alarmed. "I will check the outside. Keep an eye on her, Gunnar. Make sure she doesn't run away."

"Excuse me?" I say indignantly.

Gunnar, sensing my anxiety, pulls me closer and kisses the top of my head. "Hey, it's all right, Lena. You're safe here with us. Even if anyone *did* manage to break in, they'll need to go through me. And do I look measly and small to you?"

He flexes his arms, and I smile as I touch his biceps.

"It could be a little bigger," I say sarcastically, and he growls as he scoops me off the couch in one swoop.

"It's time for your bath, little omega," he mutters, sounding miffed that I didn't play along, and I smile to myself.

Gunnar carries me to the main bathroom just off the living room, where a beautiful clawfoot tub sits in the middle. He turns the taps on full, adds some bubble bath, and fills the tub about three-quarters of the way. After checking to make sure the temperature is just right, he removes the bandages from my sprained ankle and then lifts me into the bath.

Even though I plan to leave eventually, I need to get clean.

I moan as I sink into the water, the heat and bubbles easing the aches in my muscles.

"Mhm," I sigh, closing my eyes and tipping my head to rest it on the back of the tub. Gunnar doesn't say anything, and when I open my eyes to see if he's still in the bathroom, I find him watching me with an intense look in those steel-gray eyes. "What?"

I instantly feel self-conscious about the way he's looking at me.

"You sound so fucking sexy when you moan," he says, and I feel my face heat from his praise. Gunnar grabs a loofah, dips it in the water, and begins to wash me. I relax further into the water as he swipes the loofah over me in long, slow strokes around each breast. "Such beautiful tits."

I close my eyes, relaxing back against the tub.

But suddenly, I feel something long and hot being pressed in the middle of my chest.

"What the...?" I open my eyes in alarm, seeing Gunnar's cock placed right between my boobs.

"Squeeze your tits around me, babe," he says huskily. I'm shocked to see that he's now standing in the water, completely naked, with me. He rubs my shoulders with the loofah as I press a palm against my breasts, squeezing tight around his heavy cock.

Squeezing harder, I watch as his pre-cum slides down my chest, disappearing into the water.

"Do you like it like this?" I ask him.

"Enough," he says, and my cheeks heat with embarrassment when he pulls himself away and steps out of the tub.

*Did I mess it up for him in some way?* I'm confused, but I don't want to show it as he aggressively reaches between my legs in the water, spreading them apart.

His feral alpha side is taking over as he rubs my pussy with the loofah with fast, hard strokes. His breathing is heavy, and I'm getting a little worried.

"Why are you quiet?" I ask him in a squeaky voice as he drops the loofah and inserts two fingers into my pussy. "Are you mad at me or something?"

"You're not leaving me. You're *my* omega. Our omega," he says, pushing his fingers deep inside of me to prove a point.

"Oh, moons," I moan, my head falling back against his muscular arms as he penetrates me deeper and deeper.

"Say you won't leave me," he growls, and my heart beats faster when I hear the possessiveness in his tone.

"I won't," I gasp, and he kisses my neck deeply as he withdraws his fingers from my aching hole. I have no idea why I'm promising him this when I vowed never to be with another pack. "I'll at least give it a few days. To give you a chance."

"I won't disappoint you. I promise you, babe," he says eagerly. He lifts me out of the water and sets me gently onto the tiled floor as he grabs a towel. "Just give us a chance."

Once I'm dry, he carries me into one of the bedrooms and lays me gently on the bed, grabbing a bottle of lotion and squirting some onto his hand.

He begins to rub it into my skin, massaging me as he does so.

I allow myself to relax into the mattress, grateful for all the pampering I'm receiving. My old pack never did anything like this for me, and the difference between the alphas is striking.

The smell of mango-peach lotion fills the air. Gunnar's touch turns me on, and I can feel my pussy getting wet as his hands softly squeeze my thighs, making them jiggle while I lay on my back.

"I can smell your sweet pussy," he growls, looking up at me. There's a fire in his eyes that only makes me feel hotter. "Is my touch making you feel good, sweet girl?"

I nod, not breaking eye contact with him. "Yes."

"Then why don't you spread your legs and let me taste you again?"

Spreading my legs willingly for him while not in heat scares me that I still want him. Dipping his head between my thighs, he's already licking me- his tongue on my pussy.

He licks around my opening, sucking on my clit before pushing two fingers inside me.

"Oh, Gunnar," I cry out, grinding myself onto his hand so his fingers could go even deeper. He blows on my clit to heighten the sensation.

"You're enjoying this too much, baby," he growls excitedly. "You need me to make you cum. Don't you, sweet Lena?"

"Yes!" I cry, arching my back when he curls his fingers up and hits my G-spot, making me see stars. "I need it. I need it so bad."

"You need it, huh? Well then, I guess I'd better give it to you."

He lowers his head and sucks my clit with his mouth, his fingers pumping into me furiously as he drives me closer and closer to orgasm. It doesn't take me long until I shatter, coming hard on his hand and screaming his name. He draws my orgasm out, continuing to lick and suck my clit while he fingers me until I can't take it anymore and push his head away.

"No more," I beg. "It's too much."

"Mmm, but you taste so delicious. I want every drop."

I watch him suck my juices off his fingers through half-lidded eyes, relaxed and sleepy from being thoroughly fucked and cared for. He smiles when he's done, rebandaging my ankle and draping a comforter over my naked body.

"Sleep now, love," he murmurs, kissing my forehead. "We'll all be here when you wake up."

# CHAPTER 18

**Damon**

"Is she asleep?" I ask Gunnar as he steps into the living room, dressed in fresh clothes.

"Yes," Gunnar replies, flopping onto the couch and staring at the television screen beside me.

An action movie plays, but I'm not focused on it.

I'm preoccupied with thoughts of Lena and the stranger she encountered in her apartment this morning. I have a bad feeling about it, which only intensified when we heard that strange noise at the door earlier. It could be a coincidence, but I rarely believe in those.

"Did you find anything outside?"

I shake my head. "No, I didn't. But I really believe someone was here trying to break in."

"But I checked the perimeter when we got home, and you did too. I don't understand how they could have gotten in when the gate to the property is access-controlled, and so is the front door," says Gunnar.

"If someone did follow us in, they must have been very sneaky. There's no other explanation."

"I don't like it," Gunnar says, rubbing his chin in thought. "I promised Lena she'd be safe here. I think we should search the perimeter again. If any intruders are idiotic enough to stick around, we might be able to catch them."

We head outside, making sure to close and lock the front door securely behind us. Max is still at Lena's place, searching for clues and gathering her belongings, so I don't want to leave her unprotected and vulnerable while we search the property.

The shadows of the trees and bushes lining the front lawn stretch across the grass, and the solar-powered garden lamps flicker to life.

My eyes adjust to the semi-darkness as my wolf senses take over. I scan the garden for anything strange or out of place. I glance at Gunnar and nod to my left, indicating we should split up. He nods and quietly moves to the right, careful not to make too much noise. If someone is still lurking outside, we'll catch them by surprise.

I stalk around the property's border, checking under hedges and in low-hanging branches for anyone who might not belong there. There are no visible footprints, and the scent lingering in the air is my own. I take another deep breath, trying to decipher any unusual smells, but I can only detect faint whiffs from the flowerbeds and cut grass.

When I round the side of the house again, Gunnar is standing by the front door, fiddling with the access pad.

"Anything?" I ask.

He shakes his head. "Nothing. No unfamiliar scents, footprints, or anything disturbed around the perimeter existed. Not even the access pad looks like it's been tampered with. If someone was here, they were a professional."

Unease coils in my gut at Gunnar's assessment. Everything is far too clean for my liking.

"Let's go inside and check the CCTV," I suggest. "Maybe it picked up whoever was out there."

Once inside, Gunnar checks on Lena briefly while I pull out my laptop and open the camera feed.

"She's still out," he says with a wry grin when he joins me at the dining room table.

"Must have been one hell of an orgasm you gave her," I chuckle, and he laughs. I would love to hug and cuddle her right now, but her safety is my priority before I can relax.

I rewind the CCTV recording to the afternoon from when we arrived home from the hospital.

Everything appears calm until the camera picks up someone on the western side of the property creeping through the bushes. They disappear from sight until another camera captures them walking along the front of the house and peeking through windows.

Right around the time we heard the noise at the front door, the camera showed a person right outside twisting the doorknob.

I squint at my laptop screen, and Gunnar leans close behind me to get a better look. The picture is grainy, but I can zoom in on the person's face. It's a dark-haired man, but I can't make out much else about his features. The facial recognition software linked to the CCTV cameras identifies him as Zorin Marlow.

"Who the fuck is Zorin?" Gunnar asks incredulously. "And why the hell is he on our property?"

"Good question," I murmur. "Save this picture and put him on our radar. We need to find out more about him before we do anything else. I'm going to check on Lena."

Lena is awake when I walk into the bedroom. She's wrapped in the comforter, her hair tousled from sleep. She looks so adorable that I want to kiss her all over her beautiful face.

"Hi, Princess," I greet, smiling as she looks up at me. "Did you sleep well?"

"I did," she says, stifling a yawn. "I feel better now, though."

I chuckle. "You needed it." I sit on the bed and tuck her into my side, her soft breathing soothing my soul as the curve of her breast presses against me. "I don't want to scare you, love, but I saw the intruder on the property earlier."

She pulls back to look at me, her eyes wide with fright. "What?!"

"Gunnar and I searched the area earlier, and whoever was here is long gone."

"Do you have a picture of him... or?"

"Yes," I say, nodding. "We're going to research him before we do anything else. We need to figure out why he's here and if he's after you."

"Can I see who it was?"

Her question takes me aback.

I don't want to worry her, and I'm unsure how she will react to seeing the person trying to break into our home. I suspect this Zorin person might also have broken into Lena's apartment.

"Damon, please," she begs when I take too long to answer. "I need to see who it was."

"All right," I sigh, standing up from the bed. "Give me a minute."

I return a moment later with my laptop and the picture of Zorin pulled up on the screen. I sit again and turn the screen to face her.

Lena's face pales instantly, and she slams the laptop shut. *What the hell?*

"Lena? Is everything okay, darling?" I ask tentatively,

wondering why she had such a visceral reaction. She ignores me, turning away and tucking the comforter more tightly around her. "Sweetheart, what's wrong?"

She remains silent, her gaze fixed firmly on the comforter. Concern wells in my chest as I watch her.

"Do you know him?" I prod again, unable to let this go. "Is he the one who was in your kitchen this morning? Does he—"

"No, I don't know him," she snaps, pushing my hand off her waist.

I sit back and watch her roll onto her side, completely shutting me out. Her reaction to the picture of Zorin confuses me, and I want to push her for answers, but I know she will only isolate me further if I do. A dozen questions race through my mind, and a burning need for answers overwhelms me.

*Does she have a pack? If not, why is she so determined to be alone? Was Zorin her alpha before I found her?*

Her breathing deepens, and I realize she's either fallen back asleep or is pretending to sleep. Knowing I won't get anything from her at this moment, I sigh and leave the room, shutting the door gently behind me.

---

Hours later, I'm struggling to fall asleep, tossing and turning in my bed as I think about the day and the trespasser on my property.

I'm sure everything is linked, but I don't know the connection. Suddenly, a soft knock sounds on my door, and I sit up and switch on the bedside table lamp.

Lena stands in the doorway in her pajamas, looking at me with uncertainty.

"Lena?" I say, completely surprised to see her there.

"I can't sleep," she mumbles, fiddling with the oversized white shirt she's wearing from one of us. "May I stay here with you tonight?"

"Of course," I say, throwing the bed covers open. She climbs in and snuggles into my side.

"I'm sorry for snapping at you earlier," she says softly a few minutes later. "The things you want to know about me... they're hard to talk about. I don't like bringing them up because it's a touchy subject."

"I understand," I soothe, stroking her hair. "I'm sorry for pushing you. If you don't want to talk about it yet, I can respect that decision."

"Thank you," she says, nuzzling into my chest. "I don't like it when we fight."

"Oh, that wasn't a fight at all, sweetness," I say, chuckling softly in the dark as I pull her closer, hugging her soft body against me.

After a couple of minutes, my body finally relaxes with my omega by my side, allowing me to fall asleep at last.

## Lena

Sunlight filters through the curtains in Damon's bedroom, and I crack my eyes open, stretching leisurely when I find myself in bed alone. My ankle throbs, but the pain isn't as intense as it was yesterday, and I know that today, I should be able to walk on it a bit more.

A familiar pink suitcase sits at the end of the bed, and I sit up to look at it properly, my stomach sinking when I realize it contains the clothes and toiletries that Max had brought for me from home.

Damon was serious about me staying with them, especially since I'm pregnant. I haven't had a chance to process the pregnancy, and I place a hand over my belly, thinking about being a mother.

The thought fills me with dread. If I stay here, I'm less likely to leave eventually, and I don't want that.

I need to be on my own, where I know I'll be safer, and to keep the baby safe.

Having made up my mind, I get up and dress, determined to leave the pack house today. I wheel my suitcase into the kitchen moments later, and all three alphas stop eating their breakfast to stare at me.

"What are you doing?" Gunnar asks, pointing his knife at my suitcase. My stomach rumbles at seeing bacon and eggs on his plate, but I ignore it. I can eat at home.

I square my shoulders, stiffening my spine as I look him in the eye.

"I'm leaving," I state. "I've made up my mind, and this is the best decision for me. We've had our fun, but I know it can't last. I would rather be at home."

Max's knife and fork clatter to the table as he shoots up from his chair.

"Lena, please!" he says despairingly, breaking my heart. "We've had this discussion. You know you're better off with us."

"After your promise to me yesterday, this is what you decide?" asks Gunnar, betrayal in his voice.

"Enough," Damon says sharply, authority lacing his words. "You're not going anywhere, Lena. We are your alphas, and we must protect you as our omega. You're in a vulnerable position, and if you think I'm letting you out of my sight with our pup, you are sorely mistaken."

Panic tightens my throat with every word that leaves Damon's mouth.

"Pup?" Max says in shock, and Gunnar's eyes widen as they both look at me.

I'm trapped, with no way out. No autonomy, no choice—just an omega subject to a new set of alphas.

My breathing hitches as I remember the footage of Zorin from last night.

He's here, and I know he wants something from me. The room starts to spin as I hyperventilate, but the breaths I take do little to calm my racing heart.

I topple slightly to the left, losing my balance as I try to stay upright. Max and Gunnar are by my side in an instant, steadying me and gently guiding me into a chair.

"What the hell is wrong with you, Damon?" Gunnar snaps, jumping to my defense. "Why are you acting like such an asshole? She's carrying our baby!"

"I beg to differ," Damon says coldly, his expression softening as he looks at my belly. "Lena and the pup are safest here, where we can keep an eye on them at all times."

I try to ignore him, focusing instead on regaining control of my breathing. My stomach rumbles again, but this time, instead of hunger, I feel a wave of nausea rising.

"I need the bathroom," I gasp, scrambling to my feet. I make it just in time to vomit the contents of my stomach into the toilet.

The bathroom door is still open, and between bouts of vomiting, I can hear the worried whispers of the alphas.

"I'm here," Damon says gently from behind me. He holds my hair back and rubs my back as I continue to be sick.

Damon's presence calms me, but reminds me of the life growing inside me. I place a hand on my belly when I catch my breath, wondering what my future will look like once the baby arrives.

He may think he can keep me safe, but I know I'll be

safer if I escape the city. I need to leave when the alphas least expect it.

# CHAPTER 19

### Lena

I'm lying on the ground in the street. It's pouring rain, and the four alphas are staring down at me menacingly, their eyes glowing with rage and their teeth bared.

"You're a worthless excuse for an omega," Zorin snarls, spitting on me. I flinch as the spit hits my face, only to be washed away by the rain. "I don't know why we wasted so much time on you when you couldn't even give us a pup."

"Stupid bitch," Raul growls, kicking me in the stomach. I cry out in pain, hunching over to protect myself.

"We should just kill you now and save anyone else the trouble of dealing with you," Aleks hisses.

Zorin's wolf claws extend from his hands, and he lunges at me, slicing through my skin as I raise my arms to protect my face. The others join in on the assault, and I scream, calling for help as they continue to attack me. I scream and scream, and I—

"Lena! Wake up!"

My eyes shoot open, and I see the concerned face of Damon looming over me as I scream into wakefulness. There are three alphas on my bed.

"Lena, baby, it's just us!"

Eventually, the scream dies in my throat when my brain registers that the figures on my bed are Damon, Max, and Gunnar. I burst into tears, relieved to be in the safety of Damon's home but scared senseless by the dream lingering in my mind.

"Shh, sweetheart, it's okay," Max soothes, holding me against his bare chest. He's only wearing a pair of grey sweatpants.

I'm shaky and sweating after the dream.

Damon and Gunnar are also in various states of undress, and Damon's dark hair is sticking up in all directions as if he had been fast asleep when startled awake.

Sudden embarrassment hits me because I woke the alphas with my screaming, and they had to see me like this, but I know there's no hiding anything from them.

"What were you dreaming about?" Max asks, holding me tighter. "You gave us the fright of our lives."

I shake my head, trying to get my bearings.

Zorin's face is burned into my mind's eye—the cruel smile he wore when attacking me is so vivid that it feels as if he was actually here.

*How is it that after four years, I'm still haunted by him?* I should have moved on and been free to live my life, but he's a ghost that haunts my every move, both awake and asleep.

A few more tears leak from my eyes. I wipe them away angrily, determined not to cry about him anymore.

"Talk to us, darling," Damon presses gently, softening the moment by tucking a strand of my hair behind my ear. He's never seen me like this. "Please tell us what's going on."

I sigh and wipe my nose with my shirt sleeve. I know I

can't fight this anymore, and now that I'm pregnant, it's impossible to hide my past.

"This is a lot for me to share," I start quietly. "So please be patient with me."

"Take all the time you need."

Max, Damon, and Gunnar are watching me attentively, which makes me a little nervous, so I take a deep breath.

"Let me start from the beginning. I'm not really from DC," I say. "I only moved here a couple of years ago. Before I came here, I had a pack of my own. We were happy for a time before it all fell apart."

"What do you mean?" Gunnar asks, but I can hear the defensiveness in his tone about my previous pack. I mean, I wasn't exactly a virgin when he knotted me in the library.

"My life with the pack started years ago. I was their omega—to Aleks, Raul, Thomas and…" I hesitate. "Zorin."

"So you know him?" Damon asks carefully.

"You were his omega?" Max asks in shock.

"Yes, I was," I admit nervously.

"You said Thomas,'" Damon says slowly. "Fuck- I know why Zorin's here now."

"Why?" I ask, alarmed.

"Is he tall, broad shoulders… tattoo of a sun on his neck?" asks Damon.

"Yes," I confirm, wondering where this is going and how the hell Damon knows about him.

"We killed him."

"Oh, what?" I say, my eyes widening as I look at him. My heart is beating wildly, and I don't know if he's telling the truth, but it looks like he is by the grim look on his face. "How do you know him?"

"This might be hard for you to hear, but he was an abuser. Abused kids," Damon says, and my stomach sinks. "We received a tip from a civilian and we… took care of business."

"Oh my god," I whisper, feeling sick. I had slept with a total psychopath who deserved to be killed years ago to stop him from hurting anyone.

"Tell us about them. Your old pack," prodded Gunner, his jaw set in a stern line.

After their shocking news, I try to gather my thoughts. Taking deep breaths, I pause for a moment, trying to find the best way to explain.

"It started well enough," I eventually say. "My family didn't approve, but I still left home to be with them."

"Why didn't they approve?" Gunnar asks, and I turn to him, finding his gaze locked on mine.

I shrug, attempting to appear nonchalant despite my nervousness. "They didn't like Zorin. They thought I could do better. And I thought it was true love."

"So what happened when you left home to be with them?"

Panic claws at my chest as the memories overwhelm me, and I swallow hard, trying to push them down. "The four of them courted me, showering me with love and affection, and I fell for it. But once they had me, that was where it ended."

Max takes my hand, and I squeeze it gratefully. I take a deep breath and continue.

"Why did it end?"

"Nothing I did was ever good enough for them. I was useless. They tore down my self-esteem, breaking me, and said I was useless for not producing a pup for them."

"You're not useless," Damon growls quietly, and I glance at him, afraid of the tightly controlled anger simmering in his eyes. "Don't ever say that about yourself."

This is the hardest part to get through, and tears well in my eyes as I reflect on that fateful night.

"The very last night I was with them, everything went wrong. We were on our way back from an event when they stopped by the side of the road and beat me, leaving me for dead. I would have died that night if it weren't for a kind stranger who found me and took me to the hospital."

I pull up the sleeve of my pajama shirt, showing them my long scar.

"It's how I got this scar," I say quietly. "Zorin scratched me. When I was finally well enough to leave the hospital, I moved here and never looked back. They probably thought I died, but now Zorin is here."

Hot tears spill down my cheeks, but I'm too exhausted to wipe them away. I got through my story, and that's enough for me.

Damon, Max, and Gunnar are quiet. Each of them has their fists tightly clenched, their knuckles white. Their anger is palpable, but I know it's not directed at me.

"I'm the person who found you in the rain," Damon admits quietly. "I took you to the hospital. Even though you were wearing a mask at the time, I knew you were injured."

"I know," I say. "Max—I also want to come clean. You and I met at the ball before all this."

Max shakes his head in wonder. "This was meant to be. For us to be together."

"Zorin will never come near you again," Damon says quietly, each word clipped with fury. "I will always protect you, Lena. To my dying breath."

Max nods, echoing Damon's sentiment, but Gunnar is still too angry to speak, his gray eyes glowing in the dark with rage.

Damon lies down on the bed behind me, and I follow suit, allowing him to spoon me. He wraps an arm around my middle and pulls me closer.

"I need to hold you, sweetheart," he murmurs.

Max lies down in front of me as Gunnar fixes the blankets around my legs. I feel safe and protected, surrounded by these alphas, and I finally begin to relax after my nightmare.

"I'm going to check the perimeter quickly and keep guard," Gunnar says. "I need to make sure that Zorin stays away."

"If he shows up, you know what to do," Damon growls ominously, and I shiver.

"You got it," Gunnar replies, leaving the room and closing the door.

Damon and Max sandwich me between them.

I can hear their hearts beating, and the sound soothes me. The feel of their rigid, muscular bodies against mine ignites a spark of desire. Damon plays with my hair while Max strokes my arm tenderly, whispering comforting words.

"You're safe here with us, little omega," Damon murmurs. "No need to worry. We'll always protect you."

I hum in agreement, closing my eyes to soak in the feel of their touch. With every caress of their hands on my body, I feel myself loosen up and become aroused. My pussy begins to throb, and I can sense myself growing slick between my thighs.

Damon stills and sniffs the air, then growls hungrily in my ear.

"Looks like someone can't help her hungry pussy from needing to be filled," he says, slipping a hand down my pajama shorts and caressing me.

I whimper at the sensation and try to spread my legs a little wider for him. Max chuckles when he sees me struggling and helps to remove my shorts, slowly trailing his hand up my calf and inner thigh until he reaches my mound, where he begins to rub my clit in slow, torturous circles while Damon focuses on my entrance.

"This feels so good," I whisper when Damon slides a finger into me and then out again, dragging my wetness to my asshole.

"It's going to feel even better when my cock is in your

ass," he groans and swipes his wet finger around my asshole as he uses his other hand to hold my ass cheeks apart.

I clench when I feel his warm finger soothingly rubbing around my sphincter, slowly loosening me up for his huge cock, which I know is coming.

Max is rubbing my clit, "so wet, sweetheart. Is your little pussy ready for me?"

"Yes," I whisper just as Damon pushes his finger into my ass while I'm distracted by Max. My eyes roll back as I moan with both their fingers wiggling inside of me in both holes. The room soon filled with loud smacking noises coming from my pussy and my ass, which makes my face redden. "Oh, *moons*."

"She likes it," says Damon, pushing a second finger into my ass, making me cry out as I feel my asshole stretching around his thick fingers. Max has three fingers inside of my pussy, stretching me more and more. The two of them tease me, rubbing me and fingering me, until my thighs glisten with slick, and I'm ready to be filled.

"We're going to properly tuck you in tonight, my love," says Max, pulling his fingers out of my pussy while Damon did the same. The slick dripping from Max's fingers makes me blush. "So fucking wet. Taste yourself, sweetheart."

Max pushes his three fingers into my mouth, and I'm breathing hard with arousal as I suck my juices from his finger, feeling his hardness against me.

"Good little omega," says Max, pulling his fingers out of my mouth and stroking himself, preparing to enter me.

"I'm going inside your pretty little ass now," says Damon, as he slowly pushes in first- sliding his stiff cock into my asshole and stretching me open.

Max follows suit and gently pushes into my soaked pussy, stretching me wider than his fingers. I'm stuffed, so full of both of them, and I whine with pleasure when they begin to fuck me slowly.

Every thrust and every pull from the alphas rips a moan out of me.

"Fuck," grunts Damon as he pushes his cock deeper into my ass, and I clench around his girth. Feeling both of their cocks thrusting in and out of me has me clenching and spasming.

A sudden orgasm takes me, and I cry out as my thighs shake while Max holds my legs up. They pound into me even harder as I feel the aftershocks of my orgasm and slick rushing down my legs.

"I can't hold back anymore," Max says as he explodes straight into my womb. He pistons into me in one last thrust. "Feels so fucking good."

*Oh god*. His cock pulsating and releasing all his hot semen is right where I need it to be. My eyes roll back as his cock begins to knot at the base, stretching me fully just the way I like it.

"You like that, honey?" asks Damon as he continues to pound into my ass while gripping my ass cheek with one hand.

"Yes, I do," I gasp, feeling helpless, with Damon pounding into my ass while I'm pinned to Max's cock. Closing my eyes, I focus on the sensation of him shoving into my tiny hole wet with slick, and I suddenly clench again from arousal.

"I can feel how horny you are," Max whispers, caressing my clit while I clench around both of them. He's rubbing my clit harder.

"I already came, though," I whine to Max as Damon continues to take my ass.

"Again," he says softly, and I moan as a second orgasm rips through me. This orgasm time is more powerful than the last, and Damon also reaches his climax at the same time.

"You're ass...so good," he says, panting as he kisses my shoulders and my back rapidly while his cock begins to swell inside of me.

"Such a good little omega. We'll never hurt you," says Max as we all try to catch our breaths.

"Mhm," I moan as I feel Damon's knot straining against my asshole. "I know that, but I still can't trust you all yet. We hardly know each other."

"Don't say that," murmurs Damon as he yawns sleepily like a lion after taking his mate. "You can trust us."

Just because someone tells me to trust them doesn't mean I should. I stay quiet since I know they're sleepy now, and if I want to go through with my plan to leave them, it's better not to protest.

---

I wake up slowly the next morning, finding Max asleep beside me, but Damon is nowhere to be seen.

A dull throb in my ankle makes me hiss in pain as I sit up, prodding it gently to see exactly where it hurts. My ankle felt fine yesterday morning, but I wonder if the unusual angle of Damon's and Max's lovemaking last night somehow made it worse.

Gunnar peeks around the door and smiles when he sees I'm awake.

"Good morning, baby," he says quietly, not to wake Max. "How was your sleep after all the screaming I heard last night?"

My face reddens as I hide behind a pillow. "I slept well. Did you get any sleep?"

"I did for a little bit," he replies, leaning down to kiss me.

Instinctively, I pull back, not wanting him to kiss me. I

notice the confusion on Gunnar's face and immediately feel bad.

"You can't kiss me with morning breath," I joke softly, shuffling off the bed. "Only after I've showered."

I'm still too scared to be kissed by anyone in the pack. Kissing is serious, and if I'm not careful, it could lead to marking, which I cannot afford to do.

"Hmm," Gunnar growls, looking at me. But then, realization crosses his face when he remembers my past. "I understand, Lena. How about I make some breakfast while you get ready?"

"Sounds good," I chirp, and he smiles at me kindly before leaving the room. I suddenly feel more relaxed knowing he understands, and I don't need to explain.

Once in the bathroom, I turn on the shower and quickly brush my teeth while I wait for the water to heat.

I've just stepped into the shower when Max appears at the door, completely nude.

"Mind if I join you?" he asks with a sly smile.

"I don't mind," I reply, and he steps in behind me, breathing into my neck as he presses himself against me.

"I brought you something," he says, one arm behind his back. I raise an eyebrow in interest, wondering what Max could possibly have for me.

"Ooh, what is it?" I ask curiously.

He brings his hand around, opening his palm to reveal a small object resembling a plug. It's made of stainless steel, with a pretty pink jewel at the base.

My eyes widen, not expecting this at all from him. Usually, Gunnar would play freaky games with me while Max plays it safe.

"Is it okay if I stretch you out a little?" he grunts in my ear, and my face heats with embarrassment at the thought.

"Um, s-sure," I stutter.

He lets out a pleased chuckle. "First, I've got to get you ready."

Max sets the plug down on the soap rack in the shower, then grabs a loofah and squirts some body wash onto it. He begins to wash me, soaping up my arms, legs, and back.

He spends a lot of time on my breasts, washing them around and around until my nipples are hard and aching.

"Does that feel good?" he chuckles, flicking the tight point of my nipple.

"Yes," I respond breathily, my pussy clenching. I can feel myself getting wet, and Max must smell it, too.

"You're ready. Go ahead and bend over for me, beautiful," he orders. "And spread your ass cheeks for me."

"Oh my god, are you serious, Max?"

"Yes, I'm waiting," he says as I feel his cock poking eagerly against the middle of my back. Bending for him, I reach back to spread myself.

Max grabs the plug again and, with his other hand, begins to rub around my asshole and down to my pussy. The smooth metal feels so good against me as he slowly rubs around and around my anus.

"Oh, Max."

"Yes, moan my name," he groans softly with desire. "You're going to look so pretty with my plug in your ass."

I feel slick shoot out and coat my anus, ready for a good knotting. Just at that moment, he pushes the plug into me slowly, and I gasp at the sensation. It's so different from having one of the alphas stretch me open with their fingers. The plug is heavy, and once the base is nestled snugly against me, Max lets go of my ass cheeks and pulls me upright.

"Oh!" I sigh in pleasure once the plug has settled inside me. "That feels so... weird."

"In a good way or bad?"

"In a good way," I confirm, wiggling my hips as my pussy

clenches with arousal. All this did was make me extremely horny.

"Fucking perfect," he murmurs, squeezing my ass. "You're going to be nice and ready tonight."

"But is this necessary?" I ask shyly. The weight of the plug fills me with a different feeling, and I'm so turned on despite feeling self-conscious.

"Of course it is," Max replies, picking up the loofah to rub around my pussy. "I want you to be excited for me tonight. Ready for three alphas. Every night, baby."

"You're making me very horny," I say, clenching my thighs together, but he walks around until he's in front of me, kneeling before my pussy.

"I know, baby, I can see it," he murmurs, dropping the loofah and tracing my pubic hairs with his thumb. "I need to shave you and get you ready for the pack."

My face reddens, and I look away as he grins wickedly while standing to reach for something outside the shower. He's holding an electric shaver, and my face heats with embarrassment.

"No, Max," I squeak. "I can shave myself."

He squats down until his face is level with my pussy.

"You're so hairy, sweetheart," he says softly, running his fingers through my pubic hair. "All this hair is hiding such a pretty pussy from me."

"You don't like it?" I ask, feeling ashamed because I hadn't had time with everything happening lately.

"I love it. I love everything about you, honey," Max replies, kissing my pussy and prodding my legs open. "But I want to watch my knot sink into this tight cunt with nothing in the way."

He looks up at me, kisses my clit in one long smooch, and then turns the shaver on, bringing it to my pussy. It's strangely erotic, watching him shave me and trim my pubic hair. I love the look of concentration on his face as he shapes my hair into a neat landing strip.

I feel naughty and sensual, so aroused by him shaving my pussy.

He holds the inside of my right thigh apart from my other leg to shave me thoroughly, making my heart pound wildly in my chest. Each stroke of the shaver and its vibrations intensify my arousal, jostling my anal plug.

"Oh god," I moan as he sets the shaver down and rinses my pussy, sliding a finger between my folds.

"You deserve a reward for being such a good girl," Max says, pushing his finger inside me. I gasp and use a hand to steady myself against the shower wall as he thrusts deeper. "Yes, baby, come for me."

"Oh!" I scream, gripping his shoulders to steady my shaking legs. He thrusts faster, fucking me with his finger and making sure to hit my G-spot. My belly clenches, slick spilling all over his hand as I cry out.

"Mhmm, you're delicious," he says, tasting his fingers while maintaining eye contact with me. "Tonight is going to be so much fun."

# CHAPTER 20

**Lena**

I absentmindedly rub the wrapping around my ankle while watching a movie with Max in the living room after our morning shower. My pussy is still throbbing from his attentions, and my ass is filled with the plug he put inside me.

Gunnar has gone to nap, and Damon is preparing snacks for us. It all feels so domestic, and my heart aches at the realization that this is what life could be like with them if I weren't in so much danger.

I know Zorin won't stop until he finds me. I have too much baggage to drag Damon, Max, or Gunnar into my life.

Tears well in my eyes as I contemplate my plan to leave the pack. I sniff, trying to wipe my eyes discreetly, but Max notices and pulls me to his side.

"You okay?" he asks, rubbing my shoulder.

"Yes," I whisper. "Just scared and overwhelmed."

It's not technically a lie, but I can't reveal the full truth of wanting to leave them. I need to be smarter about it this time.

"Hey, it's all right, sweetheart," he soothes. "We'll never let Zorin get near you again. He's not going to hurt you again, babe."

"I wish I could believe that," I sigh as Damon approaches with a steaming mug of tea and a bowl of granola, fruit, and yogurt. "No thanks, Damon. Just looking at that makes me feel queasy."

"Yesterday was a long day, and you didn't eat much. You need to keep your strength up for our pup."

"It looks gross," I say, my stomach turning at the smell of green tea. Suddenly, I rush to the kitchen trash can and vomit whatever little I have left in me.

"Oh fuck," Damon says worriedly, rubbing my back as Max hands me paper towels.

"Sorry," I groan, rinsing my mouth in the sink. "I was feeling fine this morning…"

"Don't apologize ever. You're carrying our babe," Damon says, watching me with a concerned look as if I might break at any moment. "Why don't we take you out tonight? Everything at home doesn't seem to be sitting well with you."

"I can try," I mumble, leaning against his chest to calm my racing heart.

"There's a beautiful French restaurant across town that I think you'll love," Damon offers.

"What do you say, Lena? Are you up for it?" Max asks while caressing my waist.

"Sure," I reply, hoping I can keep everything down. "We can try it out."

"Consider it your first date with us," Damon adds, rubbing my cold arms.

"It's not a date," I protest, pulling away from him.

"So, are we just friends with benefits? Is that what we're telling our baby?"

My cheeks flush under his gaze of possessiveness and passion.

"I don't know, okay? But this isn't a date."

"I'll reserve a table for us," Damon says without another word, kissing me on the forehead before leaving the kitchen.

Max senses my distress when he places a hand over my rapidly beating heart.

"Hey, this doesn't mean anything," he whispers, hugging me as panicked thoughts race through my mind.

I don't want to lead the alphas on, and every day it'll get harder to leave them. Each passing second would encourage them to mark and claim me forever.

---

Later that afternoon, I got dressed in the only dress I had in my suitcase.

It's an off-the-shoulder, sparkly black evening dress with a sweetheart neckline. There's a long slit in the skirt, showcasing my legs. My sprained ankle feels much better, so I pair my outfit with black heels, knowing I'll be sitting for most of the evening anyway.

I do a smoky eye and bold red lips for my makeup, and when I look at the final ensemble in the mirror, I can't deny that I'm glowing tonight despite my fears of being marked. I plan to enjoy my last moments with these wonderful alphas I met at the library.

The anal plug tugs at my ass, and the naughtiness of that, combined with my sexy attire, makes my lower belly clench and my pussy slick with arousal. Now I'm craving the alphas badly. Maybe one more night with them, and then it'll be over. My nausea always seems to disappear when I think about intimacy with the alphas.

Damon whistles lowly when I walk into the living room.

His eyes rake over my body, growing darker with desire the longer he looks. I squirm under his smoldering gaze. The plug Max left inside me was feeling heavier by the moment.

"You look good enough to eat, baby doll," he growls, and I blush.

Gunnar smiles at me, his eyes glowing with pure affection for me.

"You look beautiful, love," he murmurs, taking my hand and kissing the back of it. "Are you excited?"

"Yes, let's go," I reply, despite the anxiety churning in my stomach.

Max sits with me in the back of the car, holding my hand, while Damon and Gunnar sit up front. Damon is driving, and I watch the city lights fly by as we travel across town. If I know anything about the alphas, it's that they have some elaborate plan in place to spoil me tonight.

My heart aches at the thought of leaving the pack forever.

I don't understand my reaction to them, but I know I can't stay. They've been nothing but kind, watching out for me when I least expect it, but my past makes it difficult to move on.

They will never meet their baby.

A tear drips down my nose and onto my dress, sparkling under the light of a streetlamp we pass. I dab it away quickly, acting as if nothing is wrong.

I don't want them to see me cry.

Max notices and squeezes my hand despite my best efforts, prompting me to look up at him. "What's wrong, sweetheart? Why are you crying?"

I shrug, embarrassed to have been caught mourning the loss of these alphas.

"It's nothing," I murmur, grabbing a tissue from my purse to wipe my cheeks. "I'm just being silly."

"You can tell us," Gunnar growls, meeting my eyes in the rearview mirror, and I quickly look down.

My mind whirls as I think of an explanation, finally settling on something as close to the truth as possible.

"I'm so grateful to you all for your care and protection," I say quietly to everyone. "I've never experienced this before. It feels so…nice."

"Lena, honey," Damon replies, his eyes glinting. "You're precious to us, and we will do anything to make sure you know it."

I nod, trying my best not to cry at his sweet words. Leaving will be much harder than I anticipated.

I haven't allowed any of them close enough to mark me or kiss me on the lips, even though I almost caved the night before. When Damon and Max were making love to me, I desperately wanted to turn and kiss Damon, but self-preservation held me back. That urge scares me, so I know it's time to leave now.

---

Ten minutes later, we finally arrived at the restaurant.

Damon parks in front and gets out, rounding the car to open my door. He hands the keys to the valet, and the four of us make our way inside.

"Welcome to La Belle Époque," the hostess greets us warmly. "Do you have a reservation?"

"Yes, it's under Lovel," Damon replies, and the hostess leads us to our table.

The restaurant is beautiful, with tall, arched windows framed by soft gold accents and gauzy curtains. Crystal chandeliers hang from the ceiling, casting a warm light across the room. Soft classical music plays from hidden speakers, and the hushed conversations of well-dressed patrons fill the space. The thick carpet mutes our footsteps as we walk to the table, and my eyes widen at the elegant yet welcoming décor—plush velvet banquettes in jewel tones and crisp white linens draped over the tables.

"This place is beautiful. I've never been here," I whisper, still in awe of the sheer luxury and elegance surrounding me. I don't think I've ever visited a restaurant this fancy.

"Just wait until you try the food," Damon says with a chuckle, winking at me as he caresses my knee under the table.

The waiter comes to take our order, and the alphas engage in easy banter that reflects their long-standing friendship. I smile as I watch them over dinner, wishing I didn't have to leave. Despite my reservations, being with these alphas feels effortless.

The food is delicious, featuring chicken alfredo and several fancy dishes whose names I don't know, but they taste scrumptious.

Once I finish eating, Gunnar orders dessert. "Could you please bring a Vanilla Bean Crème Brûlée for the lovely lady?"

"Of course, sir," the waiter replies, nodding as he hurries off.

"Aren't you going to order something for yourself, too?" I ask in surprise, and he shakes his head.

"No, babe, I already know what I want for dessert," he says with a devilish grin.

I feel his hand on my leg under the table, caressing my thigh, and my skin prickles with pleasure as that familiar tingle grows in my belly. He growls softly.

"Not here, Gunnar," I whisper.

"I can smell your slick, baby. You're an eager thing, aren't you?" His hand begins to creep higher up my thigh, pushing the fabric of my dress up and exposing my skin.

Max and Damon glance at Gunnar and then at me, a

knowing smile on their faces. I press my lips together, trying to act normal and remain silent. The restaurant has too many people, and I don't want to embarrass myself by moaning.

Gunnar cups my mound between my legs, stroking it slowly. Slick begins to drip down my inner thighs as I struggle to keep my legs closed, but Damon grips my knee tighter, holding me open.

"Do you still have that pretty plug that Max put in your ass this morning?" Gunnar whispers in my ear, slipping a finger between my folds and over my clit.

He twirls his finger around my sensitive nub of flesh. My face heats with embarrassment at his question, and I'm sure I'm bright red.

"How do you know about that?" I gasp, trying to speak without moaning.

"He told us all. Max never keeps anything to himself," chuckles Gunnar. "But it's not time to take it out yet. Your tight ass needs time to stretch."

The waiter brings my dessert, and I blush, hoping he doesn't notice me squirming, as he sets it before me. "For you, beautiful lady."

"Thank you," I say breathlessly, trying not to focus on Gunnar's fingers playing with my pussy under the table while Damon holds my other thigh apart for him.

As I pick up the fork, I attempt to mask my arousal by taking bites of the sweet dessert.

Gunnar's hand rests on my inner thigh while I eat. He's alternating between long, slow sweeps and light caresses. He teases my entrance, brushing his fingers softly along my labia, up my slit, and across my clit.

I shovel food into my mouth, hoping it will stop me from making noise. His touch electrifies me, and when he suddenly pushes a finger inside my tight channel, I let out a soft squeak of surprise through my mouthful of dessert.

"Oh!"

He grins at me, a feral gleam in his eyes. His finger begins to move, dragging across the soft, spongy tissue of my G-spot and back out again. I can feel my orgasm building slowly, in sync with the unhurried movements of his hand.

Clamping my legs together doesn't help; it only heightens the sensation, and Damon isn't releasing my thigh. The more I struggle, the deeper Gunnar's finger pushes into my pussy.

I notice Damon's cock poking against his black slacks.

I try to focus on the dessert in front of me, determined to enjoy it while Gunnar wrings pleasure from my body. The last bite of my crème brûlée is so good that I inadvertently let out a little moan of delight, causing all three of them to stiffen in their seats. Gunnar's hand stops moving, and I notice the bulge in the front of his suit pants.

"You're hard," I say, smiling at his frustration. All three alphas are scowling at me now.

"You won't be laughing for long," Damon warns playfully as he hands his credit card to the waiter to settle the bill.

Once outside, the valet brings the car around, and Max helps me inside again. Instead of turning in the direction that will take us home, Damon eases onto the road and heads toward another part of the city.

"Where are we going?" I ask as my pussy clenches with need. Gunnar hadn't finished the job, and I need release—especially now that the anal plug is still teasing at my ass.

Damon winks at me in the rearview mirror. "You'll see."

We drive for about ten minutes before pulling up to what looks like a hotel twinkling under the night sky. I gasp when Damon helps me out of the car.

"This is the Elysian Crown!" I exclaim, awed by the grand building before me. "How did you even get a reservation here?"

All I know is that it's the most exclusive five-star hotel in the city. Damon chuckles at my excitement. "Only the best for our omega."

We check in at the front desk and are then escorted to the fifth floor.

"Enjoy your stay," the bellboy says with a smile, pushing open the room door for us.

The door shuts behind us as we enter the room. I've barely taken ten steps when I stop in my tracks, staring at the sight before me.

Romantic music plays softly from the stereo in the living area, and dozens of lit candles cover the floor, leading to what I assume is the bedroom. Rose petals are scattered across the furniture, and when I follow the candlelit trail to the bedroom, I see more rose petals covering the floor and the bed.

My stomach sinks.

Something is going on. This isn't just a fancy night for sex. The alphas didn't wine and dine me to bring me here for our usual fun. No, this might be the night when the alphas want to mark me.

"Lena."

I turn around at the sound of Damon's voice. He's staring at me intently, an uncharacteristic nervousness about him that wasn't there a moment ago. I stand rooted to the spot, panicked thoughts racing through my mind.

He clears his throat, swallowing hard.

"Yes?" I respond softly.

"Lena, I know I've promised you that I'll always keep you safe, and I want you to know that I mean that," he says, taking a deep breath. "I want to protect you forever and always. Will you accept our mark tonight?"

# CHAPTER 21

**Damon**

I stand there watching Lena, waiting for her to say something.

Max and Gunnar shift restlessly behind me, anxious for her answer. Her eyes widen in surprise, and I see the color drain from her face the longer she stares at me.

Lena looks terrified, and it breaks my heart to see that expression. I don't want to pressure her into doing something she doesn't like, but I know that marking her is the best way to keep her safe.

Deep down, I know she's mine. *I always claim what's mine.*

Her mouth opens and closes as if she wants to say something. She struggles with the words, but when they don't come, her eyes dart around the room.

It's as though she's searching for a way out, and I wonder if that has been her plan all along. She won't kiss any of us on the mouth, and while she's affectionate in other ways I've noticed she avoids being kissed or touched too intimately when we're not having sex.

Everything is starting to make sense.

"I'm sorry," she begins, her chest heaving in her sexy black dress. "Damon, as much fun as I'm having with all of you, I don't feel ready for something as permanent as being marked just yet. It's too much, too soon, and I don't think I can handle it."

Her words cut deeply, and I feel rejected to my core.

I don't understand why she keeps pushing me away. *Haven't I done enough to show her how much I care?* I don't know what else to do, but I know I can't let her go without a fight.

"Lena," I groan, trying to rein in my patience. "I just want to protect you. When you wear my mark, no other alpha can touch you. It guarantees your safety. Please, I don't under—"

"You have to understand that this is all so new to me," she stops me, her voice soft, as if pleading with me. "I want to take my time and get to know each of you better. Why rush into that? We have all the time in the world."

Sensing my disappointment, Max places a hand on my shoulder as if to tell me to stay calm with her.

"It's okay," Max says gently to Lena. "We understand."

"Take as much time as you need," Gunnar adds. "We will be waiting."

Lena lets out a sigh of relief, and I turn my head away, trying to hide the disappointment that weighs heavily on my heart and soul. I only want Lena to be happy, and if it means putting my own selfish needs aside for now, then that's what I'll do.

"Let's put on some different music," Max suggests as he returns to the main room. The music shifts to soft jazz, and I extend my hand to Lena.

She looks at it quizzically, confused by my gesture.

"Dance with me," I say quietly.

"You're not mad at me?" she asks, her voice small.

"There's no reason to be mad, beautiful," I reply, and she

smiles as I take her hand in mine. I pull her into my chest and gently sway to the music.

She's so small, her head tucked perfectly under my chin as I hold her close. I love the feeling of her body against mine. Her soft warmth pressing against my rough edges makes me feel whole, like I've finally found the puzzle piece I didn't know I was missing.

Despite my hurt feelings, I want her to know there's no pressure.

I want her to relax and ease her mind. The more we dance, the more I can see that it's working. Lena is giving in and allowing herself to enjoy the moment, closing her eyes and getting lost in the music and the sway of our bodies.

### Lena

I half-expected the alphas to get angry with me, but this is much worse without knowing what's going on in Damon's mind.

Yet, for some reason, I still feel safe with him.

Damon is solid against me, warm and stable, and the feeling is comforting. We dance for a while, letting the music transport us to a place that's just the two of us, and I sway against him.

I must be swaying a little too much because suddenly, I feel like I'm falling backward. I open my eyes, stumbling slightly as I regain my footing. Suddenly, breathless and a bit dizzy, I place a hand on Damon's chest to steady myself as I try to catch my breath.

He grips my shoulders to hold me still.

"Lena?" Damon says in a panicked voice, his eyes roving

frantically over my body. "Are you all right? What's wrong, baby?"

"I'm okay, just a little lightheaded, that's all," I reply, resting my hand on his chest for support. "I'm just feeling a bit tired because of the pregnancy."

"Okay, maybe you should lie down for a while," he suggests, his body relaxing as he breathes a sigh of relief and leads me to the bed.

I sit, and he helps me take off my shoes and dress. Then he picks me up gently and places me in the middle of the bed before undressing. He lies down on my right side, kissing my forehead softly and rubbing soothing circles on my stomach.

All the alphas get naked and join us, Max on my left side and Gunnar at the bottom of the bed near my feet.

The three alphas begin to kiss and caress me slowly, taking their time to worship every inch of my skin with their mouths and hands. Their gentle touches arouse me, and soon enough, I'm writhing beneath them, desperate for more than the soft caresses they're giving.

I squeeze my thighs together, trying to ease the ache forming between them. The plug is still deeply embedded in my ass.

"What's wrong?" Gunnar teases, kissing his way up from my right calf to my thigh, then repeating his actions on the left. His teeth graze my skin ever so slightly, and I shudder at the sensation. It feels so good. "What's got you so worked up, baby? I can smell your slick."

"Can you take the plug out?" I whine, knowing he understands what I've been craving all day.

He chuckles darkly, slipping my panties down my legs and off before flipping me onto my stomach. He pulls my hips up until I'm kneeling on the bed, my face pressed into the duvet.

"Hmm, what do we have here?" he murmurs, pulling my ass cheeks apart. I feel my face heat with embarrassment, knowing that he can see the plug snugly seated inside me. The unfamiliar weight of it has kept me horny all day, but now that he's looking directly at it, I can't help but feel shy.

Damon and Max are kissing my neck while Gunnar twirls the plug inside me.

"Pink is definitely your color, baby," he says, grabbing the base. "But now it's time for something else to fill you up."

He starts to pull slowly, dragging the plug out of me inch by torturous inch, and I gasp, my pussy fluttering at the sensation.

"Oh my god," I moan as I feel slick escape from me. I'm embarrassed since every alpha in the room is watching, and I can hear their heavy breathing behind me. Gunnar tugs on the plug, and it comes out with a small pop.

I suddenly feel strangely empty without it.

"You're so fucking sexy, Lena," growls Gunnar, groaning with desire as he stares at my clenching asshole. I can feel his hot breath on my exposed hole as he nears it.

It's quiet for only a moment before I feel his wide tongue on my backside, licking me from pussy to ass. He pants loudly as he licks around my asshole in vigorous strokes like it's his last meal. My face turns red with shame, but I'm turned on, unable to believe how incredible this feels.

"Fuck," groans Damon, and I turn my head to see him leisurely stroking his cock while pre-cum leaks from the tip.

I know Max is also pleasuring himself from the sounds to my left.

"I know how much you like to be watched, dirty girl," Gunnar rumbles from behind me. "Look how hard Damon and Max are. They can't stop themselves from jacking off while they watch me eat your ass out."

"Very true. She looks so sexy lying on her stomach, and all spread out for her pack to enjoy," Damon growls. "I love seeing how wet her pretty pink pussy gets when you lick her ass."

"I'd love to see Gunnar knot her in the ass. You'd love that, wouldn't you, Lena?" says Max, addressing me.

"I think so," I squeak, burying my face into the pillow.

Arousal and embarrassment war within me, but arousal ultimately wins as I feel more slick drip down my thighs from my pussy. I shake my hips, wiggling my ass in Gunnar's face impatiently as he continues to tease me, kissing each ass cheek gently and teasing the opening of my asshole with his fingers.

"Hurry up!" I whine crossly. I'm so fucking horny, and Gunnar keeps messing around, taunting me.

His hand cracks down on my ass, the sting reverberating through me.

"Ow!" I yell, my ass cheeks stinging which only makes me hornier.

"Have patience, little omega," Gunnar growls, "or else you won't get what you want."

"But Gunnar—" I whine, needing his knot immediately after being teased all day. His wide palm smacks me on my upper thighs, and I cry out.

"Her ass is so beautiful," murmurs Max.

"Enough," he snarls, rubbing the sting away. "Apologize, or else you'll get another."

I bite my lip, unwilling to apologize, but then I think of his thick cock knotting me and change my mind. *Fine, I'll play by his rules.*

"I'm sorry, Alpha," I whimper.

"Exactly," he says and squeezes my ass cheeks. My pussy is tingling, dripping, and soaked in slick.

"Our sweet omega looks like she's enjoying this far too much. Look how her delicious pink pussy looks. It's practically covered in slick," Damon chuckles. His fingers brush against my clit, and I jump, desperate for release. "This is a sight I like to see."

"Oh, she'll learn soon enough when I knot this sweet ass," Gunnar says, and I lick my lips in anticipation.

Ever so slowly, inch by inch, Gunnar pushes his thick cock into my asshole, stretching me wide.

"Oof," I gasp into the pillow as he continues to push inside of me.

"Can you take it, omega?"

"Yes! Keep going."

The feeling is indescribable, but I'm desperate for so much more. I need him to fuck me, to rut me until I'm coming on his cock, and he's spilling his load deep inside me.

"All the way in," he groans when he pushes his entire length into my ass.

"Gunnar, please," I beg, moving my hips. "I need you to fuck me."

He grabs a fistful of my hair and pulls my head up.

"As you wish, baby," he growls, then pulls out and slams back in again.

I scream, both surprised and pleased, as he begins to move, setting a punishing rhythm as he pounds into my ass. My thighs shake, and Damon and Max hold them open for Gunnar to get deeper between my cheeks.

"Oh fuck. Oh my god," I moan, my pussy spasming on nothing while Gunnar continues to rut me. I reach between my legs to rub my clit, desperate for some extra friction to help me come, but Damon pushes my hand aside.

"Let me do that for you, princess," he murmurs in my ear, nibbling it gently. "Let me play with that pretty cunt."

His fingers find my swollen nub with ease, and I groan as he starts to touch me, my orgasm building in the best way. Max reaches under me and begins to play with my nipples, flicking and pinching them over the fabric of my bra.

Between the three of them, my skin sizzles with electricity. I'm so close, and I need it more than I need my next breath. The pleasure crescendos until I'm pulsing, ecstasy racing down my spine and culminating in my pussy.

"Oh, I'm coming!" I scream, my hips bucking wildly. Tears stream down my face, and I'm pretty sure I've never had such an intense orgasm in my life.

Gunnar keeps pounding into me. He's fucking me brutally, grunting harshly, and squeezing my ass cheeks. He keeps me spread wide while I take his cock.

"You were made to take my cock in your ass," he snarls. "Such a good fucking omega."

I cry out as Damon continues to play with my clit, eventually sliding two fingers into my soaked pussy. He finger-fucks me in time with Gunnar's thrusts, and soon enough, I'm coming for a second time, spasming on Damon's fingers.

I feel the base of Gunnar's cock begin to swell as he speeds up, then stills, groaning loudly as he shoots ropes of hot cum deep in my ass.

He's knotted snugly against me, and he's not going anywhere.

I sink onto the bed, exhausted but satisfied. If this is our last time together, it's certainly one hell of a way to say goodbye.

# CHAPTER 22

**Lena**

The morning air is cold as I stand outside the hotel, nervously looking back. It's four a.m., and I'm waiting at the entrance for my ride.

Sneaking out was tough, but I managed to do it.

After multiple orgasms, the alphas had fallen asleep in a heap on the bed. I lay awake between them, trying to keep my breathing steady as I waited for them to nod off. Once I was sure they were asleep, I crept into the bathroom, dressed in last night's clothes, and snuck out of the room.

The hotel's front desk had been empty when I hurried into the lobby, and I did my best to avoid any visible cameras. I know that when the alphas wake up and find me missing, the first thing they'll check is the footage to see what happened.

I check the rideshare app on my phone again.

My driver is still three minutes away, so I pull my coat tighter around myself against the bracing wind and ponder my next move. I'm not exactly sure where I'll go, but I know I need to get out of this city immediately.

I need to go somewhere where neither Zorin nor Damon can find me.

A few minutes later, a white car pulls up to the entrance. I check the license plate against the one in my app and cautiously approach the vehicle.

The driver rolls the window down as I near.

"James?" I ask tentatively, and he smiles.

"That's me. You must be Lena. Hop in, and we can get going."

I climb into the back of the car, and he starts to drive. James doesn't talk much during the ride, which I appreciate.

I'm too overwhelmed with emotion to hold a conversation. The city is quiet as we pass through—at this time of the morning, it's practically a ghost town, with no cars on the road and no people in sight.

My mind drifts to the alphas, sound asleep in the bed where I left them. In just a few hours, Gunnar will be the first to wake. He'll notice that I'm missing and then wake the others. They'll be frantic and panicked, searching for me wherever they can. Or they might be relieved of any responsibility secretly. My heart breaks at the thought, and I know I won't be able to take it if they *did* forget about me.

My nose prickles with unshed tears, and I take a tissue out of my purse, blowing my nose. I can't cry for any alpha anymore.

Besides, I'll always carry a little piece of the alphas with me wherever I go. I press a hand against my belly and think of my baby.

"I'll keep you safe, little one," I murmur, stroking my belly. "Nothing will ever hurt you."

I don't even realize I'm crying until the tears drip down my nose and onto my lap.

I let them fall, mourning the life I thought I would have and the uncertain future that awaits me. I know how I must look, sitting in the back of a taxi, crying over something that must have happened at the hotel I was picked up at, but I don't care what anyone thinks anymore.

Thirty minutes later, James pulls up outside my apartment building.

"Thanks so much," I say as I exit the car. He pulls away, and I wave briefly before hurrying inside, still checking my surroundings.

I rummage through my handbag for the house keys and open my front door when I find them, shutting it quickly behind me. Max had left my space neat and tidy—my mail was sitting on the kitchen table, and the groceries I'd bought had been put away. I'm grateful for his thoughtfulness, which makes leaving much harder.

I shower in record time, changing into leggings and an oversized sweatshirt that will be comfortable for travel. I check the time and move faster, knowing it won't be long until Gunnar wakes up and the search for me begins.

Once my suitcase is packed with necessities and changes of clothes, I flick through my mail. None of it is essential, so I toss it back on the table and rush through my living room, grabbing a few photos of my sisters to put in my suitcase. My hands are shaking, my anxiety sky-high as I tuck the precious pictures between clothes to protect them.

I stop and take a deep breath, trying to calm myself down before I continue.

On a whim, I grab my scent blocker lotion and shove it in my handbag along with my heat suppressants, even though I'm pregnant. I don't know if I will use them, but I pack them anyway to be safe.

*Just in case.*

As I take one last look around my apartment to make sure

I haven't missed anything, an overwhelming sense of sadness crashes over me. This little life, the one I built from scratch, is now over.

For some reason, I feel all alone again, and nothing feels more terrifying.

I hug myself around the middle as heavy, wracking sobs consume me, allowing myself just a moment to take it all in, to grieve the parts of myself that I'm leaving behind, before taking a deep breath and composing myself.

"I can do this," I whisper as I leave the house.

※

Deciding to stop by a café first, I pull my laptop out of my backpack to buy a plane ticket to anywhere and book a rental home. Spending too much time at my apartment isn't safe, so it's better to do it here, where there were a lot of people around me.

"Hi, what can I get you to drink?" asks the barista, approaching me with a small notebook and a pen. I look up and notice a small bruise under her eye. Her name badge says 'Mia' on it.

*She must be in an awful relationship*, I think to myself instantly. Or maybe I'm just being paranoid, but I know the signs now.

"Just a coffee, extra sugar," I say, and she nods timidly. "Thank you, Mia."

"Your coffee will be right up!" she says, smiling brightly, covering the sad look in her eyes. I feel bad for her as I browse plane tickets for the cheapest deal. She must be dealing with domestic abuse of some kind.

I finally booked a one-way ticket to Little Rock, Arkansas, with no return date in sight. Once settled in and living there, I can start looking for apartments.

I sigh, knowing this has to be done. I've escaped an alpha pack before, and I know I can do it again.

"Here's your coffee," says the barista, returning to my table.

"Thank you," I say as she sets the coffee down. "I used to be in your shoes. You should leave as soon as you can. It won't be easy, but I promise it's worth it."

She pauses and looks at me for a moment before quietly walking away. So maybe I was right. A boyfriend or family member was mistreating her, but I got the message that it's none of my business by the look she gave me.

Taking a sip of my coffee, I remembered how I didn't listen to anyone but myself at the end of my relationship with Zorin until it was almost too late.

***

Hours later, I'm at the airport, and it's a nightmare.

I hadn't prepared for the sheer chaos of the airport and how many people would be in the security lines. I keep checking around to make sure the alphas haven't somehow tracked my location, but I don't see Damon's towering height, Max's mop of curly red hair, or Gunnar's steely gaze anywhere, which relieves me.

I make it through security unscathed and only breathe a sigh of relief when I'm sitting outside my boarding gate. I have a little time to kill before we board, so I buy a new romance novel and snacks to pack into my handbag for later.

Eventually, we board, and I'm one of the first people on the plane.

I tuck myself into my seat and put on my headphones, content to watch out the window until takeoff. Slowly but surely, the plane fills up, the low noise of chatter reaching me through my music. The captain has just asked the cabin crew to arm the doors and cross-check when a strange smell reaches my nose. I sniff deeply, pausing my music to try and identify the scent.

*Lemongrass.*

It's a strong, vaguely familiar scent, but I can't place it. Someone sits down next to me, and the smell intensifies.

With a jolt, memories flood my brain as the scent strengthens. I turn slowly in my seat to find a man sitting next to me with short-cropped black hair and a single earring hanging from one ear. He turns to face me, smiling widely.

It's him. Zorin.

All the blood in my veins seems to turn to ice at the sight of him. My memories of Zorin and his pack attacking me resurface, and my heart beats faster. This has *got* to be a nightmare. Or I'm in a nightmare.

But Zorin, sitting next to me, is very much real.

"Why, hello there, Lena," he growls menacingly. "Long time no see."

I jump from my chair, almost hitting my head on the overhead compartment. The flight attendants are busy going through the safety instructions and telling everyone to fasten their seatbelts, but I have to get off this plane.

My heart is beating so fast I think it might burst from my chest, but I wave at one of the flight attendants, who nods in my direction when she notices me. Once the safety demonstration is over, she approaches me with a polite yet stern smile.

"Yes, ma'am, how can I help you?"

"I need to get off this flight," I say hurriedly, glancing down at Zorin. He's observing me, his mouth curved in a smug smirk.

The flight attendant shakes her head. "I'm sorry, ma'am, but that's just not possible," she says firmly but not unkindly.

"The gate has already closed, and the captain is preparing for takeoff."

"Please," I beg, feeling Zorin's gaze bore into my back. "I can't be on this plane."

"I'm afraid it's too late for that," she says without sympathy. "It's only a two-hour flight, honey. You'll be just fine."

I'm the furthest thing from fine, but she can't know that.

"Can I switch seats then, at least?" I ask, beyond caring whether I sound desperate or not. I need to be away from Zorin as soon as possible.

The flight attendant sighs, the sound long-suffering and annoyed.

"Ma'am, the plane is full, as you can see." She gestures around, and I see that every single seat is taken. My stomach sinks at the realization that there's no way out. "Now, is there a problem here, or should I call the police?"

People are already starting to look at me and wonder what the problem is, so calling the police is absolutely off the table. I shake my head. "No, it's fine. Thank you."

She gives me a tight smile before turning around and heading back up the aisle. I sit back down reluctantly, well aware of Zorin and the malevolent smile he's giving me.

"Well, well," he says with a chuckle. "I guess you're stuck with me."

I swallow hard, fear churning in my gut. This was going to be a plane ride from hell.

# CHAPTER 23

**Gunnar**

At six-thirty a.m. sharp, my eyes snap open, and I'm awake.

My years in the military primed me to sleep on the go and wake up early, so early mornings are not unusual for me. What is unusual is how well I slept last night. I'm usually a light sleeper, but I was lights out after an intense night of lovemaking with Lena.

I smile at the thought of her as I stifle a yawn.

That little minx gets me going just by looking at her. *Her ass gives me life.* Her delicious little hole is so fucking satisfying.

Sitting up, I stretch and notice that Damon is fast asleep at the foot of the bed. Max is snoring loudly beside him, one leg dangling over the side of the bed.

Looks like Lena knocked their lights out, too.

Her scent is dwindling, and I realize she's not in bed with us, so I shuffle off to check the bathroom. She's not there, and her dress and shoes are gone. I'm still half asleep, but I snap awake as I check the lounge and kitchenette and don't find her there either.

Panic starts to seep into my blood as I approach the balcony.

We didn't go outside last night, and I don't see her sitting on one of the chairs, but I open the doors anyway, peering around the small space as if she'll magically appear. A cold feeling slides into my stomach, and I peer over the balcony railing and onto the street below, but Lena is nowhere to be seen.

*She's not here.*

I step back inside and shut the balcony door, my mind whirring with possibilities. Could Zorin have taken her? It can't be. There is no other alpha scent in here.

I sniff the air, trying to discern other scents in the room. Lena's distinct perfume of vanilla and wild honey lingers in the air, along with Damon and Max's scents, but nothing unfamiliar saturates the space.

I let my gaze rove over the surroundings, looking for anything that might be missing or broken. Everything is the same; nothing is out of place. The only thing missing is Lena.

If she wasn't taken, that means she left on her own.

*Fuck. Fuck. Fuck.*

She still doesn't trust us. My mind kicks into high gear as I consider where she might have gone. If she didn't leave too long ago, I could track her.

I rack my brain, trying to figure out if I felt her leave in the night and what time it could have been, but it's useless. I was too wrapped up in her to notice anything- I was passed out by the time we went to bed.

I head back into the bedroom and quickly shove on my suit pants and shirt from last night. I keep as quiet as possible, not wanting to wake Damon and Max unless it's vital. If I act quickly, I might be able to catch Lena, and all this panic would have been for nothing.

The hallway is quiet when I leave the room, the plush carpet of the hotel muffling my footsteps.

Sniffing the air deeply, I try to pick up on Lena's scent. I can smell it, but it's faint, mixed with the other smells permeating the hallways. My nose leads me to the elevator and into the lobby, where the night manager sits at the reception desk. He smiles when he sees me approaching.

"Good morning, sir. How can I help you?"

"I'm looking for a woman," I say, cutting straight to the point. "My girlfriend."

The word feels inadequate for what she really is. She's my *omega*, my love, and the mother of my child.

"Yes?"

"I'm wondering if you saw her leaving? Perhaps in the early hours of the morning?"

"What does she look like?" he asks.

"She's about average height, roughly five feet five, with wavy auburn hair. One blue eye, one green eye. She dresses quite modestly in muted colors. She might have been wearing a black evening dress."

The night manager shakes his head. "I'm afraid I haven't seen anyone matching that description all night."

"Are you sure? Can you ask another staff member who was on duty?"

He disappears into a room behind the front desk for a few moments, then reappears, looking apologetic. "My staff says they didn't see any women come through the lobby last night."

"May I check your security cameras?" I ask, starting to get frustrated. Someone must have seen something.

"I'm sorry, sir, but I can't allow you to do that. It's against our policy."

"But it's an emergency. My girlfriend is missing," I say, raising my voice.

"Unless you return with a warrant or a subpoena, I can't help you."

He's completely useless to me now, so I head out the front door, shading my eyes against the sun as I look for Lena. She's not outside, and all I see are desolate roads for miles.

I stalk back inside, knowing it's time to inform the pack. Lena's scent has disappeared, and I know I can't track her further. I have no choice but to wake the others and see what we can do. Worry churns in my gut.

She could be anywhere by now, and she's pregnant with our pup.

In my haste to alert Damon and Max, I burst into our room, the door slamming against the wall. Damon wakes instantly, springing up from the bed.

"Max!" I shout, throwing a pillow at his sleeping form. "Wake the hell up! Lena is missing!"

"W-what?" Max asks groggily, sitting up and staring at me in confusion. "Why are you being so fucking loud?"

"Lena is missing," I say again. Pain lances through my chest at the thought of her out there alone and vulnerable.

"What do you mean?" Damon asks, now wide awake. "She was right here all night long!"

I shake my head. "When I woke up, she was gone. I searched everywhere but couldn't find her. I asked downstairs at reception, and they said they hadn't seen her."

Damon slumps onto the bed, anguish clear on his face.

"Now I know why she didn't want to be marked last night," he mumbles, scrubbing a hand across his face. "She's been planning to escape from the start. Just when we let our guard down, she disappears this morning."

"It can't be. This is a mistake," says Max in disbelief as he throws on clothes.

Damon chuckles bitterly. "We must have scared her if she would rather be out alone than be protected by us. Do we even bother looking for her?"

The hurt on our pack leader's face cuts me to the core. He might not always show it, but I know just how deeply Damon feels. He loves Lena, and her withdrawal from his life with the pup he's always wanted has destroyed some part of him.

"Damon—" I say, reaching out to put a hand on his shoulder, but he shrugs me off.

"I don't need pity. Hell, I know you all feel the same."

"I think it's time we let her go," I say, coming to a realization. "She doesn't want us."

"She's carrying our pup," Damon snarls, getting up and approaching me. "And she is the only thing I think about!"

His eyes darken with anger, and I can feel my own eyes start to glow in response. With an irritated grunt, he turns sharply from me and begins to pick up his clothes from the floor.

"What the fuck are you doing?" I ask, confused by this sudden change in behavior.

"I'm going out to find her," he says shortly.

"The longer you argue, the further away Lena gets. Do you want to find her or not, Gunnar?" Max cuts in.

"Yes," I say finally, as Damon and I glare at each other angrily for a moment. But I feel my eyes return to normal as my temper cools.

Max is right. We don't have time to mull over how Lena feels about us.

"There's a note from her," Max says, picking up a piece of paper from the dresser.

*How can I fucking miss a note from her?*

Damon and I rush to either side of him, reading over his shoulder. The letter looks like it's stained with teardrops.

. . .

*I'm sorry I had to leave like this, but I know you would have convinced me to stay if I hadn't. Please know that my leaving is not your fault. I'm so grateful to you for being so kind and loving towards me, but I'll never feel safe as long as Zorin is out there. Not even you can protect me from him.*

*Please don't try to look for me. I promise I'm going somewhere safe for the baby and me.*

*Take care of each other.*

*Love,*

*Lena*

We finish reading the note, and I realize my worst fears are coming true. This is the second time it's happened. Another omega leaving us. Lena is gone, and she's not planning on coming back.

Wordlessly, we gather our things and make our way out of the hotel as quickly as possible. Our next stop is Lena's apartment building, where I hope we can find answers about her whereabouts.

I can smell her faintly at the apartment when we arrive, and I chase the scent into her room. Max unlocks the door with the spare keys he had cut, and we head inside. It's quiet, but there is evidence that she has been there recently.

"She's been here recently," Damon says darkly. "Do you think she went back to Zorin?"

"No, she'd rather be alone forever than be with another pack," I reply.

"This reminds me of..." starts Max, but I cut him off.

"She's nothing like Zalia," I say, cringing at the memory of the first omega, leaving us high and dry for another alpha pack. She had seduced every one of us and left during her heat when she wanted a bigger pack. "Lena is innocent, caring, and wants a peaceful life."

We check each room, looking in all the nooks and crannies where she might be able to hide, all in vain. All of her suitcases are gone, and her scent is still too faint to trace. I slump hopelessly onto her bed, my heart cracking behind my ribs.

I exchange desperate looks with Damon and Max, the pain in my heart reflecting on their faces.

# CHAPTER 24

### Lena

My knuckles turn white as I grip the armrest of my seat in a death grip when the plane takes off. It's only a two-hour flight to Little Rock, but I already feel like it's going to be the longest two hours of my life.

Especially sitting next to my ex, who tried to kill me.

The silence between us is suffocating, driving my anxiety higher as I wonder about his intentions. I stare pointedly out the window while my heart thumps like a drum.

Maybe if I act like he's not there, he'll leave me alone.

It's just wishful thinking, though, because when the seatbelt lights are switched off, and we can move through the cabin freely, I hear the click of his belt buckle and feel him lean into me.

Zorin's breath is hot against the side of my face, the stench of alcohol turning my already sensitive stomach into a writhing mess. I'm pressed against the cabin wall with nowhere else to go, and I hear Zorin chuckle as he presses in even closer.

"What do you want from me?" I ask, fighting back tears and trying to stay strong.

"Oh, Lena," he whispers menacingly in my ear. "I should have killed you all those years ago when I had the chance, preferably before I threw you out of the car that night. I'm surprised by the hold you seem to have on those other alphas. Do they have something I don't?"

"Yes, they most certainly do," I reply in a steely voice, gripping the armrest so tightly I feel it might snap. "They have love and compassion for others—traits you're severely lacking, Zorin."

He hums thoughtfully, then dismisses it with a derisive snort. "Either way, it doesn't matter. You've always been a worthless omega—the most pathetic of them all." He hisses the last part, venom dripping from each word, and I shrink inward, trying to ignore him.

Hot tears stream down my face, and I try to hide them with the scarf around my neck. I don't want him to see me crying and realize that his words still affect me. Any courage I thought I had gained in the last four years of being away from him seems to have vanished, and I feel like my old self again —the sad, defenseless omega who comes crawling back whenever he speaks to me.

For some reason, his scent is now repulsive to me; it was always alluring in the past.

A small voice in the back of my mind whispers that I should never have left Damon and his pack. I'm starting to regret my decision to leave the safety of the caring alphas I met, but it's far too late for that now.

"But why are you following me?"

"I know all about the pup you're carrying," Zorin states coldly, and my eyes snap to his face. "And I'm here because of what your pack did to mine. They killed Thomas."

"How do you know about the baby?" I whisper, horrified,

my blood running cold at the smug expression on his face. There's no way he could know about the baby.

"Oh yes," he whispers. "I can smell it on you. Why did you have to be so useless when you were my omega? Giving me and my pack a baby would have made you much more valuable."

"Why is this any of your business now?"

He taps his chin in thought, then smiles cruelly. "I might have finally found a use for you."

I swallow hard, trying to muster the strength to block him out. I can't go back to who I was before. It's not just me that I have to think about anymore. I have to protect the baby now, too.

"I'm not interested in playing your games, Zorin," I say sharply, straightening my shoulders. "I've got a new pack now. They'll kill you if you try to take me away from them."

"Where are they now?" he asks coldly. "They're clearly not interested in marking you. I'll accept you and the baby as a peace offering, even though your pack deserves to be obliterated for killing Thomas."

"Never. I'm not their omega anymore anyway," I say, trying to infuse as much bravado as possible into my voice. The more he believes that Damon, Max, and Gunnar are coming after him, the more he'll make my life miserable.

"Have you said anything to them about me, Aleks, and Raul? Did you tell them about us?" he asks suddenly.

*Oh, he's worried.*

I'm taken aback by his question, noticing the deep concern in his eyes. Is he worried that I might spill his secrets to another pack? Expose the abuse he inflicted on me? Judging by the look in his eyes, I realize it would be unwise to tell the truth, so I shake my head.

"No way. You're not worth my time," I say weakly, the strength I had mustered a moment ago slowly fading.

"Good," he replies, facing forward. I let out a tiny sigh of relief, but it's short-lived when I feel his hand on my thigh.

He squeezes my thigh, and it hurts as I hold back a cry. I wince in pain as he continues to squeeze harder, leaving what will undoubtedly be bruises behind.

The memory of Gunnar touching my thigh at the restaurant last night crosses my mind, and I can't help but think how different Zorin's touch is compared to Gunnar's. Gunnar's touch was gentle, while Zorin's is hard and aggressive, hurting me just for the pleasure of it.

There is no love, kindness, or care in him. Zorin is pure evil.

"Stop," I gasp out loud, and the stewardess glances at me.

"Am I hurting you, little omega?" he mocks, digging his fingers into my skin. The fabric of my leggings is thin, and I can feel his nails scratching my thigh.

"You are. You need to stop before I call someone."

"Now that you're pregnant, Lena, you're finally of some use to me. I want to make you my omega," he says, a maniacal look in his eye.

My heart races at the words coming from Zorin's mouth. *His omega?* After everything he's done to me?

I glance around frantically, but there's nowhere to go. I'm right at the back of the plane, with Zorin sitting next to me, blocking any escape I might have had. I'm trapped, and the realization sends me into hyperventilation.

My mind flashes back to the last night I saw Zorin and his pack, the way they beat me and left me for dead in the middle of the night. I can't allow myself to end up in that situation again, but I don't see another way out. He laughs softly at my reaction, that evil smirk returning to his face.

"Water or orange juice?" asks the flight attendant, and he releases me instantly.

"Water," Zorin replies smoothly, adopting his charming

business tone as if he hadn't just been squeezing my thigh. "Much appreciated."

"And you, ma'am?" the attendant asks.

"I'll take the same," I say, striving to keep my voice even and calm.

I sink further into my seat, trying to create as much distance as possible between myself and this deranged wolf in the cramped space. Eventually, he shifts his focus, trying to catch the flight attendant's attention, and I seize the opportunity to really look at him.

Once a handsome alpha, he now appears disheveled and unkempt. His hair is long and untidy, and his suit hangs loosely on him. A dark shadow of stubble marks his jaw, where he is usually clean-shaven. I briefly wonder what caused him to spiral like this. Was it finally seeing me happy without him and his cronies? Did he even have any mercy left in him?

Before I can stop myself, the words spill out, "How did you know where to find me?"

"I wasn't looking for you. You're not that important, my dear," he says, chuckling. "When your pack killed Thomas, I had to investigate. And what a surprise when I find out you're spreading your legs for them in that god-awful library of yours?"

I gulp, thinking about him watching me get knotted during my heat in the library. There were giant windows surrounding the library, and there was a chance he could have been watching me the entire time.

"They should be the ones you're mad at," I say, as I take a shaky sip of my water. "I'm not the one who killed him."

"The only way to get back at them is to steal something that's precious to them. Isn't that right?" says Zorin, cracking his fingers over his cup of untouched water. "So you're going to be my omega now."

"You wanted me dead," I whisper harshly. "Don't think I've forgotten that night."

"It won't happen again unless you do something out of line," he says, leaning back and closing his eyes. "I suggest you get some rest before I take you to your new home."

I take deep breaths to calm myself.

For weeks, I felt like someone was watching me until I saw the camera footage of Zorin. Initially, I thought it was Damon and his pack keeping an eye on me for protection, but now I realize it was Zorin all along.

They had been watching me for weeks, possibly months, and I hadn't known. I suppress a shiver. Nothing is as I thought it was.

The two-hour flight from D.C. to Little Rock passes agonizingly slowly.

Flying is usually my time to relax and nap, but this flight has me on edge. It feels like time is moving in slow motion.

My mind races as I try to devise an escape plan. Zorin won't let me out of his sight once we land.

I need to be smart and slip away without him noticing.

Finally, the captain announces that we're descending and will land at the airport shortly.

"Don't even think about trying to pull a fast one on me," Zorin growls in my ear as soon as we land. "You know you can't outrun me. You're an omega, and I'm an alpha. Remember that."

I nod mutely, knowing it's in my best interest to act meek and mild. Zorin is relying on my fear to ensure compliance, and that's exactly what I'll do. He has no idea I've grown stronger over the past few years without him constantly belittling me.

We disembark from the plane and head to collect our luggage. Zorin stays close, like glue.

He keeps a firm grip on my arm, watching me like a hawk.

Suddenly, an idea pops into my mind, and I seize the opportunity as I grab my luggage.

"Zorin," I say quietly, hoping my meek act is convincing. "I need to use the bathroom."

"Can't you hold it?" he grunts.

I shake my head. "No, I don't feel well. I've been battling morning sickness, and I feel like I might throw up. I feel faint." I place a hand on my stomach and wobble on my feet, trying to make my sickness more believable.

"Fine. Just go," he mutters under his breath, shoving me toward the bathrooms. He follows closely behind, keeping a watchful eye on me despite my claims of illness.

"Thank you," I say gratefully.

"I'll be right outside waiting, so no funny business," he warns.

I nod and open the ladies' room door, disappearing inside.

I quickly hurry into a stall and shut the door, digging through my handbag for my scent-blocker cream. Thank God I had the foresight to pack it in my carry-on luggage. Although I had hoped to remain hidden from the alphas, Zorin's reappearance is as good a reason to make myself invisible.

Heart pounding, I strip off my clothes as quickly as possible, furiously rubbing the scent-blocker lotion onto every inch of skin I can reach. The scar on my arm is puckered and ugly, a stark reminder of what Zorin can do if I don't escape. Not willing to take any chances, I apply more lotion to my toes.

I would rather be safe than sorry.

Once I'm dressed again, I shove the lotion back into my handbag and spot the perfume I also packed. An idea occurs to me, and I spray some on, hoping it will further mask my scent. The fragrance is entirely new to me, one I've never used before, so I'm hopeful Zorin won't recognize me beneath it.

I hurriedly put everything back in place with shaking hands and pulled my clothes on.

I don't know how long I have left to hide here. Zorin is impatient, and I know that if I take too long, he won't hesitate to barge into the bathroom looking for me.

Reaching for my phone in my purse, my heart races, hoping Zorin won't hear me. I never should have flown by myself. I should never have left the safety and comfort of my pack.

Now, there's only one thing left to do.

I dial the number and bring the phone to my ear. My heart races and my breaths come in short pants. Damon answers on the first ring.

"Lena?"

# CHAPTER 25

**Damon**

Lena wasn't in her apartment. And not at the hotel. The drive back from her apartment is quiet and solemn, each of us lost in our own thoughts.

We're at a loss for what to do next with no clues to go on, and Lena's scent is still too faint to trace.

Gunner's only suggestion was to go home, regroup, and then try to think of somewhere she could have gone.

We walk into the pack house, and suddenly my phone rings. One look at the caller ID has me fumbling to answer, my hands gripping the phone tightly in urgency.

"Lena?" I answer frantically, and Max and Gunnar stop in their tracks, their eyes whipping towards me. Max's eyes are wide with surprise, but Gunnar only looks concerned, waiting to hear what our omega has to say.

"Damon!" she sobs, the sound of her voice breaking my heart. She sounds scared, and I try to keep calm, knowing it won't help if I scare her any more than she already is.

"Where are you right now, darling?" I ask, putting my

phone on loudspeaker so the others can hear. "Where did you go?"

She takes a gulping breath, trying to form her words between her tears.

"D-Damon," she stutters. "H-help, h-he's..."

She dissolves into tears again, and I take a deep breath, trying to clamp down on the panic I can feel building in my chest. Gunnar and Max are leaning toward the phone in my hand, listening closely.

"Take a deep breath, baby," says Gunnar.

"Yes, slow down," I say gently, trying to get her to calm down even though I was fucking scared right now for her. "Deep breaths. Tell me what's wrong. Where are you?"

"I'm at an airport," she whispers as if she doesn't want to be overheard. "Clinton National Airport."

Max grabs a notebook and writes down the information.

"Okay, and what's happened? What's got you so scared, darling?"

"Zorin," she breathes, and my blood runs cold. Gunnar stills, his eyes starting to glow with anger.

"What did you say?"

"Zorin," she says again, this time a little louder. "He was on the same flight as me and sat in the seat next to me. He says he's been following me for months, watching everything I do. He knows that I'm pregnant."

She starts to cry again, and I try to remain as calm as possible while my packmates are already rushing out the door, and I follow them.

"Where is Zorin now?" I ask.

"He's outside the bathroom waiting for me. I don't have much time. He'll come looking for me if I don't hurry up."

A thought occurred to me, and I hope that Lena was smart enough to have thought of it first. If she wanted to get away from us, she certainly would have wanted to disguise her scent from us.

"Do you have your scent blockers on you?" I ask, praying that she took them with her.

"Yes," she says, and I breathe a huge sigh of relief. "I already took one and rubbed my scent blocker lotion on. I'm covered from head to toe."

"Good girl," I murmur, my lips curling up in a rueful smile as I join my pack at the car.

"Hold on," says Max, grabbing my phone from my hands. "We need to draw Zorin away from the bathroom so she can escape. Why don't I call Clinton National Airport and ask a staff member to request Zorin come to the help desk to take a phone call? That way, he'll be out of the way, which gives you time to run."

"Okay," she says quietly, and I'm impressed.

"That's fucking brilliant," Gunnar mutters. "Let's do it."

"Hold on, Lena," I say when Max hands me my phone back and moves into a distance to make a call on his phone. "We've got a plan. Max will get Zorin to go to the help desk to take a call. It should give you enough time to get away from him. Try to see if you can see when he leaves. When he does, you make your move. Okay, honey?"

"Okay," she whispers, and I hear what sounds like the click of a lock on the toilet stall door. There are some quiet footsteps before a door opens, and slightly louder chatter reaches my ears. "I can see him."

"Good, Max is making the call now. I will stay on the phone with you, alright?"

"I'm scared, Damon," she admits, her voice trembling, and all I want to do is reach through the phone and hug her. "I don't want him to catch me if I leave this bathroom. He'll kill me, I know it."

"You can do it, love," I soothe, listening out for Max's voice. "You're my brave omega. You won't let him get to you."

She's quiet for a few moments, and then, faintly in the background, I hear Zorin's name being called on the loudspeaker. Lena sucks in a sharp breath, and I tense.

"He's gone," she says. "I think it worked."

"Run, Lena," I say immediately, my chest tight with worry. "Run and don't look back. Get out of there now!"

I hear the clicking of the bathroom door, a few tentative footsteps, and everything goes quiet.

My heart stops and I look down at my phone, thinking that the plan didn't work and the worst has happened, but I see that the call cut out. My phone screen is dark, only my panicked expression staring back at me.

"Fuck!" I shout, my voice ragged, breath hitching in my throat as I slam my palm against the roof of the car.

"What happened?" Max asks frantically as he returns. "Did it work? Did she get away?"

"Lena's line went dead," says Gunnar.

"I don't know," I say, running a hand through my hair. "We lost connection."

"Shit!" he snaps. "We can't just sit here. If Zorin's there, we have to move. Now."

Gunnar's expression hardens, his eyes blazing with determination. "We take the chopper—fastest way. If Lena is in danger, every second counts."

"If Zorin gets his hands on her, we're fucked. I don't even want to think about what he'll do to her. I can't lose Lena, not like this," I growl, jumping into the car.

"Then we're in agreement. Let's move," says Max sharply.

I don't want to think about what will happen if we're too late. I'm not relaxing until I see her myself and hold her in my arms. I try to shove any doubts I may have to the back of my mind. We're bringing her home, even if we have to tear the city apart brick by fucking brick.

## Lena

As soon as Zorin is out of sight, I slip out of the bathroom and hurtle down the passageway, my suitcase flying behind me.

In my panic, I accidentally dropped the call with Damon, but I don't have time to call him back as I fly past several confused travelers and toward the airport exit.

My only focus is getting as far away from Zorin as possible.

I have no doubt that by now, he's worked out that Max's call was a diversion and is looking for me. He's going to be furious when he discovers that I've escaped, but I can't let that stop me.

Freedom is just within reach.

I race through the airport, running so fast that my scarf whips off from around my neck, fluttering somewhere behind me. My suitcase is knocking into people left and right as I round corners wildly, and I can barely spare a thought for the shouts of complaint when I finally see the exit doors and the taxi bay nearby.

I burst outside and hurriedly wave down a taxi that is just pulling up, two people leaving the backseat.

The couple looks at me in alarm before grabbing their bags and hurrying inside the airport.

I fall into the backseat, slamming the door and ducking down to avoid being seen. If Zorin managed to track me outside, I don't want him to know where I'm going.

Taking a deep breath, I try to calm my nerves before I speak to the taxi driver.

"51st Maple Avenue, please," I wheeze at last, giving him the address of the home that I rented online. Hopefully, they'll allow me to check in early.

"Are you all right there?" the driver asks in concern, staring at me with wide eyes. "Do you need me to call someone?"

"I'm okay," I say quietly, wiping the tears off my cheeks. "I just really need to get going, please."

He casts me one last concerned look in the rearview mirror. "All right, but let me know if you need anything."

The driver pulls out smoothly from his parking spot, and I take one final look behind me as we pull into the city traffic to make sure that Zorin is nowhere to be seen.

*Drive faster. Drive faster.*

I'm nearly having a heart attack watching the traffic and how slow we're going.

My fingers are trembling, and I clasp them together on my lap, trying to keep it together for just a little bit longer until I can get to safety.

Things could not have gone any more haywire.

Remembering the plane ride from hell, I'm just grateful I was able to escape him one more time. With Zorin, it was complicated. He was my ticket to escape my hellish mother and the hope for freedom.

But I was so wrong. So very wrong.

The taxi driver drops me off in front of my rental home, and I tip him generously for his promptness.

"Now you take care of yourself, miss," he says. "If you need a ride anytime, call me."

Grabbing my carry-on from the backseat, I lumber out of the car with shaking limbs, and the taxi drives off. I walk up to the house, rolling my suitcase behind me.

The home is a modest light green color, giving me cozy vibes. Punching in the code the landlord emailed, I walk inside and immediately lock the door.

I'm a little paranoid right now.

I double-check every window in the townhouse to make sure that they are closed and locked. I check the kitchen pantry, the bathroom behind the shower curtain, the bedroom closet, and even under the beds.

I didn't tell anyone where I was going, but Zorin scared me badly enough that I think he's already in the home waiting for me.

To make matters worse, Zorin never said whether he had acted alone in his stalking of me. Aleks and Raul could just as easily be part of his plan, and I would be none the wiser until they showed up. The thought terrifies me, and I feel a violent wave of nausea pulse inside me, desperate to be let out.

I rush to the bathroom and puke into the toilet.

This time, there's no Damon sitting beside me to hold my hair and rub circles on my back, and I cry as I battle through my nausea, occasionally hugging the toilet as my body expels the little I've eaten today. I know that my vomiting is partly due to morning sickness, but I also think that it's partly due to stress. Damon isn't here to keep me calm with his purring.

Hopefully, I'll be safe here for a while.

Panting, I slowly get up with shaky limbs and flush the toilet. I wonder when this nausea will stop.

I wash my face and rinse my mouth, then head to the living room to sit and relax for a moment. My phone is still in my bag, where I had thrown it in my haste to leave the airport, so I grab it to see if I've missed anything.

It was on silent, so I was surprised to see that I had several missed calls and texts from the alphas.

**MAX**

Did the plan work? Were you able to get out?

**MAX**

Is everything okay, Lena?

**MAX**

Call me sweetheart. We're worried sick about you. I love you, and I need to know you're safe.

My heart aches at the declaration of his feelings, and tears roll down my face.

**DAMON**

Please let us know that you're all right, baby.

**GUNNAR**

Lena, I'm desperate. Call me. I love you.

*Why did I ever leave when I had the love of three phenomenal alphas right in front of me?* I feel like a moron, but it's too late for that now. All I can do now is let them know I'm okay and where I am.

I send the alphas a group text.

> The plan worked, and I'm okay. I'm safe. I'll send you my location.

My message has only just been delivered when my phone rings, Damon's name flashing on the screen.

"Damon?" I answer, surprised that he's calling me within seconds of me sending the message.

"Did you make it home safe?" he asks loudly over the sounds of a whirring engine.

*Was he in some kind of helicopter?* My face heats with embarrassment at the urgency he and his pack are taking to get to me.

"I'm fine," I say, raising my voice so he can hear me. "I just texted you all back. Where are you? It sounds like you're flying."

"That's because we are!" he shouts over the loud engines. "We're on our way to you. Max has got your location. Hang tight, okay? We're coming for you. Don't answer the door for anyone except us, and we'll let you know when we're there. Promise me you won't open the door no matter what."

"Okay, I promise," I say, not wanting to go against his order this time. *I need him.* I need his pack to keep our baby safe. "Thank you, Damon."

There's a long pause, and I wait for him to say something more. Max and Gunnar told me they love me. Is Damon going to do the same? My heart skips a beat at the thought.

"We'll be there soon," he says gruffly and hangs up.

Disappointment wells in my chest, but I swallow it down.

I can hear in his voice that he's upset with me. He doesn't trust me now and thinks I'm like his ex. Dropping the phone onto the couch, I sigh as I close my eyes, and tears roll down my face. Loud sobs fill the living room as I break down.

Damon's trust in me is gone. It's my fault.

Thirty minutes later, my shirt is drenched with my tears, and my face is wet.

Leaving my phone on the couch, I shuffle into the kitchen to make something to eat. I grab the few snacks I'd bought at the airport and scrounge some ramen from inside one of the kitchen cupboards.

My stomach rumbles hungrily, and I chuckle softly through my tears, patting it gently.

"Don't worry, we'll get you fed, little one," I murmur and start cooking while thinking about the baby that will be here in months. There's no point beating myself up over messing up everything Damon and I had between us. There's a baby, and I need to protect him or her from the threat outside these walls.

My hands are busy preparing the meal, but my mind is going a hundred miles an hour. I head back into the living room and turn on the TV, hoping it will drown out the noise in my head. I check the time on my phone, wondering where Damon, Max, and Gunnar are.

Slurping my noodles, I watch the comedy show on the screen without smiling. I can't relax until Damon and his pack are here. For some reason, a part of my soul is also missing them. My heart aches as I think about every one of them.

The thought alone is scary, but it makes me giddy that I could fall in love again. And maybe I'm not as damaged as I think I am.

# CHAPTER 26

**Damon**

The moment Max, Gunnar, and I arrive in Little Rock, we're on high alert. We don't know if Zorin is still in the area since Gunnar couldn't trace him using our usual channels.

Not wanting to take any chances, we hire a car as soon as we land at Clinton National Airport and head to the destination Lena provided. From the looks of our GPS, she's staying in a small townhouse just outside the city center.

I drive while Max navigates from the front seat, and Gunnar continues running recon on Zorin from the back.

"Still nothing," Gunnar sighs, setting his laptop beside him. "How much longer until we arrive?"

"About ten minutes," Max replies, glancing at the GPS.

Thankfully, the roads are nearly empty, and I speed through the city, eager to reach my omega. I had wanted so badly to tell her that I love her over the phone, but I didn't want to scare her. She's already been through so much, and the last thing she needs is me trying to stake a claim on her. If she's not ready for what we have to offer, I need to respect that.

Ten minutes later, I park outside the townhouse.

It's quaint, with green-trimmed walls and a neatly manicured lawn. There's no car parked in the driveway, so I assume Lena must have taken a taxi instead of renting a car.

We jump out of the car, and Gunnar looks around, his brow furrowed in concentration.

"We need to secure the area," I bark, and he immediately nods, walking toward the townhouse to search the perimeter. Max checks the nearby townhouses and their gardens. After a few minutes, we reconvene.

"There's nothing," Gunnar says, sniffing the air deeply. "I don't smell anyone else and no other alphas."

"Zorin?" I ask tersely.

Gunnar shakes his head. "No scent trails and no disturbances around or near where Lena is staying. I don't think he's found her."

"Thank God," Max mutters, and I nod in agreement.

My heart isn't at peace yet, and I don't relax. I need to see Lena before I even think about letting my guard down.

Quietly, the three of us approach the front door of the townhouse. I can see into the living room to my right, where I faintly hear the TV on inside. I sniff the air, hoping to catch a whiff of her delicious perfume to confirm she's there, but I smell nothing.

"She's taken her inhibitor," Max reminds me. "We won't be able to smell her until it wears off."

I raise my hand and knock sharply on the door. The TV plays quietly behind the wood, but there's no answer.

I knock again, this time with a bit more impatience.

"Maybe she's sleeping?" Gunnar suggests. "It's been one hell of a day for her."

"I want to see her now," I snarl, grunting in frustration.

"How do we know she didn't get kidnapped? We need to make sure, ASAP."

"Let me check around the side of the house and look in the bedroom," Max interjects before I get too fired up. "Maybe she thinks it's someone else. You *did* tell her not to open the door."

"Fine," I growl, and he jogs around the side of the house before I lose my temper. He returns a few minutes later.

"No, she's not there," he says, and I pull out my cell phone.

Maybe she'll answer her phone instead of the door. I dial her number, tapping my foot impatiently as it rings. When it goes straight to voicemail, I shove my phone angrily into my pocket.

"This can't be happening," I growl in irritation, breathing harshly with worry. "If she won't open this fucking door, I'll kick it down."

Gunnar and Max exchange worried glances as I prepare to kick the door down.

### Lena

My eyes snap open, and I'm suddenly wide awake.

I had fallen asleep on the couch after eating lunch. The TV is still on, and a random show is playing in the background. I sit up gingerly, listening for any sounds. It wasn't a nightmare or a noise that woke me, but something deep inside told me it was time to wake up.

My anxiety instantly skyrockets, and I'm on high alert, trying to figure out what it was that disturbed me. A strange smell reaches my nose, and I take a deep breath.

There are alphas outside my front door.

Panic rises within me, worried that Zorin has finally found me, but the scent becomes clearer.

*Smoked cedarwood and black pepper.*
*Pine.*
*Fresh earth.*

There are alphas outside my door. *My alphas*. Damon, Max, and Gunnar are here. Smiling, I leap off the couch and rush to open the front door.

Damon's massive form stands in the doorway.

His eyes are dark with fury, and he looks ready to kick the door down.

"Oh," I say, startled as I step back in alarm.

His shoulders soften and he has a sheepish look on his face, "you weren't answering the door."

"I'm so sorry," I say, bursting into tears and throwing myself into his arms. He catches me effortlessly, and I cling to him, overwhelmed with emotion that he is finally here.

I can hear the pounding of his heart even through my sobs and smell the adrenaline radiating from him in waves. He's furious with me. I know he is, but he still holds me close, and I'm grateful he hasn't thrown me off yet.

"It's okay," he chuckles. "It's not a big deal. I got a little impatient and almost broke the door down. You must have been in the bathroom or something."

"I'm sorry I left," I cry into his chest as he scoops me up to carry me into the house.

"Shh, Lena darling," he soothes, the gravel in his voice calming me. "It's okay. I've got you." He rubs my back gently, easing me into him.

Max and Gunnar follow us inside, closing and locking the door behind them. Damon walks through the house and into the bedroom, gently setting me on the bed before kicking off his shoes and climbing in beside me, settling against the headboard.

I curl into his side immediately, not wanting to distance myself from him. After the hell I've been through today, I need the security of his solid form next to me. Max and Gunnar join us, surrounding me protectively.

It's quiet for a few moments, and I allow myself to relax fully for the first time all day, content to soak in my alphas' warm and comforting presence.

Gunnar is the first to break the silence.

"We need to know," he says gently, brushing a strand of hair away from my face. "What happened today? Why did you leave like that?"

I sniffle, tears leaking from my eyes and dripping down my cheeks.

"I'm sorry," I whisper hoarsely. "I got scared."

"Did we scare you?" asks Max. "Was there something that made you worried?"

I shake my head.

"My life has been..." I search for the right word. "Difficult, to say the least. I've been alone for so long that I've never felt I could trust or rely on anyone but myself."

"But why did you leave us?" Damon growls, and I can hear the heartbreak in his voice. "Leave me? I've done everything I can to show you that you can trust me. Was it not enough?"

I left him, just like his last omega did.

I can hear how hurt he is. I can feel the slight tremble in his body as he sits next to me, and shame washes over me.

"I'm sorry," I sniffle. "I never meant to hurt you. Or Max and Gunnar. I'm just scared that what happened with Zorin and his pack will happen with you, too."

"We would never hurt you," Damon declares.

"Zorin made me believe that all alphas had to mistreat their omegas to comply," I whisper. I take a deep breath, steeling myself for what I have to say next. "When I met you guys, I thought you would be the same—flattering me to get me to stay with you, then abusing me once you had me marked."

Tears roll freely down my cheeks, but I don't wipe them away.

"I thought it would be better to get away, to escape," I continue, my heart aching, "than to be stuck in a situation I could never change once marked by alphas. I just wanted to be free."

"Lena," Damon says, turning his body toward me and placing a tender hand on my face, tears in his eyes.

It's so unlike him that my heart aches at the sweet gesture. He dips his head until we're at eye level and wipes away the tears on my cheeks with his thumb.

"I'm so unbelievably sorry for everything you've been through, darling," he murmurs, his dark eyes earnest. "No one should ever be treated that way. You deserve so much more, and I want you to be happy. I'll understand whatever choice you make, whether to stay with us or to leave. But more than anything, I want you to know that I would never hurt you. You will always be safe with me."

My heart soars at the sincerity on his face. His words are simple yet heal a part of me I didn't know was still bleeding. It feels as if I've been waiting my whole life to hear them.

I lean in, my heart racing as I close the distance between Damon and me. The warmth of his breath mingles with mine, and I can hardly believe I'm about to do this.

I place my lips gently against his. Our lips touch, and my heart flutters wildly at the contact.

I haven't kissed anyone on the lips since I was with my last pack, and I've avoided it every time the alphas wanted to try.

Damon seems surprised for a moment, but then I feel him relax against me, and his lips respond to mine with a soft warmth that ignites something deep inside me.

As we kiss, my heart swells. It's tender, unlike anything I've experienced before.

A connection sparks between us, the taste of hope mingling with the lingering uncertainty and fear of my past. I lose myself in the kiss, savoring the feeling of being wanted and cherished—something I had almost forgotten was possible.

Eventually, I pull away, slightly breathless but feeling like I could do anything now. Damon looks taken aback, and a rush of shyness washes over me.

"Wow," he says simply.

"I've wanted to do that for a while now," I whisper, my cheeks heating with a blush. I feel both vulnerable and exhilarated by my boldness. A giggle bubbles up from my chest and catches in my throat as tears build up in my eyes.

To break the tension, I lean in again, planting a quick, playful peck on his lips. He kisses me back hard until my breathing accelerates. After the kiss, his smile widens, and instinctively, I try to hide my face, overwhelmed by the surge of emotions.

Damon gently lifts my chin, refusing to let me shy away.

"It was worth the wait," he says softly, his gaze steady and sincere. His usually dark eyes are bright with emotion, a warmth in their depths that I haven't seen before. "That was the best kiss of my life."

"Really?" I ask, my heart lifting.

He pauses for a moment, then speaks the truth he had previously hesitated to share, "I love you, Lena. With all my heart."

"Oh," I breathe as Max and Gunnar chuckle softly around me. Warmth spreads in my heart as I turn to Max and kiss him on the lips. Our kiss is gentle, with him cupping my face as if he's treasuring every moment.

"I love you," Max says softly, and my heart soars.

Gunnar turns me toward him with a finger under my chin. "May I?"

I nod and close my eyes as he leans in for a kiss. Our lips mesh as he kisses me while Max and Damon caress my body. His kiss is fierce and passionate; I can feel how much he has been wanting and waiting for this moment.

I pull away breathlessly, and his eyes are glowing.

"I love you, Lena," he growls, and I look down, blushing. A warmth spreads through me at his words, making me feel cherished.

I take a deep breath and pull their hands over my belly.

"You can feel our baby," I say quietly, my voice shaky with excitement. I want to laugh at the expression that cross their faces, of excitement, love, and reverence, as their large hands cup my stomach.

Damon looks up at me, his eyes sparkling with hidden joy.

"I'm so excited to meet our baby," he says, a wide grin on his face. Max and Gunnar nod in agreement, their expressions mirroring my joy.

All the pain I endured has led me to this point in my life. It might have been hard, but it was worth it. I have everything I've ever wanted—a baby on the way, a pack that loves and protects me, and a bond that feels unbreakable.

Zorin is still out there trying to make my life miserable, but in this moment, surrounded by my alphas, I finally feel at home.

## CHAPTER 27
### SIXTEEN WEEKS LATER

**Lena**

Light filters in beneath my eyelids, and I wake slowly, stretching my arms above my head. After my little escapade to Little Rock, Damon and his pack brought me back home to D.C. in a helicopter.

I was grateful not to have to board another plane.

Seeing Zorin in the seat next to mine had made me wary of flying alone for quite some time. He seemed to have vanished from the city, but I didn't want to risk it if he was still nearby.

Max and Gunnar had helped me pack up my apartment, and I had moved in with the alphas.

Tonight, Damon and I shared the main bedroom with the en-suite, and I was thankful to snuggle up to him each night, knowing he would protect me at any moment.

I blink slowly, trying to adjust my eyes to the light in the room.

My sleep had been deep and peaceful, and I felt warm and snug in the blankets of the king-sized bed I shared with my pack leader. Life as their omega had been relatively tranquil, and I loved every minute of it. I would take turns sleeping in each alpha's room since it was more comfortable long-term.

"Good morning, gorgeous," Damon rumbles from beside me.

I turn and give him a sleepy smile. He watches me the way he always does when he wakes before I do, his eyes glowing affectionately.

"Good morning to you, too," I mumble, stifling a yawn.

"Did you sleep well?" he asks, a smile tugging at the corner of his mouth.

"I don't remember waking up screaming from nightmares last night," I reply. "Being with you is helping me."

His brow furrows as he scoots closer, wrapping a comforting arm around my waist. "You've been through a lot, love. Don't be too hard on yourself. These things take time."

"Probably," I say, nuzzling into his chest.

The house feels unusually quiet.

By this time, the aroma of breakfast cooking would typically waft through the open bedroom door, and the sounds of the morning news would be coming from the TV in the living room. It's too still, and I sit up in a panic, worried that something is wrong.

"Where are Max and Gunnar?" I ask, alarm rising in my chest.

"They've gone out for the morning. They're looking into Zorin. We need to find him before he finds you."

My heart races with fear at the mention of his name. I've been trying not to dwell on him and his mysterious disappearance. Part of me feels that he isn't truly gone from my life.

"What if he comes back?" I ask, fearfully looking at Damon with wide eyes.

He shakes his head. "I dare him to. And if he does, I won't

hesitate to tear him limb from limb. I'm not joking about that, baby."

"Don't worry, I don't have feelings for him at all," I say, relaxing against him as he slides a hand across my stomach. My belly is gently rounded, just beginning to show my pregnancy. I haven't gone for a scan or a check-up since Doctor Roman told me I was expecting.

Life has just been too hectic.

Damon rubs my belly gently, his gaze tender as he looks at me.

"Our baby is growing so fast," he murmurs. "Do you want me to take you to the doctor today for an ultrasound and check-up? You've been under so much stress lately- I just want to make sure everything is okay."

My heart softens at the concern on his face.

"That would be wonderful," I say, leaning up to kiss him gently on the lips. "I just need to get ready, and then we can go."

As I stand at the bathroom sink, brushing my teeth, I can't help but smile at the thought of the alphas in my life stepping up to protect our baby and making sure that I'm okay. It's a comforting realization, and my heart swells with gratitude as I reflect on how different this feels compared to my old pack.

Zorin, Aleks, and Raul would never have shown me such care or concern.

They were far too wrapped up in controlling me to spare me a second thought. I shudder at the thought of what might have happened if I'd had a baby with them instead, but I push it away. That was in the past, and I've moved on.

Even though Damon and his pack haven't marked me yet, I know it will happen soon. I can feel it in my heart and soul.

I rinse my mouth and wash my face. Once I'm done, I stare at myself in the bathroom mirror for a moment. The omega staring back at me is a stranger in all the best ways—my eyes are brighter, my skin is clearer, and there's a happiness about me that I haven't seen in a long time. I smile, thinking about my alphas and the glow they bring me.

I don't feel so alone anymore.

Lost in my thoughts, a shadow at the bathroom door catches my attention, and I feel Damon's presence behind me.

"I love you," he says, hugging me from behind, his warm breath brushing against my ear. He envelops me in his arms, his scent surrounding me.

My body awakens as he kisses my neck.

"Oh, Damon," I moan as he sucks and licks my skin. Watching our reflection in the mirror is turning me on. I can see his eyes dark with passion as he worships my body, kissing along my shoulders and arms.

"I love it when you say my name, sweetheart," he says, pushing my legs apart with his bare foot. He reaches between my legs from behind. "I want you to watch in the mirror as I please you, my love."

My belly flutters with arousal and it feels so freaking good. My heart races at his words, and a rush of slick drenches my underwear.

"But we need to go to the doctor's," I protest, breathing hard, even though I've missed this.

The alphas haven't been demanding intimacy since I've been afflicted with morning sickness. But I've been doing well this week, and Damon has patiently waited.

In the mirror, I can see his pointer finger rubbing around my pussy in long, slow strokes. My face reddens.

"The doctor can wait," Damon growls, his fingers sliding beneath my panties. "I need you now."

I gasp as his fingers find my wet folds. In the mirror, I

watch as his eyes darken with desire, his gaze locked on my reflection as he begins to stroke me.

My lips part, breaths coming in short gasps as his fingers work their magic on my pussy until it squelches with slick.

"Sorry about the sound," I whisper, my face flushed, looking away from the mirror.

"I love it. Look into the mirror," he commands, pushing my underwear to the side for a better view. "Look how beautiful you are when you're aroused for me. All that slick sliding down your legs."

I can't tear my eyes away from our reflection—my flushed cheeks, parted lips, and how my body arches into his touch. Damon's fingers glide through my folds, circling my entrance before sliding up to tease my clit.

"Oh god," I gasp as he drags his finger back down to push into me.

"You're so wet for me already," he murmurs against my ear, his free hand cupping my breast through my nightgown. "I love how responsive you are, how your body knows exactly who it belongs to."

My legs tremble as he adds another finger inside me, thrusting in and out until I'm moaning in his arms.

He circles my clit with deliberate strokes.

"Damon," I whimper, my hips rocking against his hand.

"Ah, Lena," he growls, his voice rough with desire. "I want you to watch what I do to you. I want you to see how perfect you look when you're desperate for my cock."

His crude words send another flood of wetness between my thighs, and Damon groans appreciatively when he feels it coat his fingers.

"Such a good, needy omega," he praises, withdrawing his hand. I whimper at the loss, but then I feel him lifting my nightgown, bunching it around my waist. "Hands on the counter. Keep watching."

I obey instantly, placing my palms flat on the cool marble as I lean forward slightly.

In the mirror, I see Damon behind me, his eyes predatory as he shoves his pajama pants down his hips. His cock springs free, thick and hard, the head already glistening with pre-cum.

"Is this what you want?" he asks, stroking himself slowly as I watch.

"Yes," I breathe, unable to look away from his thick cock. "Please, I need you inside me."

He positions himself behind me, the blunt head of his cock teasing my entrance. "Tell me who this pussy belongs to."

"You," I gasp. "All yours."

With one powerful thrust, he buries himself inside me, and I cry out at the delicious stretch. Our eyes lock in the mirror as he begins to move, his hands gripping my hips with bruising force.

"That's right," he growls, his pace steady and deep. "Mine to fuck, mine to breed, mine to protect."

Each thrust pushes me forward as I feel him stretching me.

"Oh!"

"Touch yourself," Damon commands, his voice a thick growl. "I want to see you pleasure yourself while I'm inside you."

My breath catches in my throat as I meet his intense gaze in the mirror. His eyes are almost black with desire, pupils dark as he continues to thrust into me with measured strokes.

"But I'm shaking so much," I whimper.

"Do it," he urges, slowing his pace slightly. "Show me how you like to be touched."

With trembling fingers, I reach between my legs, finding my swollen clit. The first touch makes me gasp, my inner walls clenching around Damon's thick length. His answering groan vibrates through me.

"That feels so fucking good," I moan as I circle my sensitive, swollen clit.

"Good librarians, don't swear," he growls, his hands tightening on my hips as he thrusts into me faster in a punishing rhythm. He pulls my hair back, so I'm looking into the mirror again. "You are going to watch me take you, omega."

The dual sensations—my fingers on my clit and Damon's cock stretching me open—are overwhelming. My legs quiver, threatening to give out beneath me as the pleasure increases in my core.

"This is hot," I gasp, watching him fuck me from behind in the mirror.

"You're so fucking tight," Damon says, his voice strained as he watches our movements in the mirror.

His pace increases, each thrust harder and deeper than the last. The sound of skin slapping against skin fills the bathroom, echoing off the tiles along with our labored breathing and desperate moans.

I can feel his cock throbbing inside me, growing impossibly harder as I—

"Damon," I cry out, my fingers moving faster against my clit. "I'm close...oh my god."

"Come for me, baby," he demands, his thrusts becoming erratic. "Let me feel you come around my cock."

The pressure inside me builds to a crescendo, and when Damon angles his hips to hit that perfect spot deep inside, I shatter.

My orgasm crashes through me in violent waves, my inner walls pulsing and clenching around him as I cry out his name. My vision blurs at the edges, but I force myself to keep watching in the mirror, captivated by the raw pleasure on Damon's face as he experiences my release.

"Fuck," he grunts, his movements becoming more forceful and desperate. "You feel so good, so tight around me, hugging my cock."

He thrusts once, then twice more, before burying himself to the hilt with a hoarse shout. I feel his cock pulse inside me, his hot seed filling me as his knot swells, locking us together. The sensation triggers another smaller orgasm, leaving me gasping and trembling in his arms.

Damon collapses against my back, his breath coming in harsh pants against my neck. His lips find my skin, pressing urgent, open-mouthed kisses along my shoulder and ear.

"That was so good," I say, gasping as he hugs me tight, his knot pulling me in closer.

"I agree, my love. My *omega*."

# CHAPTER 28

**Lena**

Later that same morning, we arrive at the hospital and Doctor Humphrey, the OBGYN, greets us in the waiting room.

"Miss Lena, it's wonderful to meet you," he says with a smile, his eyes warm. "I'm glad you've come in today, as you are quite far along in the pregnancy."

"It's nice to see you, Doctor," I reply, smiling, excited at the prospect of having my first ultrasound and seeing my baby. "I'm sorry I haven't been in sooner. Things have been a bit crazy."

Doctor Humphrey glances at Damon, who stands close to me with one arm wrapped possessively around my waist.

"And this is the...father, I presume?" he asks hesitantly, unsure whether his assumption is correct.

I swallow a laugh at the expression on Damon's face. He looks sheepish as if embarrassed by his previous reaction the last time someone referred to him that way.

"That's me," he says gruffly, shaking the doctor's hand.

"Follow me, and we'll set you up for an ultrasound."

I'm giddily excited as we follow him into the sonar room, and I get comfortable on the bed. Damon sits in the chair next to me, grabbing my hand and giving it a small squeeze of comfort. The doctor pulls my shirt up and pushes my leggings down a little, giving him enough space to rub some warm jelly on my stomach.

He grabs the wand and switches the machine on.

"Right," he says, angling the screen toward us. "Let's see how this baby's doing."

The wand is cold against my flesh initially, causing my skin to prickle, and I can feel the flutter of nerves in my stomach. When the screen lights up and the first image forms, I lean closer, my heart pounding like a drum.

Suddenly, Doctor Humphrey's eyes widen in disbelief, and my breath catches in my throat.

"This can't be right," he mutters.

"What is it?" I ask, my heart racing with worry.

"Hmm, one sec," he says, pressing the wand harder against my belly to get a clearer view of what's happening.

"Tell us, Doctor," Damon barks, losing patience, but I can hear the panic in his voice.

"It looks like you're expecting... four babies!" he exclaims, and the words hang heavily in the air.

I stare at the screen in disbelief, not quite believing what he's saying, but there, right in front of my eyes, are four little movements on the ultrasound monitor.

I turn to Damon in shock. He looks stunned, but his eyes sparkle with excitement.

*Four babies.*

"Wait, are you *sure*?" I ask, turning back to the doctor. This can't be real, but I've heard of omegas producing many pups at the same time, so it's entirely possible.

"Pretty sure," the doctor says with finality in his tone.

"You're going to have one big family. Is this your first pregnancy?"

"It is," I reply, my heart racing as Damon squeezes my hand. Images of juggling four crying babies fill my mind. "What are we going to do?!"

"We'll love them. And we'll raise them to be respectful members of our pack," Damon growls, leaning over me.

"Pack?" the human doctor asks.

"He means family," I say quickly, smiling as Damon kisses me deeply, and I know he's one happy pack leader.

---

We return home a couple of hours later with pictures of the ultrasound. I can't wait to share the news with Max and Gunnar—I know they'll be over the moon when they hear about our tiny quadruplets.

A pang of sadness shoots through me when I think of my family.

My sisters would be beside themselves, already planning a baby shower and putting together the nursery of my dreams. Despite her coldness toward me growing up, my mother should probably know that she will be a grandmother one day.

My heart aches. I miss my sisters so much, and I wonder how I can get the news to them all the way on Howl's Edge Island.

"We only have one crib."

Damon's voice interrupts my train of thought, and I turn to him, not understanding what he's saying.

"What?" I ask in confusion.

"I bought a crib a while ago when we found out you were expecting," he says, "but now I'll have to buy three more. Four babies," he chuckles, shaking his head in disbelief.

"Maybe we should set this one up and see if it's a good brand," I suggest, standing on my tiptoes to kiss him. He pushes his tongue into my mouth with a low growl. I pull away breathlessly. "Don't worry, I'm not going anywhere. Go ahead and set it up. Afterwards..."

"Ooh, I like the sound of where that's going," he grunts, watching me with dark eyes as he quickly springs into action.

Minutes later, Damon is sitting in the living room, trying to set up our only crib.

I sit cross-legged on the floor, watching him struggle with the crib parts scattered around him. His brows are furrowed deeply, frustration clear in every tense movement. He sighs and glances around, clearly irritated. I want to laugh—it's quite something to see my big, bad alpha get defeated by a piece of furniture.

"I'm sure I had a screwdriver here somewhere," he mutters, moving crib pieces around in his search.

"I can get a spare one," I offer, pushing up from the floor.

He waves me off, shaking his head. "Don't worry about it, darling. I can manage."

"I don't mind," I insist, determined to help because watching him struggle with putting the crib parts together is turning me on, but I'm not about to let him know that I'm wet for him right now. "I'm up now anyway."

He pauses, still gripping one side of the crib, then reluctantly nods. He sniffs the air. "The toolbox is in the basement. But I can smell that you're ready..."

"No, I'm not!" I squeal, running toward the basement. I hear him chuckling, but I escape so he can be productive today.

The door creaks when I open it, and a damp smell reaches my nostrils. It's a little dark and dingy down the stairs, so I reach for the light switch on the wall. There isn't one, so I assume there must be a switch at the bottom of the stairs.

Grabbing the wooden handrail, I make my way down slowly, careful not to trip on my feet or any debris on the steps. When I reach the bottom, I fumble around for the light switch. The darkness is oppressive, and my eyes take time to adjust to the gloom. I finally find the pull cord, and light floods the space when I sense something behind me.

A familiar scent pulls at my senses- lemongrass.

*Zorin*.

My eyes widen, realization rushing through me, but before I can react, Zorin's arm is around my throat, and his other hand covers my mouth. I claw at his hand, desperate to get away, but he only tightens his grip, cutting off my air supply.

"Make one sound, you stupid bitch, and I'll fucking kill you," he growls menacingly in my ear. "No one gets away from me."

I'm terrified.

All the blood in my veins has turned to ice. I want to beg him to stop, to leave me alone, but his grip against my windpipe is crushing.

Even if I wanted to, I can't make a sound to call for help.

"You think you're so smart, don't you?" he hisses, spittle flying onto my cheek. "You think your little plan saved you from me? Well, you're wrong." I whimper at the malice in his voice. "I've caught you now, bad omega, and I'm going to mark you before your new pack even gets the chance. That way, you'll be forced to be mine."

I scream against the hand covering my mouth in vain. Not one sound escapes as he chuckles darkly behind me.

# CHAPTER 29

### Lena

Zorin's grip on me is so tight that it borders on painful. His fingers dig into my skin, nails clawing at my flesh. I struggle against his hold, terrified of what he might do to me and my babies. He has already threatened to kill me if I make a sound, and I fear he will follow through on his sickening promise if I'm not careful.

"Stop moving, or I will kill you," he whispers heavily into my ear, crushing me against his chest. "I can smell your arousal."

I can't scream, so I stop moving to calm down. I need to think clearly. *Why is he doing this? What is his endgame? And where are Aleks and Raul?*

A lone alpha out here is confusing to me. A pack usually stays together. He was in Little Rock alone, and now he's in the basement of my pack's home alone. Aleks and Raul are nowhere to be seen, and I can't smell them nearby. A shiver runs through me as fear spikes my blood even more. If they aren't here, they could be anywhere, and the thought terrifies me.

Zorin may be deranged, but Aleks and Raul are just as unpredictable.

"I think it's time to leave, little omega," Zorin mutters. The soft, controlled way he speaks sends goosebumps prickling across my skin. "I don't want to mark you here in this dingy basement."

The thought of being marked by him and claimed forever makes me sick. I can't believe I craved it years ago, and their acceptance of me.

He hums as if in thought, then chuckles ominously in my ear.

"Mhm hmph," I try to scream, but his hand over my mouth blocks any noise from escaping.

"I think I'll take you somewhere nice and secluded where I can knot you, then mark you. That way, you'll be thoroughly compliant to your true alpha."

He takes a step backward, dragging me toward a small hatch in the corner that I hadn't noticed before—a hidden exit leading into the back garden.

Pure panic explodes inside me.

Adrenaline pulses through my bloodstream, pushing past fear. I know instinctively that if he gets me outside, I'm done for.

My feet scrape against the concrete as I kick, twist, and claw at his hold, desperation giving me strength. His grip only tightens, cruel and relentless, as he drags me faster toward the exit hatch.

*Protect yourself.* A voice in my mind screams at me. *Protect your babies.*

I scream beneath his fingers. My scream is muffled but loud enough to ring in my ears. I frantically bite down hard on his palm, tasting blood and sweat.

He hisses sharply, clamping his hand more fiercely over my mouth.

"You fucking bitch!" he snarls, his voice seething with menace.

Ignoring him, I thrash even harder, my vision blurring from fear. I dig my nails into the hand around my throat, clawing at his skin. Warm liquid runs down my hand, and a savage sense of satisfaction settles over me at the realization that I've drawn blood.

"I've had enough of you, you pathetic waste of space," Zorin hisses. He turns me around roughly, the hand I've scourged going straight to my throat. His face is thunderous, his eyes squinted with malice, and his lips pressed into a hard, cruel line. "You will obey me!"

He draws his other hand back, and I brace myself, ready for the hard slap I know is coming. But before it does, something catches my eye—a pair of glowing eyes watching from the shadows behind him, their eerie gaze fixed upon us.

My heart pounds violently, relief flooding through me upon seeing Gunnar.

Zorin notices the movement, too, but before he can react, there's a low growl, guttural and fierce, and suddenly, a flash of dark blond fur streaks across the basement. Gunnar, in his powerful wolf form, lunges directly at my captor.

Zorin releases me in shock, lurching backward, his arms raised defensively.

I stumble backward and out of his grasp, desperate to get out of the way before any harm comes to me or my babies.

The last thing I need is to get in between these fighting wolves.

Gunnar's jaws clamp down, ripping fiercely into Zorin's shoulder. A scream of pain tears from Zorin's throat.

From behind me, another wolf emerges—large, muscular, and covered in thick black fur.

*Damon.*

He growls at Zorin, the sound reverberating in the small space, and then lunges at him from the opposite side, sinking his fangs deep into Zorin's neck, the impact knocking them both sideways.

Zorin lets out a shrill yell before he fully transforms as well—an enormous white wolf standing in his place. Blood drips from his shoulder and the wound in his neck, but he struggles to his feet, snarling menacingly.

Damon stands in front of him, his chest heaving, and Gunnar comes to stand at his side, blood dripping from his maw.

His eyes glow, fury rolling off his tightly coiled body in waves.

My pulse races, relief mingling with fear as I watch the horror unfold before me. I want to scream, to tell Damon and Gunnar to be careful, but before I can, I'm picked up by a pair of strong arms.

I thrash wildly, thinking it must be Aleks or Raul. I need to escape and get as far away from them as possible.

I'm being carried toward the stairs, and I fight harder at the realization. If I go down, I'm going down where my men can see me.

"No!" I scream, at last, finding my voice. "Put me down!"

I writhe in the person's arms, more determined than ever to escape.

"Lena! Sweetheart, it's just me! It's Max!"

"Oh, thank God," I whisper, recognizing his voice and scent. I immediately stop moving and look into his eyes.

"I've got you, baby. We need to get you out of here."

I cling to him instinctively, allowing him to carry me up the stairs and away from the chaos of the basement. He puts me down in the living room, far from the basement door, and grips my shoulders possessively.

"You should help them," I say.

"Okay, stay here," he urges. "Don't get any closer to the basement. I don't know what Zorin is capable of, but we'll take care of the scumbag."

I nod, my body still shaking with adrenaline.

"If anything happens, leave and run. Call the police," he continues firmly. "And do not come near the basement until we give you the all-clear. I love you."

He briefly kisses me and then returns to the basement to join the fray before I can say anything else. I watch him go, my heart beating frantically with fear.

The sounds of growling, snarling, and furniture breaking reach my ears, and the only thing I can do is pray that my alphas come out the other side unscathed.

# CHAPTER 30

**Damon**

I'm furious that this deranged monster broke into our home and threatened my omega and my pups.

One way or another, my pack and I are ending this today.

I can feel the fury radiating off Gunnar as we both bare our teeth at Zorin, snarling for him to stay back and away from the stairs.

There's no way in hell I'm allowing him to get past us and touch our omega again. I messed up by allowing her to come down here by herself, and now I will set things straight.

To my surprise, despite his bleeding injuries, he manages to shift into his wolf form and struggles to his feet, the white of his fur stained red from our attack.

He growls at us, a deranged look in his eyes.

With a feral snarl, Gunnar lunges forward first, snapping his jaws viciously toward Zorin's already wounded shoulder. Zorin twists away, narrowly avoiding the attack, then retaliates with savage fury, driving Gunnar back with a swift swipe of his paw. Gunnar tumbles sideways, crashing heavily into a wall with a painful grunt as the breath is knocked from his lungs.

I surge forward now, my tightly coiled muscles propelling me onto Zorin's back.

I sink my teeth into his ruined shoulder, determined to incapacitate him while Gunnar catches his breath. Zorin lets out a fierce howl and thrashes wildly, trying to throw me off and dislodge my teeth. Blood flows freely from his wounds, staining both our fur and the floor a deep red.

With renewed vigor, Zorin throws himself sideways, slamming me into the basement wall. I let out an involuntary yelp, releasing his shoulder and collapsing onto the floor. Zorin staggers upright, preparing to attack again, baring his teeth at me.

My body aches as I struggle to my feet and glance around momentarily, checking to see if Lena and Max made it to safety.

*Damon, watch out!* Gunnar yells telepathically.

Suddenly, I feel a burning pain in my side. I howl in agony, fire consuming me from the inside out. Glancing down, I see a silver dagger buried in my flank.

*Fuck.*

The dagger is made of silver, with an intricate skull carved into the handle, and Zorin stands not far away. He's shifted back into his human form, wildness in his eyes as he stares at me, blood dripping from his mouth as he cackles.

"If I can't have her, you won't either," he says, laughing maniacally even though he knows it's his last moments on earth.

Summoning whatever strength I have left, I throw myself at Zorin and slash his throat with my claws. He yelps, the sound gurgling as blood spurts from the wound. He grabs at his throat, desperately trying to stem the flow.

I collapse onto the floor, watching as Gunnar finishes him off.

Gunnar shakes himself off before propelling himself at Zorin again, clamping his teeth around the gaping slash at Zorin's neck.

Zorin's incapacitated form lies not far from me, his eyes blank and unseeing as he stares at the ceiling, a pool of blood slowly forming around him.

"Damon!" shouts Max as I slip in and out of consciousness. The fire from the dagger spreads through my body, causing me to black out.

I can't shift back, drained of energy. My body feels spent.

*I need to see Lena before it's too late.* And it's the last thought I have before the darkness consumes me again.

---

Blinking, I wake up in a bright room I don't recognize.

Sharp, sterile smells assault my nostrils. The lights on the ceiling nearly blind me, and the rapid beep of a heart monitor rings in my ears. The smell of disinfectant stings my nose, clean and clinical, and I realize I'm in a hospital room.

Gunnar is beside me, and I hear him exhale sharply when he sees I'm awake.

"He's awake," he announces urgently. "Thank god."

I'm groggy, my body heavy as I try to turn my head. I see Max and Lena standing behind Gunnar.

Max has his arm around Lena's shoulders, her face tear-stained and pinched with worry.

"Lena," I rasp. "Are you okay?"

She steps forward and cups my face in her hands. Her touch is warm and angelic, and I thank all my lucky stars that I'm awake for just one more moment to experience it.

"I'm fine, Damon," she says, but her voice trembles with

fear, and her eyes are glossy with tears. "It's you I'm worried about."

"I'll live, sweetheart," I chuckle, then hiss in pain as the movement aggravates the wound on my side.

I glance down at my body and swallow hard when I see the blood-soaked sheet covering me. The stain is dark red and seems to spread further out the longer I look. My lower half is numb, and I'm glad about that since I see the dagger sticking out from the sheet.

"I know you will," she whispers, sniffling as she wipes away a lone tear that has leaked onto her cheek.

"Excuse me," a doctor says, approaching us with urgency. "I'm going to have to ask you all to leave now. We need to wheel Damon into surgery to remove the dagger. If we don't act now, he'll bleed out."

Max and Gunnar nod and step back from the bed.

"We'll be outside waiting for you, man," Max says, giving me a reassuring smile. "You got this."

"You're one tough son of a bitch," Gunnar adds with a wry smile as my head starts to spin from the medication in my IV line. "You'll be just fine."

Lena stares at me, looking like she's about to cry.

She opens her mouth to say something, but no words come out. I look back at her beautiful face, warmth settling in my chest. Even though I'm weak and can't comfort her the way I want to, I'm happy she's here.

*She is everything to me.*

Gathering the last bit of my strength, I grab Lena's hand and squeeze weakly.

"I love you," I say softly. I can feel my strength fading with the effort of speaking, but I need to reassure her. "No matter what happens, I will always love you. If I don't make it, Gunnar and Max will take care of you. I promise."

"You *will* make it," she sobs, cupping my face in her hands again. "You can't talk like that, Damon. You have to come back to me."

"I will."

She kisses my face, her salty tears splashing onto my skin as she plants soft kisses.

"And I love you, too," she whispers. "Nothing will happen to you, my love. You're going to be all right."

My heart soars at hearing her finally say the words.

It's taken her some time, but I've known she loves me through everything she does. It means so much more to hear it. I give her a weak smile, the love in her eyes imprinting onto my memory.

The doctor finally ushers Lena aside, and she steps back into Max's embrace. I watch them as I'm wheeled out of the room, my eyes never leaving hers until the swing of the operating room doors blocks her from view.

# CHAPTER 31
## FOUR MONTHS LATER

### Lena

I stare at my naked reflection in the tall bedroom mirror, twisting and turning to admire my now eight-and-a-half-month pregnant belly.

I'm huge, my belly protruding almost obscenely from my body, but it doesn't bother me in the slightest.

I'm excited to meet my sweet babies, due any day now.

The doctor was surprised that I've carried to nearly full term. He had strongly advised against it, but I can't exactly tell him that werewolves are built differently and that omega bodies are designed to carry our offspring full term for the best chance at life.

I wince when one of the pups kicks at my ribs.

"Ouch," I murmur, pressing my hand over my stomach. "Mind your manners, little one. That hurt."

"Everything okay in here?"

I perk up at the sound of Damon's voice and turn to see him standing in the doorway of our bedroom, a broad smile on his face, fully recovered and alive after his major surgery.

"Just the babies acting up again," I say, giggling as he leans down and cups my face tenderly for a kiss. Our tongues tangle as he groans in desire.

I'm grateful that he's home alive and well. Zorin may be dead, but the damage he inflicted on Damon with his dagger took months to heal. The silver in the dagger caused blood poisoning, severely compromising his healing time.

The only reminder of that terrifying period in our lives is a thick scar on Damon's side.

It reminds me of the one Zorin gave me, and through a wild twist of fate, it has made Damon and me even more connected.

"Okay, we should stop," Damon says, pulling away and adjusting the front of his pants. I can see the bulge of his cock pressing against the zipper of his shorts and eye it hungrily. "Baby doll, if you don't stop looking at me like that, we'll never get to the surprise."

"What surprise? The only surprise I need is your knot," I moan, grabbing the front of his shirt and pressing my naked body against him.

"Put on some clothes, little omega," he growls, trying to maintain a stern expression. "And then I promise you will have my knot after the surprise."

"Fine," I mutter, frustrated by the throbbing in my pussy as I hurriedly slip into a red flowery dress that stops just above my knees.

"Fuck, you look even more delicious in that," Damon says, eyeing me as he takes my hand to lead me out of the house.

After Zorin snuck in through a hole in the fence, Gunnar increased security around the property tenfold. He wanted to ensure that nothing like that would happen again, especially with the threat of Aleks and Raul's revenge still looming. We still don't know exactly where they are, which makes me anxious.

The backyard is adorned with lounge chairs and a table overflowing with food. Max stands at the barbecue, the smell of grilling meat filling the air. Gunnar lounges in one of the chairs, his shirt off, soaking in the afternoon sun.

The sight warms my heart; all my alphas are relaxed and happy at home.

"This is for you," Damon says, hugging me from behind. "We figured this might be one of the last times it's just the four of us together before you have the babies, so we wanted to throw a little barbecue to celebrate you."

Tears well in my eyes at the sweet gesture even though it's just a damn barbeque. I'm much more emotional than usual these days, but my alphas have grown accustomed to it.

"I love it, and I love you all," I choke out, kissing each of them in turn.

---

I settle into one of the lounge chairs to enjoy the relaxing afternoon.

Damon and Max are in the garden, casually tossing a football to each other while Gunnar oversees the rest of the cooking. Occasionally, he joins in, and the three race around the garden, laughing and joking as they pretend to tackle each other for the ball. Watching them makes me smile. They would make great fathers to our pups.

"I'll feed you," says Gunnar, bringing over a plate piled high with barbecue meat and pulling me onto his lap with his other hand.

"I feel like I'm squashing you," I say, rubbing my belly.

"What if I *want* to be squashed by you?" he whispers, offering me a slice of the tender meat.

"Mhm," I moan as I savor the delicious flavor of the lamb. "Whoever marinated this did a great job."

Gunnar lets out a soft chuckle as he feeds me another bite, his other hand stroking my thighs with deliberate intent, making my pussy throb.

"Gunnar, hold off on touching her like that," Damon barks, and I blink in shock.

He's never told any of his pack members to stop touching me—ever.

"Damon?" I say, my voice a low hiss. Gunnar doesn't respond.

I can't let Damon bully the others, even though he's the pack leader. I quickly jump to my feet, my heart pounding with adrenaline.

"I don't want you making rash decisions," Damon says, brushing off his hands on a napkin as he approaches me. He looks uncharacteristically nervous as he stares down at me, fiddling with something in the pocket of his shorts.

"Decisions about...?"

"Lena, my love," he says, dropping to one knee before me. He clasps one of my hands, his thumb tenderly stroking my skin. "Don't be upset. I just didn't want anyone to turn you on or make you feel aroused. I need a clear decision from you about what I'm about to ask."

My heart starts to race. I know where this is going, and a happy flutter goes through me.

"What... what are you about to ask?" I whisper.

"The day you came into my life changed me for the better. I didn't know what I was missing until I found you. You are our omega, the mother of our pups, and the love of my life. I would be lost without you, and I can't imagine going another day without making you mine. Will you marry me and my pack?"

He reaches into his pocket and pulls out a beautiful ring.

The band is platinum, with a huge square-cut diamond in

the center, flanked on either side by sapphires. It's stunning and sparkles brilliantly in the fading afternoon sun.

"Yes," I sob, happiness radiating from me in waves. "Of course, I'll marry you! I love you so much!"

Tears stream down my face, but they're the good kind—the kind that's an excess outpouring of love with nowhere to go. I launch myself at him, throwing my arms around his neck. My belly gets in the way somewhat, but he still catches me easily, laughing as he holds me.

He captures my lips in a searing kiss before kissing the tears on my cheeks and then sliding the ring onto my finger. It's a perfect fit, and I hold up my hand, admiring how the diamond shines and sparkles in the sun.

"It's so pretty," I whisper, my heart bursting at the adoration on his face. "I'm so lucky."

"I think we're the lucky ones," he murmurs, kissing me again.

"Phew, she said yes," says Gunnar, laughing as I hug him next. "I thought Damon was in for it after what he pulled."

"I'm okay," I reassure him. "I'm more than happy."

"I can see that," he says, nibbling my neck and making me blush. Pulling away, I turn to Max next, and his eyes glow with joy at our engagement.

"Our fiancée," says Max, kissing me square on the mouth, and I kiss him back.

***

After the barbecue, the alphas led me into the bathroom so we could wash up.

Damon has installed a large hot tub-like bathtub in the main bathroom—big enough to fit the four of us if we want to bathe together, which is often the case. He starts filling the tub when Max and Gunnar join us.

Each of them starts lighting a few candles and placing them around the bathroom.

Damon adds some bubble bath to the water, ensuring it's suitably fluffy, then checks that the water is at the perfect temperature before turning it off. I undress, and he helps me into the tub before undressing and getting in himself.

I sigh in contentment when the other two join us, and the four of us settle in to relax in the hot water together.

"I could get used to this," I murmur, and Max chuckles.

"Good thing it's forever, then," he replies, winking at me.

The alphas begin to wash me gently, each taking a loofah and scrubbing it across my skin. Their hands on my body both soothe and arouse me, and I wriggle in anticipation as they start to kiss me everywhere, their mouths roaming greedily across my lips, neck, and breasts.

Max kisses my neck, gently sucking and nibbling on my skin before whispering in my ear, "You're going to be our pretty little omega wife soon, sweetheart. I can't wait."

"I can't wait to show everyone that you're mine," Gunnar murmurs in my other ear, his hands drifting down to touch my clenching pussy beneath the water.

"My beautiful fiancé," Damon agrees, his eyes blazing.

A thrill shoots through me at the term, leaving me giddy with love and excitement. I can hardly believe I get to share forever with these alphas who care about me.

Gunnar's fingers gently stroke, deftly parting my folds to find my clit. I gasp at the sensation, and he grins, pulling me in for a kiss while he rubs small circles around my clit. I can feel myself becoming more aroused, slick gathering at my entrance despite the bath water.

"Does that feel good?" he growls lowly, and I nod breathlessly. He inserts a finger into me, and I clench around him, craving so much more.

"I think she needs a little more," Max chimes in, a wicked

grin on his face. His hands sink into the water, and soon enough, I feel him spreading my ass cheeks, his fingers searching for my rosebud.

"Oh!" I gasp when Max pokes a finger into my asshole, pumps it twice, and then adds another.

"Mmm, you're going to be so tight around my cock," Max groans, kissing the shell of my ear.

I can only pant and rock my hips in time with their movements, bringing myself closer to climax. Damon watches with dark eyes as Max and Gunnar pleasure me. I can see the desire burning in their depths, making me hotter.

He leans forward and takes one of my nipples into his mouth.

My nipples are puffy and sensitive from my pregnancy, and when he starts to suck and nibble on them, I just about lose my mind. The sensation of having my holes filled while Damon sucks and plays with my nipples, is almost too much, and I orgasm with a loud moan, my hips bucking and causing the water to slosh around us.

I whimper when Gunnar and Max withdraw their fingers.

"Don't worry, baby. That was just a warm-up," Gunnar chuckles, kissing me on the mouth.

I can feel his hard cock pressing into my leg as he deftly lifts me onto his lap with me face-forward, and I open for him willingly. He spreads my pussy lips and pushes his cock in slowly, taking his time before he's fully seated in me.

"Oh god," I whimper when he bottoms out. He stretches me to perfection, and when he starts to thrust into me, I can't hold back my moans of pleasure.

"Oh yes, baby. Let me hear you," he growls. He picks up the pace, fucking me in earnest. Water is splashing out of the tub and onto the bathroom floor, but I only care about the way Gunnar drives into me, demanding my pleasure.

I can feel him swell at the base of his cock, and I know that he's close to coming.

"Oh, Gunnar," I moan.

"You're mine, Lena," he growls. "My omega."

His canines extend, and just as he's about to come, he sinks his teeth into my skin and marks me just below my right clavicle.

I scream, an orgasm so intense rushing over me when I feel his teeth pierce my skin.

Everything is electric, and my pussy spasms in pleasure around his cock, drawing him into me, and I feel him grunt against my skin as he finally knots inside me.

"Fuck," says Max before I can barely recover from my powerful orgasm. I feel Max slip behind me and spread my ass cheeks again.

He doesn't give me any warning before he pushes inside my asshole slowly, stretching me around his thick cock. The pleasure is almost too intense, and I cry out when he thrusts against me, firmly seating his cock inside my ass.

"Oh, *moons,*" I moan, trying to catch my breath. "It's too much."

"It's never too much," Max rumbles in my ear. "I know you can take me like a good omega. We've all rutted you before, sweetheart."

My face reddens as he thrusts into me repeatedly, and the tightness from being knotted by Gunnar only heightens the sensation. My core tightens, bringing me closer to what I'm sure will be another earth-shattering orgasm.

Max brushes a few loose tendrils of hair away from my neck.

"All mine," he murmurs before biting down on the left side of my neck and marking me. I scream in ecstasy again as my orgasm rushes through me. Both Gunnar and Max groan when they feel how much I tighten around them, my pussy pulsing in time with the waves of pleasure crashing over me.

Max knots my asshole, grunting into my ear as he orgasms hard.

I'm stuffed to the brim, breathing heavily after being taken by two alphas at once.

"That was intense," I gasp, and the alphas chuckle softly. Gunnar kisses me fully on the lips while Max kisses and licks the spot he marked. "I'm your omega now."

"Damn right you are," says Max, and I can feel his chest vibrating against my back. He's purring with happiness, and his knot inside me begins to vibrate, making me gasp.

Gunnar starts to purr with darkened eyes, pushing his tongue into my mouth. His knot inside me is vibrating as well, making me moan out loud.

"That feels so amazing," I gasp, as the vibrations from their dicks buried inside me make my center clench and my asshole tighten.

"Lena baby, you look so beautiful, knotted, and loved by my pack," Damon says in a low voice as he watches me breathe hard and pant against Gunnar's muscled chest.

"She does," mutters Gunnar, kissing my neck while Max runs his hands down my waist from behind.

***

The water cools as we lie together in the tub, waiting for Max and Gunnar's knots to subside.

They stroke me and kiss any part of me they can, and I've never felt more loved than I do in that moment under their undivided attention.

Eventually, they manage to slip away gently, but not before kissing me thoroughly as they pull out. I should feel satisfied after being perfectly pleasured by two of my alphas, yet I only feel more aroused when I see Damon leaning against the side of the tub, watching me with hungry eyes.

"Come here," he says, opening his arms for me.

I wade across the tub and into his embrace, straddling his thighs. His cock is like steel, slightly protruding from the water, and my mouth waters at the sight of it.

"Ride me," he orders, and my heart races.

Cum drips down my thighs as he lifts me by the hip, guiding me to his entrance. Slowly, I sink onto him, feeling his delicious girth stretch me wide.

Damon lets out a low groan as my heat wraps around him, tightening his grip on my hips.

"Fuck yes," he growls, and I push myself up before dropping down again, setting a steady rhythm that he soon intensifies, lifting and lowering me on his cock in rapid succession.

Water sloshes around us, splashing onto the already-soaked floor, but I don't care, only focusing solely on how Damon makes me feel and the heat of his gaze on my skin. My core clenches tightly around his thick cock, and he groans as he digs his fingers deeper into my hips.

"Give me your arm," he says.

"What?" I ask, confused, hesitating as I pause my movements.

"Your arm, Lena. The one with the scar. Give it to me," he growls, pushing me back onto his cock.

I suck in a sharp breath, resuming my movements as I extend my arm to him.

"I'm going to mark you here," he grunts, thrusting forcefully, burying himself deeper inside me. "Let's remove what your ex did to you."

My heart swells at his words, love overflowing between us where we're joined, but I have only a moment to absorb it all before he bites down on my arm.

"Oh!" I cry out, overwhelmed by the pain and pleasure of

his mark. My pussy throbs and tightens around his cock almost instantly as he explodes inside me.

He thrusts faster as I bounce on his cock wildly.

"Fuck," he groans as he begins to knot snugly inside me, stretching me wide. I slump against him, feeling his heart beat erratically beneath his ribs.

He takes my arm again and licks the burning bite, cooling the wound. Our hearts beat as one as I lay on him.

"Mate," I whisper, and he grunts in approval.

"And you are my omega. Forever, baby."

# CHAPTER 32

**Lena**

A month later, I'm back at the library, trying to get back into the routine of things before I'm due to give birth.

I adjust the pillows behind my back for the fourth time in about ten minutes, attempting again to find a comfortable position in my office chair. The babies have been restless all morning, moving and shifting and poking me in ways that make focusing on cataloging the library's index more challenging.

Today is my last day before I go on maternity leave, and I have to make sure I get a few things done before I go. I don't want to leave Paige and Annabelle with mounds of my work to catch up on after the birth.

I shift in my chair again, a delicious soreness pressing up from between my thighs. My alphas had taken turns knotting me half the night, even though I protested that I had to get up early for work.

"What's got you smiling like that?" Annabelle asks with a knowing grin as she and Paige approach the front desk.

"Thinking about that man? Gunnar Thorne?" Paige teases, wiggling her eyebrows suggestively.

They knew about Gunnar since they'd met him several times as he visited the library. But they had no idea about the other two men in my life, which is good since they'll never understand our wolf dynamics.

"Yes," I say, smiling bashfully.

"Girl, those babies will be here before you go on maternity leave if you carry on like that!" Paige jokes, fanning her face. Annabelle and I let out whoops of laughter, the sound carrying across the library.

"Can you keep it down?" someone says, and I turn to see an elderly woman at the nearest bookshelf staring at us reproachfully.

"Sorry!" I whisper loudly, and Paige giggles.

"Well, we can't let you leave without giving you something special."

"You didn't have to get me anything," I say, touched by their kindness. My babies shift again as though they can feel the warmth radiating from my friends.

"Of course we did," Paige says gently, handing me a large cream-colored gift bag tied neatly with a pastel pink bow. "It's not every day that your best co-worker goes away on maternity leave."

I place the bag on the desktop, carefully unwrapping the bow. Inside is a large hand-knitted blanket in delicate shades of ivory, pastel green, and pastel yellow, all woven beautifully together. Beneath it lie four small, plush elephants, each with a different-colored ribbon wrapped around their tails.

My throat tightens with emotion at the thoughtfulness the two women put into their gift.

"Aww! I love it," I say, my fingers grazing the blanket's softness. Annabelle grabs my hand and gives it a gentle squeeze.

"You deserve every bit of happiness," she says sincerely. "We'll miss you around here."

"I'll miss you both, too," I say.

"We're excited to meet your four babies," Paige says, easing the sad mood just enough to make me laugh softly. "They're certainly going to keep you busy!"

"Oh, I'm sure they will," I say, grinning. "I get scared sometimes that I might not be a good mom."

"Wait, why would you say that, Lena?" asks Annabelle.

"My own mother wasn't great," I admit softly. "One of the reasons why I stayed with an abusive boyfriend for years before I met Gunnar."

"I'm sure you're nothing like her," says Paige softly, hugging me. "Even though we're co-workers, we love you and we both know you're going to be great."

A profound sense of wholeness deep in my core starts flowing through me. She was right. No one had liked my mother anywhere she went, and she never had friends.

The moment is fleeting, however, when I feel a gush of liquid rush down my legs. I glance down and see that my maternity pants are soaked, a puddle of water collecting at my feet.

"Oh shit," I say, too stunned to do anything except stare at the growing puddle.

"What?" Annabelle asks anxiously. "Are you okay?"

I look up at her and Paige with wide eyes, panic starting to creep in. "I think my water just broke."

Annabelle and Paige glance down at the floor and then back up at me, their expressions of shock mirroring my own.

"Oh my God," says Paige.

"I can't believe this is happening right now!" I say in a panicked squeak.

"You shouldn't have been messing around with your man so much," says Annabelle, panicking, making me laugh and then groan in pain, my hand flying to my stomach as the first contraction hits.

"Do you need me to call an ambulance?" says Paige frantically.

"No, it's okay," I gasped, shaking my head. "The contractions literally just started, so I have time. I need to call Gunnar."

Annabelle hands me my phone, and I dial his number, grimacing as another contraction rolls through me.

"Hey, baby," he answers smoothly. "I missed you."

"It's happening!" I whisper-yell into the phone, trying to be mindful that we're still in the library. "My water broke!"

"Oh fuck!" he exclaims. "Okay, just hang tight, love. We're coming to get you."

"I've got the hospital bag!" I hear Max yell as Damon curses in the background, urgently barking out orders.

Gunnar ends the call with a quick "I love you" and then hangs up. I smile at their readiness. In the last few weeks, we've practiced our 'go' moment about a dozen times. I want my delivery day to be perfect, and my alphas have been more than accommodating, catering to my every need.

"Do you want to sit down?" Annabelle asks nervously, touching my elbow. "We can go to the break room? Or you could just wait here?"

"Here is fine," I say, giving her a reassuring smile. Paige wheels my chair around the desk to where we're standing, and I've barely taken one step toward it when the library doors burst open violently, slamming against the walls with a resounding crash. The people at the bookshelves nearest us cry out in alarm, the books in their hands dropping to the floor.

I turn in the direction of the doors, and my heart stops. It's not my alphas.

Aleks and Raul are standing in the doorway. Their gaze is

locked on me, their eyes cold and cruel, and I barely notice the silver daggers in their hands until Raul waves one at me.

"My, my, little omega... how you've grown," he sneers and takes a menacing step into the library as the people dash for the exit, screaming.

"Aleks... Raul..." I croak, my voice tight with terror. "W-what are you doing here?"

"Did you think we wouldn't know what happened to Zorin?" Aleks snarls, approaching me. "We came to finish the job that he started."

I feel my pulse race frantically, panic flooding through my veins, and my eyes dart toward Annabelle and Paige. They're standing frozen in fear beside me, their faces drained of all color.

"Why now?" I ask, stalling for time. Maybe keeping them talking long enough will give Damon, Max, and Gunnar enough time to get to the library.

"Why not now? This is the perfect time to destroy your impending happiness."

"We've been watching you for quite some time," Raul says. "Your pups will belong to us after you give birth. You owe us that."

A sense of déjà vu passes over me so strongly that I feel like I might vomit. I can't believe this is happening again. Raul and Aleks have always been cold and cruel, but seeing them again chills me to the bone. A pack isn't supposed to be without a leader, so Zorin's death must be affecting them negatively.

They're coming apart at the seams, and there's no stopping it.

Raul moves swiftly toward Annabelle and Paige, and the women shrink back in terror. He grabs them both roughly by the arms and pulls them away from me.

"Go with Aleks," he snarls at me, his canines extended. "If

you don't, I'll kill your friends here—and everyone else in this fucking library."

"Let us go, you bastard!" screams Paige. Annabelle lets out a small whimper of terror and begins to tremble.

"Shut up!" he hisses, then points his dagger at me. "Do it, Lena. Now!"

My breathing hitches, dread settling in my bones at the fear on my co-workers' faces.

"Please," I beg desperately, hoping he'll hear me out. "Let them go. They have nothing to do with this!"

Raul laughs bitterly, unfazed by my pleas. He draws closer to Annabelle and points the dagger at her throat. Tears roll down her cheeks as she eyes the dagger carefully, trying not to let it touch her.

"They do now," he spits viciously, the threat clear in his eyes.

"Don't," I plead again, my voice cracking with fear and anguish. "I'll go with you, just don't hurt them."

Aleks waves me over.

"Well, come on, then," he mocks. "We don't have all day."

Despite my words of acquiescence, my feet refuse to move, rooting me to the spot with terror and dread.

"Enough!" Raul shouts. "You will come with us!"

He drops the dagger, and Annabelle lets out a small sigh of relief when it clatters to the floor, but it's short-lived when he reaches into his pocket and pulls out a gun. The cold, gray metal gleams in the overhead lights of the library, and Annabelle sucks in a sharp breath. My eyes widen when he points the gun at her, the barrel pressing against her temple.

"Time to move," he seethes, "or she gets her pretty head blown off."

The remaining people in the library had frozen in fear when Aleks and Raul barged in through the doors, waving their daggers, but once Raul pulled out his gun, they began to scream.

The old lady who had shushed us earlier drops the book she's holding and hobbles toward the back of the library, far out of reach of the crazy gunman. Two other people who had been working on the computers in the corner make a dash toward the door, but before they can escape, Raul points the gun straight in the air and fires it.

"Not so fast, motherfuckers!" he screams, and in the silence that follows, the clink of the empty round hitting the floor echoes throughout the library. "You'll leave when I say you can leave!"

The two people closest to the door drop to the floor and shuffle back until their backs hit the wall, watching the rest of the scene unfold with terror.

Aleks walks closer, and I can see the deranged look in his eyes as he stares us down. He points his dagger at Paige and Annabelle.

"On your knees, you stupid bitches!" he growls, and the two women comply, terror etched in every line of their faces.

"Aleks, don't hurt them!" I yell loudly, shaking with adrenaline and fear for all the innocent people here who might die because of me. It's all my fault for getting involved with the wrong alphas in my past.

"You!" He swings toward me and grabs a fistful of my hair. I yelp in pain, my hand automatically going to his to try and pull him off of me. "Let's fucking go!"

"Let me go!" I scream, but Aleks's fingers only tighten in my hair, pulling at my roots. He starts to drag me by the hair toward the library door, but I dig my heels in.

I'm not going anywhere with him.

"Move it, you useless whore!" he shouts.

"Aleks, please," I sob, beyond caring that I'm begging.

"Just let me leave! If you won't let me go, at least let the people in the library go."

"I don't think you get to ask for favors," he sneers. He pulls my head up so that we're at eye level. "Now shut the fuck up, or I will kill you."

He carries on dragging me forward, and I kick and scream with all my strength, but it's in vain. He's so much stronger than I am, and even with the weight of my pregnant belly, he still manages to handle me easily.

Pain lances through me, and I cry out.

I look down, thinking for a moment that Aleks has had enough of me and decided to stab me after all, but when I don't see a dagger sticking out of me anywhere, I'm confused. Another stab of pain rocks through me, making me curl into myself, and then it hits me—it's my contractions; the stress is making them come faster.

I look at Annabelle and Paige, kneeling on the floor not far from me. Their wide-eyed and fearful expressions tell me they've realized the same thing.

I can't have my babies now. *Not here!* I start to cry as another contraction rolls through me.

My babies are coming, and there's nothing I can do to stop it.

# CHAPTER 33

**Damon**

*Our omega is in distress.*

I can feel her every emotion through our bond, specifically from the mating mark I gave her.

The moment we pull up to the library, I feel the hairs on the back of my neck stand on end. I don't know what it is, but I do know that we need to get to Lena as soon as possible. Max and Gunnar feel it, too, and the two of them tense up, anticipation rippling between us.

"Something is off," Gunnar murmurs, his eyes starting to glow as he surveys the surroundings out the car window. "I don't like it."

"Agreed," Max says and opens his car door. "Let's get Lena and get the fuck out of here."

Exiting the car, I close the door, and at that moment, I hear a gunshot ring out.

"Was that from the library?" I bark, panicking and shifting into my wolf form without thinking.

Adrenaline surges through my veins, and I nod my head in

the direction of one of the library windows, angling my body toward it. We need to take whoever is in the library by surprise, and the best way to do that is with an unexpected entrance.

Max and Gunnar pick up on my meaning, and we launch forward, crashing through the building's window.

Glass explodes around us, shards falling like rain, and whatever controlled calm there had been before evaporates in a second. People are screaming and running toward the back of the building, desperate to get away from us.

I only care about Lena.

My eyes immediately lock onto a strange alpha holding Lena by the arm. There are two strange alphas I've never seen before. They must be Aleks and Raul. Suddenly, they looked familiar to me from the pictures Lena had shown me of them.

Aleks grips a silver dagger, his stance menacing.

Lena is struggling against his hold on her, her expression terrified.

I growl lowly. *No one hurts my mate*. Behind him, Raul raises a gun, his expression cold and calculating. I notice the empty shell casing on the floor. I snarl, baring my teeth.

Max and Gunnar spring toward Raul, who starts firing the gun aimlessly at them. The shots echo in the library, and more screams can be heard from behind the bookshelves.

Max and Gunnar dodge the bullets that whistle past them, and Gunnar positions himself between Raul and the terrified bystanders, shielding them with his massive frame while Max charges Raul head-on.

I surge towards Aleks, launching myself at him with explosive force. My body slams into his, knocking him off balance.

He hits the floor hard, the breath rushing from his lungs, and the dagger skittering away across the tiled floor.

Lena takes the opportunity to duck onto the floor,

crawling on her hands and knees towards Paige and Annabelle, who are watching the scene unfold with wide, fearful eyes.

Aleks stirs, and shock at being attacked momentarily registers on his face before it transforms into pure rage. He stands, and I watch as he shifts into his wolf form, eyes blazing red with hatred. He growls furiously at me, and I bare my teeth, showing him that I'm not afraid.

"You fucks think you're slick, huh?" Raul shouts, his eyes gleaming wildly. He waves the gun in the air frantically.

He starts to fire relentlessly but inaccurately, bullets embedding into the walls, books, and splintering furniture.

Max, Gunnar, and I dodge every bullet, keeping low to the floor and rolling out of the way. I keep one eye on Lena, watching as she curls into herself, Paige and Annabelle surrounding her protectively. When the gun finally clicks empty, he lets out a growl of frustration and tosses it aside.

Raul shifts into his wolf form, muscles bulging and thick, dark brown fur shooting out from his skin as he joins the battle on equal footing. His hackles are raised, and he lets out a bark that sounds almost like a rough laugh.

He glances to the left, toward where Lena and her friends are cowering, and grins wolfishly at me.

Before I can react, he darts toward her.

"Let go!" Lena screams as he drags her dress by the fangs, placing her between us, forcing me to hold back to avoid hurting her.

*Dirty fucker*, I growl in frustration.

Every time I make a move, he dashes behind her again, keeping me at bay. It won't be long, though, and soon enough, I'll beat him at his own game.

Suddenly, Aleks lunges at me from the side, teeth bared, aiming for my flank. It forces me to twist hard, putting distance between Lena and me for just a second. That moment of movement breaks the deadlock, and it's all Lena needs.

## Lena

The second Damon twists to avoid Aleks's teeth, Raul's attention slips. His jaws loosen from the fabric of my dress, and instinct takes over.

I drop my weight to the floor like a stone and roll away from both of them, my heart slamming in my chest.

Paige doesn't hesitate—she grabs my hand and yanks me into a crouch, pulling me backward fast.

"Now, Annabelle!" she cries.

Annabelle darts forward, pushing the table to block Raul's path, buying us precious seconds. I stumble as another contraction hits me, nearly toppling to the floor, but they catch me—one on each side—and we rush across the main hall.

Aleks roars behind us, realizing too late that I'm no longer his shield. The moment I'm clear, Damon charges forward like a bullet, smashing into Aleks with a snarl of pure anger.

Paige looks over at me, then at Annabelle. "Holy shit. Lena. Are those guys—your mates—wolves?"

I let out a strangled sound between a cry and a laugh. "Yes. Long story. Later."

Annabelle's face is pale. "They shifted. Oh my God, Paige—they're real wolves. Is this even—what the fuck is even happening?"

"They're protecting us," I whisper. "Please. Don't be scared. Just help me."

Annabelle snaps out of it. "Right. Right. We've got you."

"The contractions!" I gasp as pain tears through me again.

We're in the storage room now, and I'm suddenly reminded of the time I was in heat, being knotted in this very same room to conceive my babies.

More pain lances through me, and I curl forward in agony, placing a hand over my belly.

My contractions are coming closer together, and I know there's no way I'm going to be able to make it to the hospital—not with the current state of things.

Annabelle and Paige exchange worried glances. They must be terrified, but they've been holding it together so well.

"We should be okay here," Annabelle says, her voice trembling.

My contractions are coming in quicker now, and I can't stop the cries escaping my lips. Fear grips me, not just for myself and my babies but also for my pack.

The thought of losing my alphas is unbearable, and a sob wracks my body at the idea.

"Paige," I choke out between contractions. My voice is raw and desperate, and I swallow back the wail, threatening to escape. "Paige, I need you to check on them. Are they okay? What's happening?"

I can hear snarls and grunts, the sound of massive bodies colliding as they try to tear each other to shreds.

"They're okay," she says, peeking out the door. "The evil wolves are bleeding a lot. Your men have the upper hand."

I nod weakly, gripping Annabelle's hand tightly as another wave of pain crashes through me.

"They're coming!" I wail, panic mounting. "I don't have my bag. This isn't supposed to happen like this!"

"I'm going to call 911," Annabelle says frantically. "Hold on for me, Lena. I promise we'll get your babies here safely."

She dials the phone and puts it on loudspeaker.

"911, what is your emergency?" the dispatcher says coolly.

"We're at Willowstone Library," Annabelle says smoothly,

guiding the emergency services to our location. "There's a woman here in active labor. It's multiples—four babies. We need help immediately."

"How far apart are the contractions?" the dispatcher asks.

"Three minutes, I think," I say, groaning and grimacing in pain as another one hits.

"Okay, honey, I'm going to need you to breathe," the dispatcher says calmly. "I'm going to talk to your friend through the birth. The ambulance is on the way as we speak."

Annabelle's eyes meet mine, and I can see the panic within her gaze. "Lena, listen to me. I know this isn't your plan, but we'll get through it. Breathe with me."

I nod, desperately trying not to freak out. Anything might happen. Panicking only makes the contractions speed up.

"You can do this, Lena," Paige says with conviction, gripping my hand as I scream. "We've got you. We'll make sure everything is all right."

"Make sure there's nothing in the way when you start to push," says the dispatcher.

I scramble to push down my maternity pants and panties, and Annabelle grabs them, tucking them away safely for me. I spread my legs wide, not even bringing myself to care that my vagina is on full display to my friends.

I just want to deliver these babies. Tears stream down my face as the pressure below increases.

"It's almost time. Listen to me carefully, honey. I need you to do exactly as I tell you, okay?" the dispatcher says.

Another contraction grips me, stronger this time, tearing through me with such intensity that I scream. Sweat beads on my forehead, dripping down my temples as my body instinctively pushes.

Annabelle ducks her head between my legs to see what's happening.

"The first one is coming, Lena. Push now," Annabelle

urges. Her calmness soothes me, giving me courage even though I'm scared out of my mind.

"That's it!" Paige says. "Push, girl, push!"

I bear down, pushing with all I've got until the pressure relieves. Moments later, a shrill cry pierces the air, and tears come to my eyes, overjoyed that one of my babies is safely out. The chaos of the fight behind us fades into the background as Annabelle hands the squirming bundle to Paige, who wraps the baby girl in her cardigan.

"There's one baby," the dispatcher cries happily over the phone.

Another powerful contraction takes hold of me, and I scream in pain. It's like a ring of fire stretching me, and I can't do anything to stop it.

"You need to push, Lena. You're doing amazing," Annabelle coaches me softly, still talking urgently to the dispatcher.

Closing my eyes, I bear down as hard as I can while I scream. I never wanted it to be this way. Not at all.

Suddenly, a shrill cry sounds, and I know the second baby is here. I open my tear-drenched eyes, crying and laughing when I see the baby boy.

"A boy!" Annabelle declares and lays him against my chest.

During the brief respite, I turn to Paige. "Paige, what are my men doing right now?"

"They have the guy with the gun cornered. They're going to finish this," she says as she looks out the storage room's door.

The update gives me strength, and I bear down again as I get ready to deliver the rest of my babies.

The third and fourth babies arrive swiftly, another girl and boy, one after the other, and their sweet cries are like music to my ears amidst the snarls and growls from the library.

My body trembles with exhaustion, and tears stream

down my face as I clutch one of my newborns protectively to me, hoping against hope that their fathers make it out alive. Annabelle and Paige work together to clean off the babies using the blankets they've gifted me.

The snarling and growling have suddenly stopped, and fear grips my heart, hoping the worst hasn't come.

An eerie silence settles over the library, and then I hear the soft padding of paws as Damon, Max, and Gunnar approach the storage room in their wolf forms.

Damon lets out a long howl when he sees that our babies are born already and crying. Annabelle and Paige scoot away from him, intimidated by his massive size and the fierce look on his face.

I'm elated to see them safe and alive.

"Don't worry, he doesn't bite," I say, smiling as he gives them a wolfish grin before stepping closer to sniff his pups. Max and Gunnar join him, their big bodies crowding me as they tenderly sniff their offspring and lick my face and neck.

The three alphas transform back into their human forms, naked as the day they were born. I bite my lip to keep myself from laughing at Annabelle and Paige's expressions, but the alphas don't notice. Max tenderly picks up one of his sons and Gunnar the other, cooing at them softly and kissing their tiny faces.

"My beautiful, strong Lena," Damon whispers, dropping to his knees to cup my face. His gaze is soft as he looks at me. "You've given me the most precious gift I could ever ask for."

He kisses me tenderly before picking up his daughters and holding them close to his chest. The sight makes my heart swell.

"You're in trouble," I murmur, and he looks at me sharply.

"Why?" he asks in confusion.

"Those little girls are going to have you wrapped around their fingers," I say.

"They already do," he says, chuckling.

The sound of sirens cuts through the ringing in my ears. It starts faint but grows louder by the second until it drowns out everything else.

Lights flicker red and blue across the broken library windows, casting eerie shadows across the ruined bookshelves and glass-covered floor.

They're here. The sound of the front doors slamming open.

"EMS!" someone yells, their voice echoing through the chaos, fast, heavy footsteps rushing through the library.

"In here!" barks Max.

Three paramedics storm in, uniforms dark, eyes alert, and scanning the situation. One speaks into a radio clipped to his shoulder while another has gloves on.

"Where's the mother?"

Annabelle steps forward, waving frantically from the doorway. "In here! She just gave birth—quadruplets! It happened fast. She didn't even make it out of the room!"

I can hear them moving closer into the dark storage room, the sound of their boots on tile mixing with the softer, faster breaths of my babies. My arms are full, one baby against my chest, the others safe in the arms of my alphas as pain throbs in my center.

"She's right here," Paige says, her hand on my shoulder.

A medic kneels next to me. His hands are warm and steady as he checks my pulse. "Hey there, Mama. Can you tell me your name?"

"Lena," I whisper. "They're okay, right? My babies..."

"We're checking them now," he says gently, nodding toward them. "Small, but stable. You did good."

Another medic begins checking the babies, clamping cords, and wrapping them in clean, warm blankets pulled from a supply bag. He speaks quietly, calmly, but efficiently, and I catch words like "heart rate good," "pink color," and "neonatal transport."

"We're going to take you all in," the lead medic tells me. "County Sun Hospital. NICU is ready."

I nod weakly, too tired to speak. My body feels like it's made of glass and sand—fragile and heavy, all at once.

Damon leans over me, brushing the hair from my damp forehead as the medics lift me onto a stretcher.

"We're coming with you," Damon says, voice low and fierce. "We're not letting you out of our sight."

# CHAPTER 34
## LENA

***One Year Later***

My hands tremble as I clutch the bouquet, the delicate white veil fluttering against my face with each anxious breath. The wedding march begins, and my stomach ties itself into knots as tight as the ones my alphas will give me later tonight.

I shouldn't be this nervous.

These alphas have seen every inch of me, claimed every part of me, and even fathered my beautiful babies—but walking toward them now, about to become officially theirs forever, has my omega instincts in complete overdrive.

"Ready?" my sister Carmen asks, squeezing my arm gently.

I nod, unable to form words as we take our first step onto the petal-strewn aisle.

The setting sun casts a warm orange glow over Howl's Edge Island, transforming the simple outdoor ceremony into something magical. Rows of white chairs fan out on either side of us, filled with people whose faces blur together through my veil. I can only focus on the three tall figures waiting for me at the altar.

"Oh God."

"Breathe, Lena," Carmen whispers.

"I'll try," I whisper back, my voice little more than a squeak. "This doesn't feel real."

The gentle breeze carries the scent of ocean salt and wildflowers, mingling with the unmistakable alpha pheromones emanating from the front of the aisle. Even from this distance, my body responds instinctively to my mates, a rush of warmth spreading between my thighs as memories of their touches flash through my mind.

My thoughts drift to just months ago when my family flew to D.C. after hearing about the birth of the quadruplets. I'd been terrified they'd judge me for disappearing, for the relationship with the three new alphas, and for the mess my life had become after Zorin.

But the moment Carmen stepped into the hospital room, tears streaming down her face, all those fears dissolved.

"Oh, Lena," she'd whispered, reaching for one of the tiny bundles in my arms. "They're perfect."

Mom had followed, then Francine, all of them cooing over the babies while eyeing my three hovering alphas with a mixture of curiosity and caution.

Damon had been the first to win them over, his protective stance softening as he explained how they had found me, cared for me, and loved me. Max had made them laugh with stories of my pregnancy cravings, while Gunnar demonstrated his devotion through silent vigilance, always watching me and the babies.

And now, here we are a year later at my wedding, my family fully supporting me as they walk me toward the rest of my life.

"I'm freaking out," I admit to Carmen, my legs wobbling beneath my flowing white dress.

Carmen slows our pace slightly, her fingers tightening around mine.

"Listen to me, Lena. Those alphas up there? They worship the ground you walk on. I've watched them with you and the babies. They're nothing like Zorin."

The name sends an electric shock through my system, memories of cruel treatment flooding back.

"I know."

"Zorin broke you," Carmen continues, her voice fierce but quiet. "But Damon and his pack put you back together. They won't hurt you like he did. I wouldn't be giving you away if I thought otherwise."

I swallow hard, focusing on the three figures coming into clearer view with each step.

*My alphas. My protectors. My mates.*

"I know they wouldn't hurt me," I whisper as I lock eyes with Damon, my heart stopping at the intensity of his gaze.

"Besides," Carmen adds with a small smile, "if they ever tried anything, I'd rip their throats out myself."

This startles a laugh from me, earning curious glances from nearby guests. My heart hammers against my chest as soft music plays in the background.

We're halfway down the aisle now, and I can finally make out the expressions on my alphas' faces. Damon's dark eyes lock with mine through the veil, intense and possessive. To his right is Max, looking at me with pure adoration—his red curls catching fire in the sunset. Gunnar, stoic and powerful on Damon's left, watches me with such hunger that my knees nearly buckle.

"Oh god," I whisper to Carmen. "They're looking at me like they want to devour me right here."

"That's how alphas look at their omega," she responds. "Especially on their wedding day. Trust me, it's a good thing."

*Three more steps.*

My pulse races faster, the bouquet clutched so tightly in my trembling fingers that I'm surprised the stems haven't snapped.

*Two more steps.*

I catch a whiff of their combined scents, and my omega wolf responds with a rush of slick between my thighs.

One final step, and I'm now standing before them.

"Who gives this omega to these alphas?" the officiant asks, his voice carrying across the gathered crowd.

"I do," Carmen replies, placing my hand in Damon's waiting palm. His skin is warm against mine, his grip firm and reassuring. Carmen gives me one last look of encouragement before releasing me completely and taking her seat in the front row.

I turn to face my three alphas, and my breath catches in my throat.

Damon's eyes are suspiciously bright, a sheen of moisture making them glitter in the fading sunlight. Max is less subtle, a single tear tracking down his freckled cheek as he beams at me. Most shocking of all is Gunnar, whose usual stone-faced expression has cracked open to reveal raw emotion, his eyes swimming with unshed tears.

These powerful alphas are reduced to tears by the sight of me in my wedding dress. The realization makes my own eyes well up.

"You're so beautiful," Max whispers, lifting my veil and revealing my face to them fully. "Our perfect omega."

I offer them a shy smile, still unable to believe that in moments, I'll officially belong to these three incredible alphas who changed my life. My gaze drifts from their adoring faces to the guests, scanning the crowd until I find what I'm looking for- my babies.

They're in the front row, all four dressed in adorable matching outfits. Phoebe and Amelia, with their tiny bows and red frilly dresses, are nestled in my mother's arms, while Rhett and Luke, handsome in miniature gray suits, are being gently bounced on the knees of Carmen and Francine. At one year old, their little faces light up as they see me.

Tears spill over my lashes as I give them a tiny wave, my heart so full it might burst. The quadruplets wiggle excitedly in response, causing a ripple of affectionate laughter to spread through the guests.

The officiant clears his throat, pulling my attention back to the ceremony.

Damon steps forward first, taking both my hands in his. The setting sun casts shadows across the sharp planes of his face, making him appear even more dangerous and beautiful than usual.

"Lena," Damon begins, his deep voice carrying effortlessly across the hushed gathering. His dark eyes bore into mine with an intensity that made my breath catch. "From the moment I caught your scent, I knew you were meant to be ours. I vow to protect you with every fiber of my being, to cherish what is precious to you, and to lead our pack with strength and wisdom."

The sincerity in his words and the promise of protection—it's everything I have ever craved.

"I will never let anyone harm you again," he adds softly so only I can hear, and my eyes sting with grateful tears.

Max steps forward next, his eyes twinkling with affection as he takes my still-trembling hands from Damon.

"My sweet Lena," he says. "I vow always to make you smile, catch you when you fall, and remind you every day how perfectly you fit into our pack and hearts."

Max has always known how to ease my anxiety and bring light back into my life whenever he finds me crying or waking from a nightmare.

Then Gunnar moves forward, his enormous muscular frame blocking the sunlight as he stands before me, his face is tight with concentration. His love is an emotion clearly harder for him to express in words.

"Lena," he says, his voice rough like gravel. His eyes lock onto mine with predatory focus. "I vow to fight for you until my last breath, to claim you in ways that make you remember who you belong to, and to worship every inch of your body until you can't remember your name."

A collective intake of breath ripples through the guests, and heat flares in my cheeks at his boldness. Typical Gunnar, saying exactly what he means without any filter.

"Lena, would you like to recite your vows?" the officiant prompts, and I nod shyly.

"I still remember the day you alphas barged into my quiet little library like you owned the place, tracking in about fifty pounds of mud. I thought I was just offering shelter from a storm, but who knew it would turn into a full-blown mating bond?" I say with a smile as everyone chuckles around me. "But here's the thing: that crazy, heat-induced weekend? That was the beginning of my life. You didn't just claim my body- you claimed my heart. And then you gave me something even bigger: a pack. A family. And four very loud, very adorable reminders of what we created together."

"That's beautiful," says Damon, wiping my tears with his thumb.

"I love you all so much," I continue. "Our journey hasn't always been easy, but you've been my rock. Thank you for making me better, loving me when I thought I was unlovable, and not leaving me when I constantly pushed you away."

"We'll never leave you, sweetheart," says Max, his eyes fiery.

The officiant looks at all four of us with a smile. "With the vows completed, I now pronounce you alphas and omega. Alphas, you may now kiss your omega bride."

Damon takes my hands, and I know this is the happiest moment of my life as my heart swells. His large hand slides to the nape of my neck, fingers threading through my hair as he pulls me toward him.

His lips claim mine in a kiss that's firm and possessive. His tongue sweeps into my mouth, demanding and thorough, and I melt against him, forgetting the audience entirely. When he finally releases me, I'm breathless, my lips tingling, and my pulse racing wildly.

"There you go," he growls, and I fan my face, making the guests laugh.

Max approaches me next, and I smile.

His kiss is as different from Damon's as his vows were—sweet and tender, his lips soft against mine. He places his hand over my heart, feeling my heartbeat as we kiss.

"My wife," says Max, and I smile, glowing as he looks at me.

Gunnar snakes an arm around my waist to pull me flush against his hard body while his other hand grips my jaw.

His kiss is nothing short of filthy, open-mouthed and demanding, his tongue thrusting into my mouth in a blatant imitation of what he plans to do to me later. I whimper against his lips, my pussy clenching and throbbing in response. When he finally releases me, I sway on my feet, drunk on his taste, as the officiant discreetly coughs, his face slightly flushed as he tries to regain control of the ceremony.

I hear a few knowing laughs from the audience, and even Carmen looks amused when I dare glance her way.

Damon's hand finds the small of my back, a gentle touch that sends butterflies fluttering through my stomach.

"Mine," he growls softly in my ear before suddenly bending and lifting me onto his shoulder in one fluid motion.

I gasp in surprise, my hands instinctively grasping at his suit jacket as he straightens to his full height. From this position, I have a perfect view of our laughing, cheering guests as Damon turns to carry me back down the aisle.

"Damon!" I squeal, half-laughing, half-mortified, as my dress rides up slightly.

"Better hold that dress down, little omega," Max teases from beside us, his hand coming up to pat my bottom playfully. "Unless you want to give everyone a preview of tonight."

Gunner flanks Damon's other side, his expression having returned to its usual seriousness, but I notice how his eyes keep darting to where my dress is hitched up over my thighs.

The guests rise to their feet as we pass, throwing handfuls of rice and flower petals that rain down around us like confetti. I catch glimpses of smiling faces—my mother wiping away tears, Francine bouncing little Luke on her hip, Carmen giving me a knowing wink while surrounded by her own pack of alphas.

***

We reach the waiting limousine, its sleek black exterior adorned with white ribbons and flowers. The driver holds the door open, and Damon finally lowers me from his shoulder, setting me gently on my feet.

"In you go, my lovely wife," he murmurs, his words making my belly clench with arousal.

I slide into the luxurious interior, immediately enveloped by the rich scent of leather and the combined pheromones of my alphas as they file in after me. Damon sits to my right, his thigh pressing against mine, while Max takes the spot on my left. Gunnar settles directly across from me, his knees nearly touching mine in the confined space.

As the door closes and the noise of the celebration fades, I let out a long breath and rest my head against Damon's solid chest.

"We did it," I whisper, feeling the tension drain from my body. "I can't believe we actually had our wedding day."

"Why wouldn't we?" Max asks, his hand resting on my thigh.

I shrug, playing with the delicate lace on my dress. "After everything with Zorin, the pregnancy, the babies... sometimes it feels like I've been waiting for the other shoe to drop. It seems too good to be true."

Damon's hand finds mine, his fingers intertwining with mine. "You're ours now. Officially."

"The ceremony went perfectly," Max says, his thumb tracing lazy circles on my shoulder. "Better than we could have hoped for."

"But I think our officiant nearly had a heart attack after Gunnar's kiss," I giggle, glancing at the alpha in question.

Gunnar smirks, watching me from his seat. "He's lucky that's all I did to you in public."

The darkness in his voice makes me blush almost instantly.

"The babies were so good," I say, changing the subject before the pulsing heat between my thighs becomes unbearable. "I was worried they might cry during the ceremony."

"They seem happy staying with your mom and your sisters while we're gone," Damon agrees, stroking my arm while I'm still lying on his chest.

"One week," Max says, squeezing my shoulder. "One whole week of having you all to ourselves, with no two AM feedings or diaper changes."

"Just two AM knottings," Gunnar adds bluntly, his eyes darkening as they fix on my face.

My cheeks heat at his words, but I can't deny the throbbing of my pussy.

It's been difficult finding time for intimacy with four babies demanding constant attention. The thought of one uninterrupted week with my alphas makes my body tingle with anticipation.

I feel Damon's large hand resting possessively on my belly through the delicate fabric of my wedding dress, his warmth seeping into my skin.

Without warning, his fingers begin a slow, deliberate journey downward, the pressure just enough to make my breath hitch as he finds the hem of my dress and slips beneath it. His palm is hot against my bare thigh, calloused fingers tracing lazy patterns on my sensitive skin, working steadily higher.

My heart hammers against my ribs, knowing exactly what my alphas have planned for this ride. They've been barely restraining themselves for weeks in anticipation of this night.

"Where—" I swallow hard as his thumb brushes dangerously close to the lace edge of my thong. "Where are we going?"

Damon's dark eyes meet mine, pupils dilated with desire.

"That's a surprise, little omega," he murmurs, his voice dropping to that commanding alpha tone that makes my pussy clench instantly. "But I think we need to warm you up first."

I squirm in my seat, trapped between Damon and Max, feeling their heat enveloping me from both sides while Gunnar watches with predatory intent from across the limo.

"She's already warming up," Max observes, noticing the flush spreading across my cheeks. "Her face is very pink already."

"Let's see if that pretty blush extends elsewhere," Damon smirks. He nods to Gunnar, who leans forward without hesitation.

Gunnar's strong hands grasp the skirt of my wedding dress, gradually bunching the expensive fabric around my waist. The cool air of the limo hits my exposed thighs, making goosebumps rise on my skin.

I instinctively try to press my legs together, but Damon's hand on one thigh and Gunnar's on the other keep my legs wide open.

"Max," Damon orders, "check if our bride is ready for her wedding night."

"But the driver," I whisper harshly. The beta driver stares straight ahead and suddenly rolls up the barrier between us. I blush even harder, knowing that the driver knows I'm about to get ravished by my alphas.

My breath catches as Max slides from the seat to kneel on the limo floor between my forcibly spread legs. His freckled face is level with my most intimate parts, his warm breath fanning against my inner thighs as he studies the tiny white thong barely covering me.

"So pretty," he murmurs, tracing one finger along the lace edge. "White for purity."

"We all know our omega is anything but pure," Gunnar chuckles darkly.

Heat floods my face at his words, but I can't deny the rush of slick that bubbles from my pussy.

Gunnar and Damon spread my thighs wider, their grips bruisingly tight. Max hooks a finger under the thin strip of fabric and pulls it aside, exposing my pussy to their hungry gazes.

"Fuck," Max breathes, his eyes widening. "She's drenched."

I whimper as I feel his fingers brushing through my folds,

exploring my wetness with deliberate slowness. My hips buck involuntarily, seeking more pressure, but Damon's hand moves to my lower belly, holding me firmly in place.

"Tell us what you see, Max," Gunnar demands, his voice tight with restraint.

Max's fingers continue their torturous exploration, dipping shallowly into my entrance before withdrawing. "Her pussy's completely covered in slick. It's running down toward her ass."

Damon lifts my chin, forcing me to look at him. "Was the thought of our wedding night arousing you, little omega?"

"Yes," I gasp as Max's thumb brushes teasingly over my clit.

"Check her ass, too," Damon commands, his grip on my thigh tightening.

Before I can protest at the invasion, the three alphas perfectly coordinate to reposition me. Gunnar lifts me effortlessly while Max pulls my legs toward him. In seconds, I'm lying horizontally across the seats on my belly. My head is cradled in Damon's lap, my body stretched out with my legs toward Max.

The position places me directly beneath the overhead lights of the limo, exposing every inch of me to their scrutiny.

I feel Damon's erection pressing hard against my cheek through his suit pants as Gunnar and Max kneel on the floor beside the seat.

My wedding dress is bunched around my waist now, my ass completely exposed except for the thin strip of my thong disappearing between my cheeks.

"Hold her open," Gunnar growls, and I feel their hands on my ass, squeezing the flesh roughly before pulling my cheeks apart. The cool air hits my asshole, and I bury my face against Damon's thigh in embarrassment.

"Fuck," Max gasps, and I can practically hear the grin in his voice. "Did our little omega get her asshole waxed for us?"

My face burns hotter against Damon's leg. He threads his fingers through my hair, tugging gently until I'm forced to look up at him again.

"Did you, baby?" Damon asks softly. "Did you prepare your tight little asshole for your alphas' cocks on your wedding night?"

I bite my lip, nodding slightly.

"I wanted... I wanted to be ready for you," I admit, my voice barely above a whisper. "For all of you."

A collective groan rises from all three werewolves. Damon's fingers tighten in my hair, forcing my head back further.

"Such a good, thoughtful omega," he praises, his thumb brushing my lower lip. "Always thinking about how to please your alphas."

"Look at how pink and tight it is," Max marvels, his thumb gliding over my exposed hole. The unexpected touch makes me jolt and whimper. "Perfectly smooth, not a single hair."

"I bet she had someone spread her cheeks just like this," Gunnar adds, his voice rough with desire. "Legs spread wide while they waxed this pretty little pucker for us."

His finger replaces Max's, circling my rim with torturous slowness.

"Did you think about us while they were doing it, omega? Did your pussy get wet knowing we'd be staring at your smooth asshole on our wedding night?" Damon demands.

"Yes," I gasp, unable to lie under their intense scrutiny. "I thought about you the whole time."

"I want her to slick from her asshole," Damon declares, his eyes dark with lust as he continues to hold my gaze. "Make it happen."

My heart races at his command, knowing exactly what's coming. Sure enough, I feel a slippery finger—I'm not sure whose—pressing against my rim, cold with lube or spit.

"We'll make it happen, boss," says Max, and I realize it must be his finger circling my entrance, gradually applying more pressure while Gunnar breathes heavily.

"The perfect omega deserves the perfect wedding night," Damon replies, his free hand moving to unzip his pants. The sound of the zipper seems deafening in the confined space of the limo. "And that means getting fucked in all her pretty holes."

Max's finger breaches me just as Damon finishes speaking. His finger pushes past the tight ring of muscle with careful insistence.

I arch my back instinctively, a strangled moan escaping my lips as my body adjusts to the intrusion.

"That's it," Max encourages, working his finger deeper. "Open up for us, baby. Relax those muscles; you know what to do."

A second finger joins the first—Gunnar's this time, I think, based on the thickness, stretching me wider. The burn quickly transforms into pleasure as they work together, their fingers pumping in and out of my ass with increasing strokes.

"Lena is very eager," Gunnar grunts, pushing his fingers deeper. "Her asshole is sucking us in."

"I need your knot," I moan, longing to reach our destination. I can't help the shameless moans that escape me, my ass arching higher, silently begging for more.

I'm vaguely aware of the limo driver just beyond the partition, but I'm too lost in pleasure to care if he hears me.

"Your sounds are too beautiful to waste," Damon murmurs, freeing his thick cock from his pants. It springs free, heavy, and flushed, a bead of precum glistening at the tip. "Open your mouth, omega. Let me silence those pretty moans from our driver. That's only for us, baby."

I part my lips obediently, and Damon guides his cock into my mouth, the musky, sweaty taste of him exploding across my tongue. He sighs in pleasure as I take him deeper, his hand firmly gripping my hair to control my movements.

Meanwhile, Max and Gunnar continue their relentless assault on my ass, adding a third finger that makes me moan around Damon's cock. The vibration causes him to thrust deeper, the head of his cock hitting the back of my throat.

"Fuck her ass harder," Damon orders, his voice strained as he fights to maintain his composure. "I want her coming just from that."

Their fingers drive into me with renewed vigor, curling and scissoring, stretching me in ways that send electric pulses of pleasure throughout my body. My pussy clenches on nothing, desperate for attention, but the alphas are focused solely on my ass, determined to fulfill their pack leader's command.

The dual sensations of Damon's cock sliding between my lips and the fingers pumping into my ass create a perfect storm of pleasure.

My stomach begins to clench, that telltale pressure building rapidly, my voice muffled against Damon's cock.

"I think she's close," Max observes, his free hand gripping my thigh tightly. "Her pussy is gushing with slick."

"Come from your ass, omega," Damon growls at me, his cock still buried in my mouth. "Show us how much you love being filled by your alphas."

My orgasm crashes through me with stunning force, my entire body convulsing as waves of pleasure radiate outward from my core. I feel a rush of slick gushing from both my pussy and my ass, soaking their fingers and probably the limo seat below me.

"Holy fuck," Gunnar growls as they continue to work

their fingers through my spasming hole, prolonging my pleasure until it borders on pain. "She's fucking drenched."

I whimper around Damon's cock as they slowly withdraw their fingers, the sudden emptiness making me clench around nothing.

The lewd, wet sound of their exit brings a fresh wave of embarrassment crashing over me.

"Such a responsive omega," Damon praises, finally withdrawing his cock from my mouth and tucking himself away with obvious reluctance. "And we've only just begun."

The limo begins to slow, and I realize with a jolt that we've arrived at our destination. Gunnar and Max help me sit up, adjusting my wedding dress to cover me, though nothing can be done about the mess of slick coating my thighs.

"We're here," Max announces, peering out the window. "The perfect hideaway for our honeymoon."

My legs feel wobbly as Damon helps me from the limo, my ass still tender from their attention.

We've stopped in what appears to be a secluded forest clearing, with towering pines creating a natural privacy screen around a stunning log cabin. Solar lights illuminate a stone pathway leading to the front door, and I can see the flicker of firelight through the windows.

Damon scoops me into his arms without warning, carrying me bridal-style toward the cabin while Max and Gunnar follow with our luggage.

"Do you like it?" Damon asks, his lips brushing against my forehead. "We had it built special for you."

# CHAPTER 35

**Damon**

My cock throbs painfully as I carry Lena through the forest path toward our honeymoon cabin. Her small body is cradled against my chest, the delicate scent of vanilla from her skin making my mouth water with each step.

The weight of her in my arms, knowing she's mine—our pack's—to claim properly tonight has my alpha instincts roaring with anticipation.

My erection swings heavily between my legs as I walk.

"This place is beautiful, Damon," she breathes, her eyes widening as she takes in the surrounding woods and the rustic cabin that appears through the trees.

I can barely focus on the scenery.

All I see is her- my omega, my wife, mine to claim and knot until she's crying from pleasure. My cock bobs with each step, growing harder as her sweet scent intensifies. Behind me, I can hear Gunnar and Max following, their own arousal evident in their heavy breathing.

"I've been hard since the fucking ceremony," Gunnar

growls, adjusting himself. "That dress makes her ass look perfect for breeding."

Max chuckles, a hungry sound. "Her scent's getting stronger. I think our little omega knows what's coming."

"Three knots," I reply, my voice a deep rumble that makes Lena shiver in my arms. "One for each of her holes. She'll be leaking our cum for days."

Lena whimpers softly, pressing her face against my chest. I can smell her arousal strengthening, her pussy getting wet just from our words.

"You like hearing that, don't you, little wife?" I murmur into her hair. "Knowing we're going to take turns filling you up?"

She nods, her body trembling against mine.

I shift her in my arms, making sure she can feel the hard length of my cock pressing against her through the thin fabric of her wedding dress.

When we reach the cabin, I push the door open with my shoulder, carrying her over the threshold. The interior is simple but luxurious. A large fireplace dominates one wall, already lit and casting a warm glow over the rustic furniture.

"Can you put me down? I want to look around," Lena says eagerly.

I tighten my grip on her, my fingers digging into the soft flesh of her thigh.

"You can admire the place later," I growl, my patience at its end. "I've been smelling your sweet pussy all day, watching you in this dress, knowing what's underneath. I'm not waiting another second to claim you properly, wife."

She gasps at my tone, her pupils dilating with arousal.

I carry her straight to the bedroom, Gunnar and Max following close behind. Their heavy footsteps match my own urgent pace. The bed is massive, custom-made to accommodate all four of us, covered in silk sheets.

I sit on the edge of the bed, positioning Lena on my lap so her back is to my chest. My erection presses insistently against her ass through her dress, and she squirms, teasing me with the subtle movement.

"Gunnar, Max," I command. "Remove her stockings and heels."

They kneel immediately, one at each of her delicate feet.

Max lifts her right leg, carefully sliding off the high heel before letting his fingers trace up her calf to the top of her stocking.

Gunnar mirrors him on the left, both of them reverent in their movements as they roll the sheer fabric down her legs, exposing her pale skin inch by tantalizing inch.

While they work, I begin unbuttoning the long row of pearl buttons running down the back of her wedding gown. My fingers brush against her spine with each button, and I lower my mouth to the exposed skin of her shoulder, pressing hot kisses there. I inhale deeply, breathing in the intoxicating blend of vanilla and aroused omega that's uniquely hers.

"I can smell how wet you got in the limo," I murmur against her neck, my teeth grazing over her pulse point. "Your pussy was dripping through your panties. Were you thinking about what we'd do to you tonight?"

She shivers, a small moan escaping her lips as Gunnar's hand skims up her inner thigh, stopping just short of where she's aching to be touched.

"We need an answer," Gunnar demands, nipping at her thigh.

"Y-yes," she whispers, her voice trembling. "I couldn't help it."

My cock jerks against her ass, pre-cum leaking from the tip as I continue unbuttoning her dress. I want to tear the fabric apart, to expose her to us faster, but I restrain myself. We have all night, all week, to be rough with her.

This first time as husbands and wife deserves more moments of care and attention.

She squirms again, her perfect ass grinding against my erection through the thin material of my pants. A growl rumbles deep in my chest as I struggle to maintain control.

"Feel that?" I ask, thrusting up slightly against her. "Feel how fucking hard I am for you?"

"Yes," she breathes, pressing her ass back against me more deliberately now.

I lean forward, my chest pressed to her back as I continue my work on the buttons.

"You're going to be so well-knotted tonight, little omega. We're going to take turns rutting you until you can't remember your own name. Your pussy, your mouth, your ass —we're going to fill every hole until you're overflowing with our cum. Would you like that?" I whisper, brushing my lips against her ear.

She nods frantically, her breath coming faster now. I can smell her arousal intensifying, her slick soaking through her panties.

Finally, I undo the last button. I place my hands on her shoulders. "Stand up for us, wife."

Lena obediently rises from my lap, her legs slightly unsteady.

I keep my hands on her hips as the dress slides down her body, pooling at her feet in a puddle of white silk. She stands before us in nothing but a lace thong, her perfect breasts bare and flushed pink with arousal, her nipples hard and begging for attention.

The three of us stare at her, my cock straining painfully against my pants.

The dying light from the setting sun filters through the window, casting a golden glow on her pale skin that makes her look like something divine.

"Fuck," Gunnar growls, his eyes fixated on her breasts. "Those tits are perfect for sucking."

"Look at that ass," Max adds, his voice thick with lust. "So pretty and round, just begging to be filled with cum."

"Turn around," I command, and she does, giving us a view of her round ass, barely covered by the lace thong as I palm my cock. "That ass was made for knotting."

I turn her back to face me, my hands moving up to cup her breasts reverently.

They fit perfectly in my palms, soft and warm. I squeeze them delicately, testing their weight, flicking my thumbs over her hardened nipples. My cock is getting harder, tenting my pants obscenely as I weigh her tits in my hands.

The scent of her waxed pussy is driving me wild—clean, fresh, and dripping with arousal just inches from my face.

Gunnar's hands trail down her waist, his fingers digging slightly into her soft flesh. Max stands behind her, his hands cupping her ass, kneading the plump cheeks vigorously.

I release her breasts reluctantly, my hands moving lower, skimming over her flat stomach until I reach the edge of her thong. I run my finger along the waistband before dipping lower, stroking her pussy through the damp lace.

"You waxed yourself so nicely for us tonight," I observe, my voice rough with desire.

"Yes, I did," she replies shakily, her thighs trembling under my touch.

I look up at her face, flushed pink with a mixture of shyness and arousal.

Despite having knotted her several times before, she still acts like a pure virgin whenever we're about to fuck her. It turns me on beyond belief, my cock jerking eagerly in my pants. I cup her pussy more firmly, letting my middle finger slide beneath the lace to dip into her wet, warm hole.

She gasps sharply, her inner walls clenching around my invading digit.

I push in deeper, feeling her slick coating my finger, her heat enveloping me. When I withdraw my finger, a sticky stream of her arousal follows, clinging between my fingertip and her needy cunt.

"Look how wet and eager you are for us," I say, holding up my glistening finger before bringing it to my mouth to taste her essence. "So fucking sweet. I think I'll taste you properly before I give you the first knot."

She nods quickly, her eyes glazed with desire.

"Use your words," Gunnar prompts, nibbling at her neck. "Tell your alpha what you want."

"Please," she whimpers, her voice small but urgent. "Please taste me, Damon."

"On the bed then," I command, my cock throbbing with anticipation. "Lie down for us, omega."

She moves with surprising grace despite her obvious arousal, sliding onto the silk sheets and settling in the middle of the large bed, her eyes never leaving mine.

I stand at the foot of the bed, my fingers working quickly to unzip my pants. My eyes never leave Lena's body as she lies before me, waiting for instructions.

"Spread your legs," I command, my voice thick with lust. "And touch yourself. Show us how much you want this."

As she complies, her thighs parting to reveal her glistening sex, I free my cock from the confines of my pants. It springs forth, heavy and engorged, pre-cum already beading at the tip as I wrap my hand around the shaft and stroke lazily, savoring the sight before me.

Beside me, Max and Gunnar are hastily removing their clothes, their eyes fixed on our omega as she tentatively begins to circle her clit with delicate fingers. The scent of her arousal fills the room, making my mouth water and my cock throb harder in my palm.

Her pussy is a work of art—plump outer lips, perfectly waxed, framing the glistening pink folds within. Her entrance flutters invitingly with each circle of her fingers on her swollen clit, a fresh wave of slick making her shine in the dimming light. The sight of her, spread open and vulnerable for us, has me gripping the base of my cock to keep from coming then and there.

"You're fucking gorgeous," I growl, giving myself a few slow strokes. "That pretty little cunt is begging to be eaten, isn't it?"

She nods, her teeth catching her lower lip as her fingers move faster.

A small whimper escapes her throat when I finally climb onto the bed, positioning myself between her spread thighs. I hover over her pussy, breathing in her thickening scent before placing a gentle kiss just above her mound.

"You smell divine," I murmur against her skin, letting my hot breath graze over her sensitive flesh. "I've been thinking about tasting you all day."

I lower my head slowly, maintaining eye contact as my tongue makes that first delicious contact with her slit, licking a long, deliberate stripe from her entrance to her clit. The taste of her explodes across my tongue—sweet, tangy, and uniquely Lena—and I groan against her flesh.

"Oh god," she moans, her back arching off the bed.

"Fucking good," I growl as I swirl my tongue around her clit, applying just enough pressure to make her squirm without pushing her over the edge too quickly. I want to savor this, to make her fall apart completely before I claim her with my cock.

The world narrows down to the exquisite taste of her pussy, the soft sounds of pleasure she makes, and the increasingly desperate movements of her hips against my face. I'm vaguely aware of the mattress dipping as Max and Gunnar position themselves on either side of her, but I'm too consumed with the feast before me to pay them much attention.

I alternate between broad licks across her entire sex and focused attention on her clit, occasionally dipping my tongue into her hole to taste the slick flowing from her pussy. Her thighs begin to tremble on either side of my head, and I grasp them firmly, holding her open so I can see her come.

"Oh god, Damon," she gasps, her hands finding their way to my hair, fingers tangling in the strands as she tries to guide me where she needs me most.

I comply, zeroing in on her clit with precise flicks of my tongue.

I slip two fingers inside her dripping hole, curling them to find that G-spot. I find it, and her reaction is immediate—a sharp cry and a hard buck of her hips against my face.

The taste of her becomes stronger, her arousal coating my chin as I work her toward climax ruthlessly.

My cock is impossibly hard, hanging heavy between my thighs as I feast on her pussy. I could stay here for hours, drawing orgasm after orgasm from her with just my mouth, but my need to be inside her is growing too intense to ignore much longer.

I increase the pace of my fingers, fucking her with them while my tongue works her clit in tight circles. Her moans grow louder, more desperate, her thighs quivering against my hands. When I feel her inner walls begin to tighten around my fingers, I seal my lips around her clit and suck, hard.

She comes with a scream, her back arching dramatically off the bed.

Her legs try to close around my head, but I hold them firmly open, forcing her to endure the pleasure as I continue to lick and suck through her orgasm. I can feel her cream leaking around my fingers, her body producing even more slick in preparation for what's to come.

"Damon, please," she begs breathlessly, trying to wriggle away from my relentless mouth. "It's too much, I can't—"

"Shhh," I soothe, placing one last kiss on her oversensitive clit before raising my head. My face is slick with her juices, and I make a show of licking my lips as I meet her dazed eyes. "I'm going to make love to you now, little omega. Going to fill this sweet pussy with my knot."

She moans in response, still panting from her orgasm.

I position myself between her thighs, noticing that Gunnar has moved to kneel by her head, his cock jutting toward her face. Max is at her side, his mouth latched onto one of her nipples while his hand kneads her other breast roughly.

I grasp my cock, guiding it to her soaked entrance.

The head slides through her folds, gathering her slick before pressing against her opening. Despite how wet she is, there's resistance as I begin to push inside—she's always tight, her body gripping me like a vice no matter how many times I've had her.

"Fuck," I hiss as the head breaches her entrance. "So fucking tight. Going to take your husband's fat cock now, aren't you, little omega? Going to be a good girl and take it all?"

"Yes, Alpha," she gasps, her eyes fluttering closed as I push deeper. "Please, I need you so much. You've my love and my life."

*Oh fuck.*

I press forward slowly, watching with fascination as her pussy stretches to accommodate my girth. It's a struggle to fit all of me inside her, but her body was made for this, made to take our cocks and our knots.

I pull back slightly before thrusting forward with more force, earning a sharp cry from Lena as I sink deeper.

The sensation is overwhelming- hot, tight, wet perfection gripping my cock.

"So good," I groan, finally bottoming out. "So perfect for me."

I pause for a moment, savoring the feeling of being fully sheathed inside her. I watch as Gunnar guides his cock to her lips, groaning when she opens eagerly to take him into her mouth. Max has moved to her other breast, his teeth grazing her nipple as his hand slides down to where her clit is still swollen and sensitive.

The sight of my omega being pleasured by my packmates, her body servicing all three of us at once, sends a surge of pride and lust through me.

I begin to thrust, withdrawing almost completely before driving back in with a force that jostles her entire body and pushes her mouth further onto Gunnar's cock.

"That's it," I growl, setting a faster pace. "Take it like the good little omega you are."

Each thrust is punctuated by the wet sound of her pussy gripping my cock and the muffled moans she makes around Gunnar's length. I grab her hips, angling them upward to hit her deepest spots, and am rewarded with a particularly loud whimper.

The sight of her flushed, filled at both ends, her breasts being attended to by Max's eager mouth, is almost too much. My thrusts become more erratic, more forceful, as I chase my release. I can feel my knot beginning to swell at the base of my cock, catching on her entrance with each thrust.

"Going to knot you," I pant, sweat beading on my forehead as I drive into her repeatedly. "Going to fill this perfect pussy with my cum."

Her eyes meet mine, glazed with pleasure and submission

while her mouth is full, and that's all it takes. With a final, powerful thrust, I bury myself to the hilt as my orgasm crashes over me. My knot expands fully, locking us together as my cock pulses inside her, shooting rope after rope of hot cum deep into her womb.

"You're so fucking perfect," I murmur as I catch my breath, still locked inside her by my knot. "I love you so much, Lena."

### Gunnar

"There you go, little omega," I growl as Lena's hot mouth works my throbbing cock. Her cheeks are hollowed as she sucks with surprising strength. "Take it deeper."

My fingers tangle in her auburn hair, not forcing but guiding, showing her the rhythm I need. Watching Damon brutally fuck and knot her moments ago has me on edge already, my balls tight and heavy with need. The way her tits bounced with each of his thrusts, the desperate sounds she made—it was fucking art, and now I'm desperate.

Damon is still knotted inside her pussy, his large body partially draped over hers as she lies on her back, facing my cock. His eyes meet mine over her body, a satisfied smirk on his face as he watches our wife service me. The knowledge that her pussy is currently filled with his knot and cum while she sucks me off sends a fresh wave of arousal through me.

She swirls her tongue around the sensitive head of my cock, paying special attention to the slit where pre-cum is already beading. The sensation makes my eyes roll back, a deep groan escaping my throat.

"Fuck, you're good at that," I praise, watching her eyes light up with pride. "Such a perfect mouth for alpha cock."

Her response is to take me deeper, her tongue working the underside of my shaft as she bobs her head. One of her hands wraps around what she can't fit in her mouth, stroking in time with her sucking. The other reaches up to cup my balls, gently rolling them between her delicate fingers.

The dual sensation has me cursing, my hips jerking forward involuntarily.

She makes a small choking sound but doesn't pull away, instead relaxing her throat to take me even deeper.

"Damn," I say my voice rougher now. "Take it all like a good little omega. Show me how much you want to please your husband."

She moans around my length, the vibrations sending shockwaves of pleasure up my spine. I tighten my grip in her hair, setting a slightly faster pace as I guide her head. My cock disappears repeatedly between those perfect lips, emerging slick with her saliva before plunging back into the wet heat of her mouth.

Max watches from beside Damon, stroking himself as he waits for his turn. The room is thick with the scent of sex—Damon's release, Lena's arousal, and the musky scent of aroused alphas. It's intoxicating, pushing my already heightened senses into overdrive.

"Knotted by one alpha while sucking another's cock. Such a perfect little omega wife doing her duties," whispers Max.

I see the flush of arousal on her cheeks at his words. She likes being talked to like this and reminded of her place as our shared mate.

"You were made for this," I continue, my cock growing impossibly harder in her mouth. "Made to be filled by alpha cock in every hole. You'll take all three of us tonight, won't you? Going to let us use this sweet body until you're leaking our cum from everywhere."

She nods as best she can with my cock still in her mouth,

a muffled "Mmhmm" vibrating against my length. The enthusiasm in her response nearly makes me lose control then and there.

My balls are drawing up tight against my body now, the familiar pressure building at the base of my spine. She must sense it too, because her movements become more focused, more determined. Her hand moves faster on my shaft while her tongue lavishes attention on the sensitive head.

"Fuck, I'm close," I warn, my thighs tensing as I fight to prolong the pleasure. "Keep going just like that."

The heat in my groin intensifies, spreading through my lower abdomen as my orgasm approaches. Lena doubles her efforts, her cheeks hollowing as she sucks harder, her hand working my shaft with perfect pressure.

"I'm going to come," I growl, my voice strained. "Going to fill that pretty mouth with my cum. You're going to swallow every drop like a good omega, aren't you?"

Her eyes meet mine again, and my cock pulses violently as my orgasm tears through me, cum shooting into her waiting mouth in hot spurts.

I grip her hair tightly, holding her in place as I empty myself onto her tongue.

"Fuck, fuck, fuck," I groan, my hips jerking erratically as the pleasure crashes over me in waves.

She struggles slightly with the volume, a small trail of white escaping the corner of her mouth and trickling down her chin. As the last pulses of my orgasm subside, I loosen my grip on her hair, allowing her to pull back enough to swallow properly.

She gulps audibly, her throat working to take down my release.

Before I can reach to wipe the escaped cum from her chin, she uses her finger to places it on her tongue with a wink.

"Holy fuck," I breathe. "If I hadn't just come, that would have done it."

"Oh, Gunnar," she says, giggling.

"I love you," I say, kissing her on the forehead.

"I love you, too," she whispers.

I shift to lie beside her, my body still humming with satisfaction as Damon moves. Damon rearranges her, rolling her on top of him so she's straddling his hips, her stomach to his chest.

"Your turn, Max," Damon says, spreading Lena's ass cheeks apart with his large hands. "She's nice and ready for you to take this sweet ass."

I watch through half-lidded eyes as Max approaches eagerly, his cock standing at attention, ready to claim the last unexplored territory of our omega.

## Max

My cock is hard as steel as I stare at the erotic sight before me. Lena is sprawled on top of Damon, her stomach pressed to his chest, her legs spread wide on either side of his thighs. Her pussy, freshly knotted and slowly seeping with Damon's release, is on full display.

Her ass slightly reddened from where Damon's hips slapped against her during their fucking, is just waiting for my touch. I lick my lips in anticipation, my cock throbbing painfully as I move closer to claim the one last remaining hole.

I reach out, my hands grasping her ass cheeks, squeezing the soft flesh appreciatively. Her skin is soft. I spread her cheeks apart, revealing the tight pink pucker of her asshole. I groan at the sight, my cock jumping excitedly.

"Look at this tight little hole," I say, my voice thick with lust. "Your ass is begging to be fucked, isn't it? Looks like a juicy peach just waiting to be eaten."

"It is," gasps Lena as I run my thumb over her entrance, feeling it contract under my touch.

"Do you want me to knot this tight little bud, omega? Want me to stretch it open with my cock?"

She moans, pressing back against my hands.

"Yes, Max, please," she breathes, her voice shaky with need despite having already come twice.

I lower myself between her spread legs, my face level with her ass. Without warning, I lean in and press my tongue flat against her puckered entrance. She cries out in surprise, her body jerking against Damon, who holds her steady with his strong hands on her thighs.

"Fuck," Gunnar chuckles from where he's watching beside the bed, his cock already showing interest again despite his recent release. "Max just wants a taste first, little omega. Relax and enjoy it."

I circle her rim with the tip of my tongue, savoring the clean, musky taste of her. Her asshole is immaculate.

Clearly, she prepared for this possibility, and I show my appreciation by doubling my efforts, alternating between broad licks and pointed prods against the tight muscle.

Her entrance looks exquisite as I pull back briefly to admire my work, the delicate pink ring glistening with my saliva, clenching and unclenching.

I spread her cheeks wider, exposing her completely to my hungry gaze.

"Look at this beautiful asshole," I murmur, dipping my tongue back in for another taste. "So tight and perfect, blinking at me like it's begging for cock."

My tongue pushes more insistently now, breaching the tight ring of muscle slightly. Lena moans loudly, her face buried against Damon's shoulder. As I continue to rim her, I notice fresh slick beginning to leak from her pussy and ass, dripping down to mix with Damon's cum that's already seeping out of her.

"She's starting to slick again just from having her ass eaten," I comment, pulling back to admire the glistening evidence of her arousal. "She's getting wet from having a tongue in her ass. You like it, don't you, Lena babe?"

"Yes."

I circle her rim again, one hand reaching down to stroke my aching cock. The other moves to her entrance, my middle finger pressing gently against the tight muscle.

"Going to get you nice and ready for my cock," I tell her, slowly working the tip of my finger inside. The heat and tightness that greet my probing digit make me groan.

Her inner walls clench around my finger, resisting the intrusion briefly before relaxing enough to let me push deeper. I continue working my tongue around my finger, lubricating her entrance as much as possible.

"That feels nice," she says with a moan, and I smile.

"Your ass is a work of art," I praise as her body accepts my finger to the second knuckle. "It needs to get knotted."

I curl my finger slightly, feeling the silky smooth walls of her rectum as I begin to pump in and out gently. Her moans grow louder, and more desperate, as a fresh gush of slick coats my finger dripping from her asshole.

"Please, Max," she begs, her voice breathy and strained. "I need your cock now. I'm warmed up enough."

Her desperation sends a surge of arousal through me, my cock jerking in response. I withdraw my finger slowly, replacing it with two and scissoring them gently to stretch her further.

"Not yet, princess. Don't want to hurt you."

I work her open methodically, my fingers pushing deeper,

twisting and spreading to prepare her for my knot. By the time I have three fingers sliding easily in and out of her ass, she's practically sobbing with need, her body trembling as she pushes back against my hand.

"Please," she whimpers. "I need you inside me. Need your cock in my ass."

I can't ignore her any longer.

I withdraw my fingers and rise to my knees, positioning myself between her spread legs. The head of my cock, slick with pre-cum, press against her prepared entrance.

"Don't worry baby, I'll fill your tight ass right now," I tell her, my voice strained with the effort of holding back. "Going to stretch you open and fuck you until you're screaming."

I push forward slowly, watching as her tight ring of muscle stretch around the head of my cock. The pressure is incredible- hot, tight resistance that gradually gives way as I press forward. Inch by inch, her body accepts me, her ass gripping me as I sink deeper.

"Ahh! That feels so freaking good," she cries out, arching her back for more.

"Fuck," I hiss, sweat beading on my forehead from the effort of not slamming into her all at once. "So fucking tight."

Beneath her, Damon has his hands on her thighs, keeping her spread wide for me. Gunnar has moved closer, his hand reaching under to fondle her clit as I continue my slow invasion of her ass.

The combined stimulation has her panting, small whimpers escaping her with each centimeter I gain.

Finally, my hips are flush against her ass cheeks.

I pause there, giving her time to adjust to the fullness, my cock throbbing inside her as I fight for control.

"How does it feel?" I ask, running my hands up her back, feeling the slight tremors running through her muscles.

"Full," she gasps. "So full. Please move, please fuck me."

I withdraw slowly until just the head remains caught in her tight ring before pushing back in with more force. She cries out, but it's clearly from pleasure rather than pain.

I establish a rhythm, starting with measured thrusts.

The tight grip of her ass around my cock is mind-blowing, each thrust sending shocks of pleasure up my spine.

Her legs are spread obscenely wide on either side of Damon, giving me the perfect angle to drive deeper with each thrust. My balls slap against her pussy with each forward motion, adding to the wet, filthy sounds filling the room.

"Your ass is hungry for my knot," I growl, gripping her hips to pull her back onto my cock with each thrust.

"She's wet as fuck," says Gunnar, still playing with her sensitive clit. Lena is moaning uncontrollably now from the dual stimulation.

I increase my pace, driven by the immense pressure building in my groin. Each thrust is harder, deeper, and more primal as my control begins to slip. The sight of my cock disappearing into her tight ass, and the sounds of her breathy moans all combine to push me rapidly toward the edge.

"Going to fill this sweet ass with my cum," I pant, my rhythm becoming erratic as my orgasm approaches.

Her inner muscles clench around me in response, her body squeezing my cock.

With a final, powerful thrust, my orgasm crashes over me. My cock pulses violently as I come into her ass.

I collapse forward slightly, catching myself using my palms on the bed to avoid crushing her. My cock remains buried in her ass as the last pulses of my orgasm subside, leaving me breathless and utterly satisfied.

"Wow," she gasps, trying to catch her breath.

"Fuck," I breathe as my cock begins to swell, knotting her to me. My cum leaks into her well-fucked hole, and the feeling of that makes me happy. "You're mine. My wife."

"And you're my husband. I love you," she whispers.

## Lena

I'm slumped against Damon's chest, utterly spent and full. His knot pulsates inside my pussy while Max's stretches my ass, both keeping me stuffed with their cum. Every small movement sends aftershocks of pleasure rippling through me, making me whimper softly.

My body feels used in the most delicious way—marked, claimed, and thoroughly satisfied by my alphas. I've never felt so complete, so utterly possessed, and the thought brings a dreamy smile to my face despite my exhaustion.

"I'm so lucky," I murmur, my voice hoarse from screaming in pleasure. "To be your wife. To be claimed by all of you."

The words come out slurred, my mind still floating in a haze of post-orgasmic bliss.

Damon's chest rumbles against me as he speaks, his deep voice vibrating through my body. "We're the lucky ones, little omega. To have found you, to have claimed you."

His lips brush against the sensitive spot behind my ear, making me shiver despite his body's warmth.

He traces the mark on my upper arm gently—the claiming bite he placed there during our mating ceremony. The touch sends a pulse of warmth through my bond with him, a reminder of the permanent connection we now share.

"Remember the night I marked you?" he asks, his voice soft with the memory.

"How could I forget?" I say, smiling. I will never forget the beautiful bath and riding him. Warm water scented with jasmine surrounded us, his teeth breaking the skin of my arm as he claimed me forever. The moment had been simultaneously painful and ecstatic, the bond forming between us instantly.

"You cried," he recalls, kissing the mark. "Not from pain, but from happiness."

"I never thought I'd find a pack that would love me," I confess, the vulnerability in my voice a stark contrast to the sexual activities we've just engaged in. "After what happened with...before."

"We'll never let anyone hurt you again," Gunnar promises from where he's sprawled beside us, his hand reaching out to rest possessively on my thigh.

I wiggle slightly, loving the feeling of being so thoroughly filled by my alphas. The movement causes both knots to shift inside me, drawing a gasp from my lips and a groan from Damon.

"Careful, little wife," he warns, his hands gripping my hips to still my movements. "You'll get us all worked up again before we've even recovered."

Max chuckles from my other side. "Speak for yourself. I could go again in about ten minutes."

Their playful banter washes over me, filling me with contentment as much as their knots fill my body. With careful movements, Damon and Max maneuver me so I'm lying between them now instead of on top of Damon. The shift in position tugs at where we're connected, sending another wave of pleasure through my oversensitive body.

Damon leans down, capturing my lips in a tender kiss that contrasts with the roughness of our earlier activities. I can taste myself on his lips, and I blush.

When he pulls back, his dark eyes are soft as they scan my face. "You're beautiful like this," he says. "Thoroughly fucked and filled with our cum."

"The perfect omega," Max agrees, pressing kisses along

my shoulder, and Gunnar hums in agreement, his hand trailing lazy patterns up my side.

"The wedding night was everything I hoped it would be," he says, his normally gruff voice tinged with satisfaction. "And we've got the whole week ahead of us."

"A whole week of knotting you, babe," Max adds, his lips curving into a smile against my skin.

"I love you," I whisper. "My alphas, my mates, and my home."

"And we love you too," Damon responds, pressing his forehead to mine. "More than you could ever know."

In this moment, I know I've found where I belong.

After years of fear and hiding, of using blockers to mask my scent and keeping everyone at arm's length, I've finally found my pack, my family, my forever.

As the dying light casts long shadows across our tangled bodies, I close my eyes and breathe in the mingled scents of my alphas, Damon's smoked cedar, Gunnar's sandalwood, Max's pine and cinnamon- all mixed with the unmistakable scent of satisfied omega.

For the first time in my life, I feel completely and utterly safe, held in the arms of the men who would tear apart the world to protect me.

"Sleep and rest now, little omega," Damon whispers against my hair. "We have all night, all week, and all our lives to love you."

"Okay," I whisper back, feeling safe in their embrace as I slowly drift off to sleep with a smile on my lips and my heart bursting with love for my new pack.

**THE END**

# SNEAK PEEK

MARKING MIA

## Chapter 1
## Mia

"What the fuck was that, Trevor? You're supposed to cover me when I go in!" my boyfriend, Justin, screams at the TV, his fingers jabbing frantically at the controller. "Now we've lost the whole fucking match because of you!"

I wince at the volume, my shoulders tensing automatically.

The pan sizzles as I pour the eggs in, watching them bubble at the edges. Three weeks since he lost his job at the warehouse, and this is all he does- play games from dawn until I get home, sometimes well into the night. He promised he'd look for work, showed me job listings on his phone, and even mentioned an interview that mysteriously got rescheduled twice before he stopped mentioning it altogether.

"Justin," I call over my shoulder. "Do you want some eggs?"

The spatula scrapes against the pan as I push the edges toward the center, but he doesn't respond.

The oversized headset covers his ears completely, his attention solely on the screen where animated characters move in violent bursts of color.

I don't try again. Better to be ignored than snapped at.

My stomach growls as I slide the eggs onto a plate. I hadn't had dinner last night—too tired after my double shift to do more than shower and collapse into bed while Justin had been gaming all night.

"Jesus, babe, maybe you should skip breakfast sometimes." I freeze, spatula suspended mid-air. I didn't realize he'd taken off his headset. His eyes flick from my face to my midsection before returning to the screen. "Just saying. Those jeans were already tight last month."

I bite my lip, the familiar sting of tears threatening behind my eyes. Don't cry. Not in front of him. I focus on breathing, on the simple act of transferring eggs from pan to plate without dropping anything, without showing how deeply his words cut.

"I need to eat," I say quietly, my voice smaller than intended. "I'm on my feet for eight hours at the cafe."

My hand drifts unconsciously to my stomach, pinching the soft flesh through my sweater. When did I get so... soft? It wasn't noticeable, was it? But if Justin sees it, then customers probably do, too. The thought makes my chest tighten with embarrassment. I just don't have time to go to the gym when I'm the one supporting us.

"Whatever you say." He shrugs, adjusting his headset. "You're the one who's always complaining about your clothes not fitting."

I wasn't. I'd mentioned once, just once, that my work

apron felt tighter. A passing comment that he filed away to use against me later.

The fork feels heavy in my hand as I shovel eggs into my mouth, not bothering to sit. Standing makes it faster and makes escape closer. The eggs taste like nothing, like dust. I swallow mechanically, each bite a chore, eyes fixed on the clock above the stove. Twenty minutes until I need to leave.

"You could be a little nicer to me, you know," I finally say, as my emotions boil inside me. "The comments about my weight and all. It kind of hurts Justin."

Justin sighs dramatically, pausing his game and looking at me like I'm a particularly slow child. "Mia, I'm just watching out for you. If I don't tell you, who will? Your coworkers are too nice to say anything, but I guarantee they notice, and they'll never promote you."

"That's not something..."

"It's for your own good," he cuts me off. "I'm being honest because I care. Would you rather I lie and tell you everything's fine when it's not?"

My throat tightens. "There's a difference between honesty and being mean."

"Don't be so sensitive," Justin says, rolling his eyes. "I'm trying to help you. If you don't want my help, fine. Keep eating whatever you want."

The remaining eggs on my plate look suddenly revolting. I dump them into the trash, stomach churning with hunger and shame. The clock says it's time to leave anyway. I grab my coat from the hook by the door, shrugging it on with jerky movements.

"I'll be back at three," I say, reaching for my purse.

"Can you grab me some of those cheesy pretzels on your way back?" Justin calls, already re-immersed in his game. "From the gas station."

The gas station is six blocks in the opposite direction

from our apartment. My feet already ache thinking about the extra walking after my shift.

"Sure," I agree because it's easier than arguing, easier than dealing with his mood if I refuse. "Need anything else?"

"Nah, just the pretzels," he says, not looking up. He doesn't say thank you or goodbye.

\*\*\*

The chilly morning air stings my cheeks as I pull my coat tighter around my body, but the bite of cold is welcome after the suffocating air of my apartment. This is my favorite part of the day, these twenty precious minutes when I'm neither Justin's emotional punching bag nor the cafe's smiling barista.

Each step puts more distance between me and Justin's cutting words, between me and the cramped apartment with its stale air and never-ending gaming sounds.

My pace quickens naturally as if my body can't wait to escape his orbit. The sidewalk beneath my feet is familiar-cracked concrete, occasional patches of stubborn weeds, the corner where someone's dog always leaves a mark.

I've memorized every inch of this route over the past year.

A year ago, we still had the car—a beat-up Honda that Justin claimed was "vintage" but was just old. I didn't mind. It got me to work when it rained, brought me to the grocery store, and gave me some semblance of freedom.

Then came the night when Justin, drunk after a party, wrapped it around a telephone pole. He walked away with a sprained wrist and some scratches. The car was declared totaled, and the insurance money was spent on gaming equipment rather than a replacement vehicle.

"We're close enough to everything," he'd argued. "You like walking anyway."

And I do—especially now. My fingers tingle with cold inside my pockets as I turn onto Cherry Street. The morning traffic hums beside me, cars filled with people heading to jobs they might hate but at least show up for. I wiggle my toes in my sneakers, trying to keep them warm. I should buy better winter shoes, but that would mean asking Justin for money from our shared account, a conversation I'm not eager to have.

By the time I reach the cafe, my nose is numb and pink, but something in me feels cleansed by the cold. The cafe sits on the corner, its windows already fogged with steam from the espresso machines and the breath of early customers.

The wooden sign above the door, Brewed Awakening, swings slightly in the breeze.

I push the door open, and the bell above the door jingles cheerfully.

Immediately, I'm enveloped in warmth, the rich aroma of coffee beans, and the buzz of conversation. The line stretches almost to the door, business people checking watches impatiently, college students staring blearily at phones, and everyone needing caffeine to kickstart their day.

Behind the counter, it's controlled chaos.

Alice darts between the register and the espresso machine, her short gray hair bobbing with each movement. She's sixty-two and moves faster than most of the college kids she employs. A stack of empty cups waits beside her, each marked with specific orders in her neat handwriting.

"Hey, Mia!" She catches sight of me, relief washing over her flushed face even as she steams milk for a latte. "Glad you're here early. Think you can clock in now and jump in?"

I'm not due for another fifteen minutes, but I nod, already shrugging off my coat. The extra fifteen minutes means extra pay and every dollar counts when Justin contributes nothing to our rent.

"Morning rush hit hard?" I ask though the answer is

obvious as I squeeze past waiting customers to reach the employee area.

"Like a tsunami," Alice laughs, handing off a completed drink to a suited man who barely looks up from his phone. "Todd called in sick, and Jasmine's running late. It's just been me since six."

I punch my code into the time clock system, then wash my hands quickly in the small sink. The familiar routine soothes me—hot water, soap, counting to twenty as I scrub between my fingers.

"I'll take the register," I tell Alice, tying an apron around my waist without thinking about whether it feels tighter today. Right now, it doesn't matter. "You focus on drinks."

The line of customers shifts forward eagerly as I appear at the register, my customer service smile sliding into place. It's not entirely fake—there's relief in being busy and having clear tasks and expectations. No one here will comment on my weight or remind me of my failures. They just want their coffee made well and served quickly.

"Good morning," I greet the first customer, a woman in a red coat who's been checking her watch repeatedly. "What can I get started for you today?"

As I take her order and the next and the next, my fingers flying over the register keys, I feel myself settling into the rhythm of the cafe. The morning rush is overwhelming, but in a way that leaves no room for thoughts of Justin, no space for self-doubt. For the next eight hours, I belong to the cafe and its demands—and after the quiet humiliation of breakfast, there's something like freedom in that.

## Chapter 2
## Jace

The campus is lively for a Monday morning. It's hard to believe this many college students are taking morning classes willingly.

I brush sandy blonde hair out of my eyes and wink at a passing sophomore. Kira, I think her name was. Or Kelly? It's hard to remember anymore. My flings with humans are as plentiful as they are short-lived. It's not like I'm looking for a future with them, just a bit of fun.

But suddenly, I stop in my tracks.

On the wintery wind, I catch a scent. One that I don't recognize, but it intrigues me. More than that, it pulls me in. It's light but intoxicating, like the purest honey.

It surrounds me and pulls me forward. The blonde forgotten I sniff the air, desperate to find the source of that scent. The cafe next to the college is open as customers leave happily with their morning coffee in their hands.

That's when my eyes land on her.

Even through the cafe window, I can tell she's beautiful. Chestnut hair falling down her back in gentle waves.

As she turns, I catch a glimpse of her face, all soft lines and glittering hazel eyes. She's smiling at a customer as she cleans their table, and at that moment, I want her to smile for me.

I need to know her.

I want to taste her name on my lips. I want to hear her scream mine.

The urge is so strong a growl starts at the base of my throat. I know nothing about this woman, but I know that I want to make her mine.

Time passes, and college students walk by, but I hardly notice them as I watch her.

She walks through the cafe with purpose, but there's a shyness to her movements. She looks down a lot when she passes people. It strikes me that this remarkable creature is shy.

That fascinates me. She radiates with beauty. Those eyes draw me in, and the way her hips swing as she makes her way through the cafe. It's intoxicating. How could someone like that not realize how incredible she is?

A primal desire out of nowhere rises in me.

*I need to claim her. To make her my mate.*

I want to know what her body looks like under that oversized sweater. It would be an honor and a pleasure to put my hands under that sweater and feel her silky skin against mine. Tearing off, that sweater would leave nothing between us but skin. Her soft pink lips would part with surprise as I traced my tongue down her neck and between her breasts.

I feel myself harden at just the thought.

This human female is driving me crazy from just a scent and a glance. It's unlike me, but in this moment, I don't care.

At that moment, I notice a frat guy in the cafe noticing her, eyeing her in appreciation. This time, I don't try to fight down the growl that rumbles out of me. *Mine.* I don't know her name, but I know she is supposed to be mine.

The thought startles me.

This isn't like me. I'm a one-and-done, especially with human females. This lust, though, is unlike anything I have felt before. It's almost like...

I take in a sharp breath as the reality hits me. There's no fucking way this heady honey scent belongs to a human female.

No. *It can't b*e.

I step closer to the cafe, but the truth is unmistakable.

She's an omega, passing as a human.

But why? And why wasn't she wearing scent blockers? Why was she out here without a pack?

I resolve to provide that for her. Wherever her pack

## SNEAK PEEK

might be, they have failed her. I will make her mine. I will protect, mark, and care for her, no matter the cost.

I need to let my pack leader, Kane, know immediately about this rogue omega being worked like a servant by the humans.

---

By the time I make it back to pack territory, I'm calmer but no less obsessed. I enter our lavish townhouse in the city, a secondary home we use when it becomes necessary to venture closer to the human world.

"There you are! Where the hell have you been," Kane asks, stepping out of the kitchen with a mug of espresso. His dark brown eyes narrow on me like he is all too aware of what I have been up to. He doesn't particularly approve of my human dalliances.

"Probably scouting out his next fuck," Finn answers from his place on the couch.

They both chuckle, but they stop as soon as they see the look on my face.

"Jace?" Kane's eyes are sharp with alarm. "What is it?"

"There's this woman," I start, and Finn busts out laughing already. "I'm fucking serious, Finn. This is going to affect all of you."

"How? What do you mean?"

So I tell them. Everything. About the girl and the pull, I felt.

"She has a scent like honey. And despite how beautiful she is, she has this shyness about her. It's really—"

Kane snorts. "An omega without her pack? Working in a coffee shop? Jace, if you want to have a fling with a human, have at it. You don't need to spin these wild stories. You know I don't give a fuck what you do."

I look to Finn for backup, but he just shrugs. There's a thoughtful look in his eyes like he believes me.

I glared at him, and he looked away, his long black hair falling into his face. But I could see the rise of color on his face. He was ashamed. I could work with that later.

"I'm telling you, she's an omega," I insist to Kane.

Kane shakes his head, tugging at his suit sleeves. "The 'obsession' will pass once you've had your fun. Just get her number and get it over with."

For a moment, I almost wonder if he's right. But I know what I experienced. That woman is an omega. And she needs us.

### Mia

"Bye," I call out to the last of the workers as I leave the little building. My eight-hour shift became a double when Alice had to run home for a family emergency.

Not that I had minded. It meant more money.

Of course, my feet are aching by now, and it's hard for me to walk. I really need to buy more appropriate shoes for a double shift.

Exhausted and sore, I make it back to the apartment building just as it's starting to get dark.

The winter chill is pressing in through my coat, and my hair is a little wind-whipped, but more than anything, I'm just relieved to be home.

Oh fuck, I forgot. *Justin's snacks*. After the hectic switch in my schedule and the last-minute rush at the cafe, I had completely forgotten to walk past the gas station on my way home. My eyes water a bit as I curse my forgetfulness.

For a moment, I consider backtracking. The gas station is still open, after all. I don't want to deal with him right now.

But my feet are sore, I'm exhausted, and the last thing I want is to walk to the gas station and back on a winter night. Swallowing past a nervous lump in my throat, I grab my keys and head toward my door.

*It'll be fine.* I try to reassure myself the best I can as I put the key in the lock. He might have forgotten and passed out in front of the TV.

But something in me knows better.

I turn the key in the lock and enter the apartment. It's dark in the small living room, the only light coming from the TV. Justin is in the same place I left him, smashing buttons on his PlayStation controller. His eyes are bloodshot, and I can't tell if it's from playing video games all day or if he has been drinking.

"Hey, Mia. Get those snacks?" He doesn't even look up from his game.

I stand in the doorway, twisting my purse strap in my hand. Cold dread grips my heart, and I open my mouth to speak, but nothing comes out at first.

"I..."

"Mia? Are you deaf or just stupid?" Justin finally casts me a glance.

"I forgot them," I blurt. "I'm really sorry. I wound up working a double shift and it was late, and I- I just forgot. I'm sorry."

The words all come out in a rush, and there's a certain relief when I'm done. But that relief is instantly gone when Justin sets down his controller.

"I'm sorry?" he says, "I must have heard you wrong. I asked you for one simple thing, Mia. All I wanted was that snack. I don't ask for a lot, and somehow you still manage to screw this up."

It isn't the words but the rage I hear in them that makes me flinch.

"Why don't you cook something at home? Or get your own snack?" I ask, breathing hard with adrenaline. I've never challenged him because I just want a peaceful relationship.

But Justin rises from the couch, knocking his controller to the floor. He whips off his headset and hurls it at the wall, hitting it with a CRACK. With bloodshot eyes and a terrifying snarl, he stalks toward me.

He's never hit me. Not once, but the underlying threat has always been there. But tonight, something is different, and he's taking his rage out on me.

"What the fuck is wrong with you, Mia?" he asks, and I can hear the startlement in his voice as well as anger.

Tears fill my eyes as I try to put some distance between us. "I'm sorry, Justin. Really. I was just tired and distracted."

Before I know what's happening, Justin backhands me across the face. Pain and heat instantly blooms around my right eye.

Clutching my face, I backed away from him in shock.

A look of guilt momentarily flashes across Justin's face as he reaches for me. When I pull away, though, the expression vanishes. "If you hadn't been so disrespectful, this wouldn't have happened."

I barely hear his words.

He hit me. He actually hit me.

The underlying threat had always been there. But he'd never once actually raised a hand to me. Clutching my face, I fight tears. Tears sting coming out of my right eye, and I can already feel the discoloration and swelling starting there.

Before he can say or do anything further, I flee to the safety of the bathroom. Quickly locking the door behind me, I let the tears flow freely. Vaguely, I hear Justin shouting after me to not be so immature. But I tune him out.

# SNEAK PEEK

*How did my life get here?* I had plans for the future. I was going to be a history major and get a master's degree down the road. But I just had to be the rebellious teenager. Dropping out of college and moving in with Justin it had all been an attempt to leave my abusive adoptive parents, who constantly told me that my birth parents never cared about me. My name isn't on the lease, so I'm scared of starting anything with him. He's the only person I have in this world.

Sighing, I begin washing off my makeup. It only serves to make my black eye look worse, and fresh tears spill down my cheeks.

I need to leave him. Deep down, I think I have always known that. But he was the only one to stand by me when I was alone. He had promised to take care of me.

Shutting off the water, I stare at my reflection, tears still running down my face. I barely recognize this girl. And if I'm being honest, I'm a little disappointed in her.

I stay in the bathroom for a moment, not sure if I want to face Justin. But when I hear the front door open and slam closed, I realize it's safe to exit. Still, I can't help but tiptoe to the bedroom, just in case he was still home.

The comforter feels warm and inviting as I slip into bed, my face still stinging. Tears roll onto the pillow as I cry myself to sleep, planning to leave Justin once and for all.

## END EXCERPT

Get the book here! Marking Mia

# ALSO BY LAYLA SPARKS

**Dawn of The Alphas: Omega For The Pack Series**

**Book 1: Maid for The Alphas** *(Breanna's story)*
**Book 2: Promised to The Alphas** *(Ruby's story)*
**Book 3: Denied by The Alphas** *(Carmen's story)*

**Howl's Edge Island: Omega For The Pack (COMPLETED)**

**Book 1 (*Tiana's story*):** Stolen by The Pack
**Book 2 (*Keera's story*):** Auctioned to the Pack
**Book 3 (*Lyra's story*):** Princess For The Pack
**Book 4 (*Vanessa's story*):** Betrayed by The Pack
**Book 5 (*Jade's story*):** Matched to The Pack
**Book 6 (*Alana's story*):** Knotted by The Pack
**Book 7 (*Lacy's story*):** Craved by The Pack
**Book 8 (*Olivia's story*):** Freed by The Pack

**The Librarian and Her Alphas (Standalone)**

**The Alpha's Perfect Prey (Stalker RH- Two Books)**

**Book 1:** Marking Mia
**Book 2:** Mating Mia

www.ingramcontent.com/pod-product-compliance
Ingram Content Group UK Ltd.
Pitfield, Milton Keynes, MK11 3LW, UK
UKHW040649170725
6939UKWH00019B/53